BLOOD BOUND

MAKAYLA RUNYON

I dedicate this book to Grandpa Tommy.

My friend, my family, my mentor.

You taught me how to follow my dreams,

and to always look out for #1.

Thank you for your love and your light-filled ways.

Miss you grandpa, and I love you.

Rest in Peace.

Blood Bound

©2021 Makayla Runyon

print ISBN: 978-1-09837-539-3
ebook ISBN: 978-1-09837-540-9

Contents

When I was younger, I thought the world was peaceful and perfect. Then, I saw 9/11, school shootings, and the effects of war. How they turned people inside out. War twists someone up inside so much that when they come back, it's like they are a completely different person. Deep down inside I always knew that the world was evil, but it wasn't until a few weeks before graduation that I accepted the world as it is: evil and unforgiving. In the end, it wasn't all bad, but the events that led up to it were things that I would never wish upon anyone else.

Chapter 1

Another X on the calendar. Exactly 34 days, 6 hours, 3 minutes and 2 seconds 'til graduation and I am officially an adult. Hi, I'm Alena, 17-year-old senior, excited for the world to come and greet me. Today is the day of the last high school play that I will ever star in. I play the lead role of "Sarah Ruhl" from the play *Stage Kiss*. She's an artist who thinks art captures all life and falls in love with someone she never expected she would. It is a good storyline I will admit, but not everyone likes the nerd at school getting the lead role.

They all prefer Sapphire, the most popular girl in school. Not that I care, she's a brat and a bully. I will never understand the popular life. Her father is the inventor of Post-It Notes. For her birthday, boys put Post-It Notes all over her locker declaring their crushes on her. Eventually, she figures one out, goes out with them for a week, breaks up with them, and then moves on to her next boyfriend. She has dated almost every guy in our school except the "nerdy" boys. Some of them she's even dated twice! Of course, she has a gorgeous toned body and long blonde hair. Me? I have wavy, frizzy, red-brown hair, so many freckles that my body is covered from head to toe, and big seafoam green eyes, just like my mom. Don't forget I'm nerdy, a drama major, and a freakish reader.

The one thing that I never understood was that I was beautiful, more than Sapphire apparently. At least that is what everyone thinks. I know I have some good features, but am I really that stunning?

Every day, my brother Jeremy drives me to school in his brand new navy blue 2018 Jeep, while I blast music through my Bluetooth headphones. I have my license and I could drive, but my mother has never liked the idea of me driving by myself, and there are only two cars to split amongst us three, and that means the oldest get them. No matter how much I ask my mom for me to drive or get my own car, it is always a no. However, I did make the deal that I won't ride the bus and Jeremy is forced to take me to school, which my mother all too quickly agreed to, something about trusting my brother over an old lady.

My family is wealthy, nearly as wealthy as Sapphire's family actually. My mother has a huge paying job, not that she has ever told me. My mother doesn't tell me a lot of things, much to my disappointment and annoyance. She always says that it's not my business, but I know that there is something else she's hiding.

My father, well, he died when I was a child. Murdered when he tried to stop an armed robbery.

Not that it matters to anyone outside my family. I am a loner. A nobody.

My brother parks the car and I jump out and say a quick goodbye. I run right to the stage theater on the west side of the school. My

English teacher, Ms. Broner, is already waiting there for me to have our usual morning talks. Mostly we talk about who won the spelling bee on TV, or the latest gossip on our favorite book and TV show series *Shadowhunters*.

"Morning Alena! Did you hear about how they killed off Malec? I was so hoping that they would get married!" Ms. Broner says.

"I know I am so disappointed!" I reply.

RING! Stupid bell.

"Sorry, Ms. Broner! Got to get to 1st block!" I say running out the door.

"Bye!" She yells after me.

The bell rings right as I get in the classroom.

"You're late!" Mrs. Yancey yells.

I'm not late, but it's a waste of time to argue with her. Instead I just roll my eyes. She yells at me again as I take my seat. She is the only teacher I've had in my entire life who dislikes me. I don't even know why! I always wonder how she is even married or has kids for that matter. They are sweet kids; I go over to babysit them once in a while. Mr. Yancey always pays well.

After what feels like only 10 minutes, I hear the bell.

RING! The first block is over.

The periods here fly by fast, sometimes not fast enough.

In our little town of Arran, nothing really happens that is history book worthy, or being put on the map. You can't find Arran on most Minnesota maps, only the really close and detailed ones. The only thing special about this town is that there is a big forest and lake on the edge of town, a few clothing shops, and a malt shop across from the high school. Life here is simple and quiet, and I hate it.

I want adventure and life and everything that makes the world beautiful and so difficult to understand. I want a life unlike the one that I have been given, and living in Arran would never let that life come to pass, no town in the southern part of Minnesota would. I want to travel, to see the places where empires once stood, where music and art was created, and where people found out who they were. I want that to be me, but I guess I will have to just hold onto the music and art that theater brings me.

It isn't long after school that we start our small rehearsal before the big show. Being the lead role is terrifying so the extra practice is great. It helps me to calm my nerves, which are in a frenzy because I have huge stage fright. However, whenever I start the play, the stage fright dissipates, replaced with wonder and joy. And that was what it was like as I performed for two hours until the play ended.

We pull up to the malt shop to celebrate, and also because we were all too tired to cook at home. As we sit down to eat, my mom goes on about how excellent I was in the play, and then starts crying because it is my last one. Jeremy tries to calm her so we don't make a scene, but of course she does and he just gives up. I giggle as I watch the scene. My mom is the best mother in the world; I couldn't have asked for a better one.

My brother is one that everyone crushes on. With that six pack and huge arm muscles, who wouldn't? Of course, I always get grossed out when people, mostly girls, flirt with him. Even my best friend Ava. She has had a crush on my brother since the 7th grade.

She is laughing next to me at all of his lame jokes he makes. Not that I blame her. If I didn't hear these jokes on a daily basis, I would probably laugh too. As if everyone crushing on him wasn't enough, every day I hear his name in the hallways. When I said that I was a nobody, I wasn't lying. I am not called *Alena*, barely anyone knows my name. They always refer to me as "Jeremy's little sister" or "the girl whose father died."

Ava is always there for me though. Sticking up for me when I am so annoyed that I want to choke someone. I don't know how I would've gotten through high school without her.

Eventually, Ava has to go for curfew and my family's getting tired. We part ways and I give Ava a big hug, and then we are on our way home. I fall asleep as soon as my head hits the pillow. Little did I know, this was the beginning of a chain reaction and the last time I would see my family for a long time. The last night I would be just a sweet, innocent little girl.

Chapter 2

I wake up to intruders surrounding my bed, both men and women. I can see seven, at least. One holds a knife to my throat.

"Get up. If you scream, we'll kill everyone in the neighborhood," a hoarse voice whispers in my ear.

I silently move, my body trembling with fear, from my bed. My body shakes so much that it takes all my concentration not to fall on my quaking legs, and not to get stabbed. I fell asleep so quickly last night, I still have on my same clothes. I slip on my tennis shoes, as he instructs.

Still with the knife to my throat, the same voice commands, "Go out the back door. Make a sound and it will be your last."

Not wanting to die, I listen, my mind forcing my body to relax. I silently go out the back door, being careful not to make a sound. As soon as I close the door and turn around, I realize they want not just any girl, but they want me. Specifically me. Several of their men and women surround my house.

"Move!" one of the 'gang' members commands, as others push me to my kidnappers. They split off into small groups, each moving in a different direction. One group surrounds me as if I was going to escape. They keep a knife to my throat like I am going to run, seemingly killing me in the process. At first, when I woke up, I had no idea what they wanted me for. Are they going to use me for ransom? Sex trafficking? Sell me to the highest bidder? I'm not sure what to make of any of this.

They are dressed in all black with a purple symbol I can't quite make out, but it seems like a circle with three lines going through the middle to each end with something else surrounding it. Are they a cult?

The thing that scares me the most are the weapons. Covering them from head to toe, are various types of weapons. From machine guns to combat knives to handguns. The man to my right even has a crossbow. Not to mention the full body armor protecting them from anyone who may decide to fire a gun and save me.

Before I even know what's happening, I'm planted face down in the dirt. I cough against the dirt in my mouth. Sirens sound from the house, loud enough to wake the neighborhood. I hear orders being yelled, and trampling feet. Gunshots, then fighting. There goes my wish for no one getting hurt.

"Get her out of here! Keep going until you reach the plane. I will take the men and be a distraction," my kidnapper tells a woman with short dark, black hair.

She yanks me up by my hair and tells me to move. I attempt to drag my feet as a sign of where I was being taken, until the woman threatens me with the gun on her hip. I stop my form of rescue and obey. We run until my legs give out. Up until this point, I have been holding back my fear, anger, and sadness. Now, I can't stop the tears from running down my face.

My body is racked with tremors, my fear taking over all the rest of my emotions. All the night's events flash before my eyes; being taken from my bed to this moment in time, crying on my knees. I try to think of a way out.

The only way I am getting out is through the girl with me now. I know I can't fight her. Not because I am weak, but because she has several weapons and I wish not to die tonight. My other option is to convince her to let me go. I have nothing to go on except my sorrow. I decide to use that to my advantage. I may be a good actor, but nothing I have ever done before was as good as this. The weird thing is, I am not even forcing it. I just let my feelings rush in and then I let it all out. I cry my eyes out with everything I have.

"Shut up!" the dark-haired woman commands.

But I can't. The tears won't stop coming. And to be honest, I don't want them to. Let her see my pain and my sorrow. Let her pity me so much that she might let me go. For a split second, I think of my father, and I cry a little harder and louder.

"Is this her?" a voice says coming up from behind me.

"Yes. She won't stop crying. Can you help me?" the woman replies.

She offers me a black water bottle filled with something and I drink without hesitation, my mouth dry from running. I assume it's just water, it tastes like it. It tastes kind of like the water you drink from the water fountain at school: metallic and disgusting.

In the long run, chugging down liquid from a weird looking water bottle, from a stranger—a kidnapper at that—at three in the morning in a forest, was not a very smart idea. I thought maybe if I really make it look like I am spiraling down into a deep pit of sorrow, she might even let me go. I think that's why she gave me the water in the first place. She pities me.

I finish off the water right before she takes it away and shoves it in a pocket around her waist. I stand upright as they both take one of my arms each, and practically drag me to a fence.

Beyond the fence looks like an airfield, except this one looks like one of those really small ones, only for private jets and flights for the 'rich' people. They drag me through a hole in the fence and take me to a private jet. There's no mistaking it for a commercial plane. This one is small, the size of three cars put together.

There are about two out of the four groups of the people that stand in front of the plane in a semicircle. They all look at me. I shudder from all the gazes. I am still in the clothes from the play. There's paint all over me, but the worst part is my hair is all over the place with dirt in it. I even have a ketchup stain on my jeans.

I blush with either anger or sadness or embarrassment. Which one? I have no idea, but that is not what concerns me for long. All of sudden everything around me feels fuzzy. I feel sleepy and dizzy.

"I feel funny," I pronounce.

One of them smiles as I start to sway, using the two people in the forest to balance me. Another one laughs as my knees give out beneath me. The woman and man from the forest catch me and lower me down onto the pavement. My eyes start to flutter shut and open again. I fight to keep consciousness. I start to question everyone.

"What's going on? Who are you? What did-d you give…" everything goes black.

The last thing I remember is the woman's voice from earlier, echoing in my mind. "Just relax, go rest your eyes. You'll need it for what's to come." My eyes give up trying to stay awake, as I feel someone scoop me up in their arms and carry me onto the plane.

What's to come? I wonder before drifting off to sleep.

As the plane is in flight, I open my eyes every once in a while, fighting to wake up, but am pulled back into darkness once again. In my darkness, I relive all of my life. Like the expression, 'I saw my life flash before my eyes.' It was as if I was watching a movie, but the scenes were my own memories. Everything from before my dad died to when I fell asleep. All of it just came and ran through my mind. But there was one memory that I don't remember at all. A strange man standing before me and then my mom, holding me with red paint on her face, men dressed in black surrounding us.

Chapter 3

The next place I wake up does not give me comfort, despite its cozy amenities. The first thing I notice is the massive bed and comfy blanket that I am curled up in. The next is my head. It pounds like no headache I have ever had before. *Is this what hangovers feel like?* I try to sit up, but fail and fall back on the dozen pillows behind me.

I am in what looks to be a master bedroom, but much more exquisite. I have my own bathroom, closet, and even my own dining area; a huge desk and massive windows backing it. I try to see what's outside but as I do…

"You're up! I was thinking you would be out for longer," exclaims a handsomely dressed man that comes through two double doors. "You must be a fighter, like your mother. I think had my men not threatened the entire neighborhood, you would be going to school today," his voice is smooth and full of amusement.

"Hello, Alena."

His eyes are the deepest of ocean blue, that stand out against his well tanned skin. His shirt defines the lines his muscles create. And the smirk on his face tells me of his confidence and authority.

"How do you know my name?" My voice is hoarse and sounds like I have been screaming. I swallow, trying to soothe the scratchiness I feel.

"I know everything about you. Your name, your birthday, your school, even that tiny birthmark right behind your ear," he replies. "I assume you have questions. I heard that you were asking a few before you passed out. Strong stuff we gave you, but clearly your family can take it."

"What is it that you gave me?"

"Rohypnol, it—"

"I know what it is," I interrupt. "Did you—,"

His chuckle cuts me off, "No. You mistake what I have you here for."

"What do you intend to do with me then?"

"I simply want revenge on your mother."

"What does my mother have to do with all of this?" I question. Each answer is leaving me more and more confused.

"You definitely are a curious one," he says. "All in good time, love, but for now you need rest for tonight. Wouldn't want you to miss dinner now, would we?" He shuts down any room for discussion with his tone.

He walks toward my bed, and then I realize what I didn't see before. The huge IV in my arm sapping some clear fluid into my bloodstream. That must be what was making me tired and weak.

"You need your rest."

With that, he turns a nozzle and I begin to feel weaker than ever. It isn't like the weakness before in the woods, this one is overwhelming but I am still aware of my surroundings.

"I'll have maids come right before dinner to prepare you. It's time you meet my brothers."

Once again I try to fight sleep, but fail, giving in to my exhaustion. I fall back into darkness.

When I wake, I find two guards standing at each post of the bed. Both are broad and muscular. One is shorter than the other, with dirty blonde hair, and the other is tall with dark brown hair.

Then I notice the maids, one on each side of the bed, just like that man said earlier. I try to sit up, but still feel too weak to do so. One of the guards notices and comes to the machine with the weird sleepy fluid and changes it out with something else. As soon as the new liquid enters my body, I feel a huge weight lifted off my chest.

The maids move immediately, going into what I assume to be the closet. While the taller guard returns to his post, the other stares right at me with burning eyes as I try to sit up again. I eventually succeed without falling, but not without losing my breath. Then, the two maids return.

Each holds a fancy, dinner party dress. Neither maid looks any older than 16. One still has childlike chubby cheeks and beautiful, long, flowing, brown hair. It bounces as she moves, almost alive with as much adventure as her eyes. The other's features differ only slightly. She appears to be a few years older and her eyes seem darker. They almost look like sisters.

"Which one do you like best? Master says you must look fabulous for tonight! The red or grey?" The younger, chubby-cheeked one says.

"The grey looks lovely," I reply trying to sound as cheerful as possible. I may have been forced here, but that doesn't mean I need to seem depressed in front of the young children.

"I agree completely. Although I thought gold was your favorite color?" The little one stated.

"It is, I just thought you didn't have it." I wonder how she knows that.

"We do! Let me go fetch it—"

"No! No, it's alright. The grey will do!" I blurt out.

"Alright! Guards, if you could go into another room; I have a feeling she won't get dressed with you staring at her," The quiet, older one says.

"Are you two sisters?" I ask as the guards turn to go.

"Yes!" The little one pipes up.

"Apologies for not introducing ourselves," the older one says. "I am Emily, and this is my little sister Lilly. She can get a little hyper sometimes. Our mother was a... friend of *his* before she died. He took us in and has kept us around to help. Mostly cleaning, but now we are to be helping you get ready," the older one, Emily, says as she works to help me get out of bed.

I stand up, wobbly at first, but I find my footing. They both work to get me out of my clothes, and into fresh undergarments.

"How old are you two?" I ask.

"I am 9 and Emily is 14," says little Lilly, as they slip the grey dress on. I am surprised by the beauty of it. The dress is a darker cloud grey silk material, with swirling beading at the base. As it goes up, the beading turns into crystals, all the way up to the low neck. The neck is barely above my breasts, but I have no breath to complain. The dress is absolutely stunning. It is so light, I feel as if I am wearing nothing at all.

They fasten my hair into natural looking curls, and give me plain flats, the color of the dress. Thank God for flats. I don't think I can walk far, let alone in heels. When they are finished, they nod with huge smiles and leave giggling.

As soon as the door shuts, I turn around and admire myself in the body sized mirror. I look like a princess. My hair is beautiful, matching with the swirls of my dress. There is even a small crystal beret in my hair to match the top of the dress. For children so young, I have to say I am impressed.

After a few minutes of admiring myself, the same pair of guards come in to lead me to the man I met before. Before, when I first woke up, I was thinking I was in a mansion. I even entertained the possibility of a castle, but it's no joke! I am in an actual castle. Judging by the number of corridors and rooms I pass, I would not be surprised if this place is only slightly smaller than Hogwarts. The corridors are carved with the ancient look of a castle: old torch holders, chiseled stone, and grand wooden doors.

My shoes clack against the hard wooden floors, as I walk. I try not to seem too impressed with the building. There are not many windows as we pass through the corridors. The few that do show are high above. I only guess that the rest of the windows are in the rooms that we pass. We go down a set of stairs before we arrive at our destination.

The dining room doesn't disappoint. From the marble arched ceilings to the old portraits of families on the walls, to the shining china on the table. It is quite breathtaking.

The man before stands with grace from his end of the table. He observes me looking around the room, like a lion gazing at a bouncy ball, amused and interested. Then I notice two other men in the room, also staring at me. My cheeks flush red with embarrassment. I turn around fully to see all of their faces.

The two men are different from one another in build. The one on the left, opposite of the table from the man I met before, is muscular and broad. The one in the center of the table, is lean and face lit by wisdom. He has a look to him that makes you think he is a historian. Curiosity fills the air, from the two new men.

"You are free to go, boys. Thank you for your work," the man I met earlier said to the guards.

They turn and leave.

"Sorry for ignoring you at first, I've just never been in a place this large before," I say with a shaky voice. I immediately regret apologizing, I owe these men nothing, especially not an apology.

"It's understandable. My brother had to steal it from our rivals," the muscular man says.

"You look absolutely stunning my darling, please come and sit," said the man before. That angers me, I shouldn't be here.

"I don't think it's a good idea to sit with three men, whose names I do not even know," I reply with a sharp tone. The muscular one laughs. He thinks of my anger as funny. The man I met in my room scowls but quickly recovers.

"I am James. These are my brothers, Will and David," he says pointing to the quiet one and then the muscular one.

"I would say 'lovely to meet you,' but in my situation it is very much not nice to meet you," I spat out with a clear sound of disgust in my voice.

The muscular one, David, as the man called him, burst out laughing this time, "You picked a good one, huh brother."

"You will not speak to them or me in that tone as long as you are here, Alena. You will do well to remember that." James says in a threatening, calm tone.

"I never asked to be here."

"You might not have, but your mother did when she decided to hurt my family."

"Don't ever speak of my mother in such a way!" I snap at him.

"You will not raise your tone at me, young lady. Now sit before I have to go send a team out to kill every civilian in your neighborhood," James firmly tells me.

I don't sense any seriousness in his voice, yet I obey.

With that, I sit. I would like to do anything else than sit at a table with the man that stole me from my family, but the statement about the kind people at home weighs over my head. Not to mention my growing curiosity about his comments on my mom.

"As I said before, you are just like your mother," James, the man who organized the whole kidnapping, repeats in a calm tone. "You wonder why I brought her here, brothers. It is quite simple. I want you to teach me *dawning*."

With that, I was confused, which led me to, "What is dawning exactly?"

"Something that you would very much hate," the quiet one, Will, says.

"And why is that?" I ask.

"Because it makes you do things you have no control over," he calmly says to me.

"And you mean to do this with me? I will do no such thing!" I yell, putting the pieces together.

"I don't quite care if you want to do it. After the blood is in your system, it won't matter. You will be mine to control," James says, as his anger rises. I can almost feel the room crackle with his emotion.

"I am not some 'thing' to be controlled. I am a human being. You should treat me as one." I spit the word "thing" out like it's poison.

"That is not your choice to be made, it is mine. I don't think you quite understand what a kidnapper is. I will do what I wish with you, whenever I wish to. I don't care what you think, you are just here to serve a purpose, so whatever I decide to do with you will happen. Now shut up and eat."

"How do I know there are no sleeping drugs in this as in the water?" I questioned.

James's fist hits the table, hard. "Because if I wanted to put you to sleep, I have other ways of doing it. Now eat! I will not ask a third time."

I do as he says and eat. I scoop small helpings of mashed potatoes, green beans, chicken breast, and a roll of bread onto my plate. I scarf it all down and finish it with a glass of water. Having to sit there and eat with James was like stabbing myself over and over again.

"That can be arranged if you wish it to be, Alena," Will says before swallowing a piece of bread.

"Excuse me?"

"You want to be stabbed over and over again instead of sitting here with him," he points at James. "I said that can be arranged."

The tips of James' lips curl up into a wild smile.

"How did you..."

"I can read your mind, your thoughts, and pretty much every-thing you're thinking right now."

"Can you read this?" I picture his brother lying on the floor, bleeding out, screaming to be saved.

"Yes, but I don't see how my brother bleeding on the floor and yelling is going to help you."

James and David burst out laughing.

"If you think you can kill me, you are extremely wrong, darling. I am more powerful than you can possibly imagine." James says.

So disturbed with the intrusion in my brain, I get up to leave. As I try to grab the door handle, James is already there, grabbing my wrist and turning me around to face him.

"And where do you think you are going?"

"Anywhere but here."

"I don't think so. You go nowhere without my knowledge and permission."

"I am not a puppet for you to control. Find someone else to boss around." At that, he squeezes my wrist until I bark out with pain. I still feel weak from what I guess to be the fluid they were putting in my body, before.

"You're hurting her brother." Will states as he and David stand up at the sudden turn of events.

"I know. She would not be in pain if she would just listen and obey," he says, not breaking his gaze with me. I shoot him a devilish glare.

"If you give a slave too many whippings, they might lose their sense of feeling and then you cannot control them with pain," Will responds as he starts to walk towards us.

James says, "What are you trying to say?"

"The more you try to control her, the more she is going to retaliate."

"I beg to differ, but since you are so keen on leaving," he turns back to me, "allow me to escort you to your bedroom."

"I don't need a babysitter-"

"And I don't need a problem. I am going to make sure you behave."

"Is this what you really want, brother? Do you really want to do this? Dawning is a powerful thing that is hard to control," David breaks in.

"Yes. You two have been doing it for years, messing with your play things. Now I want in," he responds.

"I said it before, I will say it again, I don't care what you want, I am not a thing. I am a person," I reply, tired of him not treating me like one. I am also tired of them talking like I am not even here.

He moves so fast I have no time to react. He yanks my wrist and pulls me out the door, back into the hallway, practically dragging me to my bedroom. As soon I try to pull away, he swings me around and…

"What did I say? Obey."

"And I said that I don't care."

With that he grabs my throat with his hand and shoves me against the wall, knocking the breath out of me. I gasp trying to retain at least a little bit of the breath lost. I claw at my throat, trying to rip his hand off my neck, if only for a little bit of air.

"Why don't you reconsider that. This is not a request."

"I take it back. I care. I will go to my room." I gasp out.

"Good girl," he says as if he were talking to a dog.

He drops his hand, and I walk to my room with no complaint, no resistance. Eventually, he lets go of my wrist and allows me to walk freely.

Finally, we make it to the doors of my room, and the guards open up the doors for us—or maybe for him, because they bow to him as he herds me through the doors.

Emily and Lilly come out of the closet at the sound of the door. When they see us they turn to bow to James. I roll my eyes. The girls giggle as they see me do so. James notices and slaps me on the shoulder. The girls snap back up with no laughter, except Lilly smiles a bit.

"What did you just do?"

"Nothing! I just…um…," I stutter not wanting to get in trouble.

"You what?"

"I rolled my eyes," I say a little more confidently. Not really caring at this point.

"Not the worst thing you have done. But you girls I expect better, no food tomorrow," James says as he turns to leave, like that is something he says everyday.

"Please don't do that to them, it's my fault. They are just kids. Punish me instead if you have to punish someone," I tell him.

"You don't have to do that Alena, it isn't the first time. We can handle it," Emily says.

James counters, "No Emily, she said she would take it. She deserves it anyways."

I look at him with pride at that. Knowing that throughout this whole night, I have managed to make him at least a little mad.

Looking at the two sisters, I instantly have a request in my mind. The worries of me getting in trouble are not in my mind.

"I want them to have the day off tomorrow, they get to do whatever they want. I will pay for it," I quickly say.

Emily said that it's not the first time, and I certainly wasn't going to let it be another. The price, whatever it was, would be worth it. They are just kids, that have probably never seen a life outside of this one.

This is worth it.

"No!" Little Lilly yells out, on the verge of tears.

"Hey, it's okay," I say walking towards her, bringing her and her sister into an embrace. "You guys have had many more days of pain than me. Let me do this for you. He can't hurt me too much. Go have fun," I reply, releasing them from my crushing hug. "Take care of each other. Have a good-"

"Alena!" Emily yells as she grabs her sister and backs away.

Whack! I feel a warm liquid fall down my face. I open my eyes to the guards looking at me. One with a wooden bat.

The girls run out the door.

My vision starts to blur and black, my head spinning equally.

James crouches down to hold my chin up as I try to sit up, "You said you would pay for it, then you shall. I was going to wait till you did something else stupid, but this is a good lesson to show you that for all the kindness you give out, there will be consequences. Remember that with each blow. Have a good night, darling. See you in the morning."

As soon as he stands up, walks out the doors and after they close behind him, they hit me back to the ground. Stomach, nose, knee, throat, everywhere they kick me. Over and over again.

I look at them with a devil stare and yell at them with my blood pooling out of my mouth. It sprays everywhere when I speak.

They pull me up by my hair, to my knees, from my place of lying on the floor. I look them in the eyes to see them smile, wild smiles.

This is worth it.

"'Nighty night, Alena. Sweet pains,'" the one holding me says as he takes my head, knees me in the face, and everything goes black."

Chapter 4

When I wake I am back in the bed I woke up in before. James and his two brothers surround me. Will has his hand on my head with his eyes closed, possibly concentrating on something that I don't know of. James and David stare at me with curiosity. I look down at the floor where I was beaten the night before, the blood is gone with no trace of last night's events.

"You're finally awake again. You were out for half the morning. Not that I am surprised. You took some hard hits," James starts.

I still look around in a daze. My head hurts a lot making it hard to concentrate. When I try to sit up-

"OW!" I exclaim.

"I wouldn't do that. You got hit so hard in the ribs, two of them broke. Best not to damage them even more."

"It wouldn't be so hard to move if you hadn't given the order."

"You're the one who said, 'Give them the day off, I will pay for it.' I didn't make you say that," James says, using his fingers as quotation marks.

"Hey! I just wanted them to have a day of freedom from you!"

"Brother, stop. Her emotions are going to lock me out," Will says, starting to stroke my neck on the jawline. I am calmed by this unusual movement.

"Sorry my brother, continue," James calmly says.

"What are the girls doing today?" I ask trying not to raise my hopes for what could have happened.

"You said anything they want. They decided to go to New York. They've always wanted to go," James replies.

"That's amazing. I am happy for those… AHHH!" I scream out in pain. Will tries to keep stroking my neck, but the pain is too much.

"Hold her down. David help me," Will quickly says. Within seconds, David's hands are on my forehead and James and his guards are holding down my legs and my arms.

"I am going to look inside her mind for a second. David keep me anchored," Will commands.

Then my worst nightmare happens. I have thought of this memory every day for a full month, when I was younger. I was so scared of it that I asked my mom if we could just cut it out. If someone could just remove it, but they can't.

It's a memory that I made. It's the memory that keeps me moving, always doing what I can to succeed. My fear is me, being too helpless that I have to be helped to do everything, and people get hurt for it.

I scream as loud as I can. I can feel my face and body boiling; I suffer as if my heart is going to explode. I can't think straight, or shake the memory from my mind. It takes over my senses, everything going blank and bright at the same time. I can't think, only hear my screams and my own thoughts shrieking in my ears.

The memory I created flashes before my eyes with the faces of those I have been taken from, the ideas of them being hurt from my helplessness drilling into my thoughts, until one thought outshines the rest. My father. He died because of me...

Will is pushed back onto the ground by an invisible force and quickly scrambles back up. He watches with concern and sadness as I scream. I scream as I have never screamed before.

Will comes back to my bedside and gently touches my cheek and says, "Somnia bona somnia."

My nightmare stops and I go into my dream. My dream of becoming a motivational speaker. Inspiring the world to help others, to care for others. I have a family that supports me, and my dad is there too. Walking me down the aisle at my wedding.

"You can let go of her, she won't be bugging anyone, anytime soon," Will says in a sad tone as I watch the guards take their hands off her body and step back.

"What is it that you saw brother?" I asked in concern, "I haven't seen you this sad since mother and father."

"That child's nightmares are something no one should think about. She needs rest. Unless you're ready to do dawning in which case, *you* will need to rest." Will says gathering his wits.

"I am ready."

When I wake, I look to see men surrounding the bed, James and Will talking to each other. The first thing I heard was "I am ready," from James.

"Men you might want to come back and help again. This time should be easier; she is weaker than before," David speaks up, "and can someone bring in the ceremonial dagger so we can do this?"

"She's waking up. See if she'll take it willingly," Will says.

My eyes open just in time to see a bunch of people, and the doors to my room flying open bringing more people in. Not to mention the scary looking knife on a pillow. It has an ancient look to it. Bright, straight, gold blade with an iron hilt. At the end of the hilt is a giant blue stone. It almost looks like it is glowing. Before I have time to say anything, David butts in.

"Brother let me see your wrist."

James gives his wrist to David. David picks up the golden blade and makes a long, clean cut into James' wrist. He grunts with pain in his eyes and then turns to me.

"What are you doing?" I ask, starting to scoot away from him.

"We can either do this the hard way or the easy way. Your choice." He replies instead of not answering my question. I continue to scoot away but I reach the end of the bed.

"Hard way then. Lovely choice." The guards start to move in and pin my arms and legs down, as James moves to come closer to me. He grabs my chin and moves it for easy access to his wrist. I struggle to move away, but their grips are too tight. I bare my teeth and then close it rapidly as I realize what he intends to do. I quickly remember him saying as soon as the blood is in my system, I won't have any control over myself. James places his wrist onto my mouth.

"Drink it, Alena. Do not make this worse for yourself," James commands.

I won't listen. I start to breathe out of my nose. James notices and covers my nose, stopping any air flow to my body. Leading me to my only source of air left in my mouth. I hold my breath for seconds which feels like minutes. David comes into view as he whispers into James' ear an idea. James' wicked smile makes me whimper as he raises his fist, and brings it down hard on my stomach, releasing all the air I had left, forcing me to open my mouth for air and blood. In which I tried so hard to avoid.

I start to see stars dancing above my vision for a brief second, then it disappears. I lose all control as soon as the blood hits my tongue. My body tingles in response to the warm liquid that trickles slowly down my throat. I try to resist the urge to drink, but it becomes too much, and I obey.

"My God. She's actually drinking it," I exclaim.

"You may let go of her now," Will says across from me.

David smiles as they let go, and Alena's hand slowly comes to meet my arm. She pulls hard on it, pushing it more into her mouth. I reach down and cup her head as I lift it up for more access. She suddenly sits upright and pulls more at my arm.

"She has two broken ribs, how is she sitting up right now?" I ask with curiosity.

"She did have broken ribs, look again," Will responds.

I reach underneath the blanket to feel her stomach. Where there once was a sharp point, is a smooth flat surface. I look up at her with disbelief.

"Your blood did that. It healed her. This is a very good sign." David states.

The guards, like me, are looking at her with both disbelief and curiosity.

"Now, once she has drunk enough, she will fall back to sleep," David says.

I smile at that.

"You boys can go treat yourself to anything you'd like tonight, you have earned it," I say to my men without taking my eyes off of Alena. With that they all file out of the room, leaving me and my brothers alone with Alena.

"Lie her back down brother, she will have her fill soon," Will suggests.

I listen and lie her back down onto the many pillows behind her. She starts to slow her drinking. I softly caress my fingers along her neck, on the jawline. She sighs at the soft feel of my fingers. Her hands slip away as her mouth falls and she lies fully back onto the pillows. I wipe away the blood running down her chin. She looks so peaceful when she sleeps.

Will turns to me and says, "This time when she wakes up, she will be a completely different person in every way. She is confident now but will be scared the next time. But the unique thing about this is you can customize her to your liking, kind of like a robot, except she is human. She'll want to do everything you wish and serve only you. The blood is what keeps her at bay. Congratulations brother, you have your own Dawn."

"About damn time," I say with a smile.

Chapter 5

W hen I wake up, I know I am not really awake. I am in a valley, lying against a tall tree. I look up to see blackish, blue sky, with pinks and greens and yellows. The ground is cold. The grass has a slight beige color to it and looks as if it is dying.

"Hello? Is anyone there?" I quietly say.

Out of the corner of my eye, I see a bright light. When I look into it, I see my bedroom, but through someone else's eyes. It's as if I am looking through a mirror onto my life. Like I am in a cage inside of my own mind. The picture moves to James' face, he looks so handsome. For a kidnapper at least. He smiles mischievously. I now understand what he did. I hear him tell the other *me* what to do and how to act.

"I will be back in an hour or two, stay in this section of the castle," James commands. He walks out the doors.

"Quite hard to see yourself from this side isn't it?" A female voice says from behind me. I turn around to see where the female voice came from. Directly behind me is a young girl with long, flowing, raven hair, turquoise blue eyes and some freckles on her cheeks and nose. She is beautiful.

"Not being able to do anything but watch. It breaks you."

I then notice the ripped, floral dress she is wearing, covered in dirt. Her broken nails covered in dried blood. There are tons of cuts on her hands. I can even see a little piece of glass sticking out of her thumb.

"Who are you?" I ask with gentleness.

"I'm Ella. I am guessing you are Alena, right?" she replies.

"Yes. How do you know that?"

"David has been talking about it with the other *me*. I assumed it was you."

"You are one of David's..."

"Dawns? Yeah. That's what they call us."

"How did you meet David?" I ask.

"I met him at a coffee shop. I was going there after school, like every day. He noticed me and we talked for a little bit. He eventually left, said he had to get home. Little did I know he was actually getting his men ready to take me. I was leaving around five like always, and all of a sudden, his men snatched me. Been here ever since."

"And how long has that been?"

"About two years." She states with calm grace.

I run over to hug her. Two years, I can't even imagine. Being stuck, watching your body be controlled by someone that is not you.

"I am so sorry," I whisper into her ear.

"Girls she is alright. She is the same as us." She yells out breaking away from our hug.

Out of nowhere, girls appear from behind trees. They all look the same as Ella. Beautiful and broken.

"You're all Dawns?" I ask with a shaky voice, hoping it wasn't true. There are nearly twenty girls surrounding me.

They all nod yes. My heart has never felt this way before. It felt as if it was going to explode. I fall on my knees crying. I am imagining what these girls have gone through. Something I am now also forced to endure. How long they have been here. Watching their lives be controlled by a stranger, being forced to watch. They all start to walk closer to me and drop onto their knees before me. Pulling me into a hug, they all look at me with sad eyes. I pull away from my tears.

I look at all of them in the eyes and ask, "Do you mind if I get to know you guys?"

They all nod, understanding why I ask. Because if this is the only life I will endure, I want to know who I am spending it with. I want to know that I am not alone.

17 girls total. We sat in a giant circle. Whenever there was silence, someone stepped in to share their story. First to speak was Natalia. She was 16 and was one of David's Dawns. She had been here for almost a full year. Then there was Nora. She was 15 and one of Will's Dawns. She had been here for almost three years. Then there was Julianna, 16; Olivia, 16; Megan, 18; Lucy, 17; Hannah, 18; Katia, 17; and Isabella, 17. They were all Will's Dawns.

Then there was Charlotte, 13; Chloe, 14; Holly, 15; Katrina, 17; Kayley, 16; Arabella, 17; and Sarah, 16. They were all David's Dawns.

No one here was James' Dawn, which doesn't surprise me because he had seemed eager with me. In the end, the girls' stories hurt me more than anything. These men were cruel and evil. Most of them had been here for many years. The longest was Hannah. She was abducted at age 13 by Will. She has been here for over five years.

"So you guys just watch our *us* control your body?"

"We call them opposites, but yes. Sometimes, it gets too hard to watch. Seeing your body used in such a way. You'll get used to it, but some of it, you can't even stand to look at," says Megan.

Kayley jumps in and snaps at Megan, "Don't act like what happens to us isn't horrible. They took us from our families, to what? To…"

Kayley stops speaking, her eyes going distant, a painful memory crossing her mind. It takes me no time at all to understand what she was about to tell me. The rest of the girls clearly know and stop, we all sit in silence as we wait for the tension to dissipate.

I know that these men are awful human beings, but this, whatever this is, is hell. How could you do this to a person?

I look back at my opposite sitting next to James, looking at Will and David. She is chatting with them like old friends, which I hate.

"I won't stand for this. I won't stay here. When I wake up, I am going to free you. All of you," I say standing up.

"We would all love nothing more than to be free, but you can't escape," Katia says.

"We'll see about that," I say, walking up to my view of my opposite. I start to pound on it. I feel her blink.

So, I hit harder, then she coughs.

I smile and I start to punch, kick, hit, and scream, hitting the mirror-like image. I can see her seizing and coughing. The brothers are trying to help her, but there is no helping her. I want my body back. So, if she won't give it. I will take it back.

"I will see you all soon," I yell to them as I break through.

I blink. I am staring at the floor. I glance down at my body and smile. I then look up, and remember what a terrible situation I am in. I gaze to my left, there are doors leading to the hallway. I bolt for them as fast as I can.

"She's awake!" Will yells out, quickly realizing what just happened.

"Guards! Guards! Keep Alena in the castle at all costs!" James yells out.

I can hear the trampling feet behind me. Guards shouting orders. I turn a corner and already know it is over. Guards create a wall blocking my exit out, there were about six of them. Two run to attack me, but I didn't come this far to give up.

In high school, particularly in Minnesota, the schools make it a class to learn to defend yourself. One specific class, we had a martial arts trainer come in to teach us basic defense techniques. She had recommended a few youtube videos after the lessons in order to perfect our technique. I jumped at the opportunity, motivated by my father's passing. Maybe it was only a few lessons, but I got a few basics down. And these assholes are going to see just how much I know.

I kick one right in the face. He falls back, holding his nose to try to stop the blood from coming out. The other one goes down after a few punches to the stomach and then the throat. He falls back gasping. Four more advance.

The guard closest goes straight down with a kick to the balls. I smile a little at that. The three advance at the same time I manage to take out one with an elbow to the throat. But the other two are already there pinning me to the ground. I try to struggle but it is no use, they're too strong. They hoist me up to face the three brothers. Will comes up to me and studies my face. I can feel the guards digging deeper into my arms. I let out a hoarse laugh.

"Was that the best you can do? I have gone through far worse. I will not be controlled by something you put inside of me!" I scream while being short of breath.

Will's eyes soften as he takes my chin in his hand and lifts my eyes up to meet his. I almost think he pities me. He looks sad when he says something, and everything goes black.

I watch as she takes out two of my strongest guards before the other two restrain her. They lift her up into our direction.

She laughs with bitterness in her voice as she says, "Was that the best you can do? I have gone through far worse. I will not be controlled by something you put inside of me," She says with a raspy breath. Will walks up to her and lifts her chin. The fire that was in her eyes earlier disappears. It is as if she trusted him, for that small amount of time at least.

"Somnum," Will says.

She goes limp in the guard's arms. Will turns around with sad eyes and nods to me.

"Bring Alena back to her room. Put her on the floor before the fireplace," I command.

I watch them walk away as one hoists Alena over his shoulder and the other leads the way. I watch them as they go. Will leaves at the same time, headed in the direction of the library. Then, I turn back to my guards that were taken out by Alena.

"How can you fall to a 17-year-old girl, who is inches smaller, and not nearly as strong?" I ask, furious.

They all shake their heads.

"I suggest then that you go and train. Become stronger. If I have to, I will come and punch you where Alena did, repeatedly, so you don't feel anything when she does that again. Do you understand me?" I ask with a sharp tone.

"Yes, sir," they all say in unison and scurry off.

I turn to the others and nod. They are all gone within seconds. I pace back and forth thinking of what was bothering Will so much. I decide to go and ask him.

I search the castle for where he might be. I finally find him in the library staring at a giant dusty, old, book. He looks up at me when I enter, then sighs and looks back to his book.

"Will, do you mind telling me what is bothering you?"

"Nothing you need to worry about, brother," he replies with sad eyes.

"Really? Because it seems that I do need to worry myself with it, seeing that you were not like this until you searched through her mind."

"Alena's mind has nothing to do with it. It's her dreams, her nightmares. The experiences that she has are far too big for someone her age. And I cannot seem to figure out why the dawning process didn't work correctly. I did everything the book said, and more."

"What is it you saw? What are her nightmares?" I ask, wanting to know what scared him so much to become so paranoid.

"Nightmare. Singular. She only has one."

"What is it then?"

"You really want to burden yourself with it?"

"Of course I do," I say walking towards him.

"Love and death. She is scared of love and death. She thinks that by living her life, she is helpless, and that costs something that she won't be able to pay. Then, everyone she has come to know or love, or that knows or loves her, will die. All because she just wanted to live her life. But she will always and forever care for others more than herself. She would rather die than let another one die, even you," he finishes with tears in his eyes.

"And her dream?" I ask unsteadily. Knowing that I have ruined any chance of her dream coming true. Keeping her here, it will break her.

"She dreams of changing the world—of saving it. She wants everyone to be equal, to be safe, and most of all to be happy, at any cost; where she didn't have to sacrifice her happiness for others' lives." Will finishes.

"I don't know why dawning didn't work. It should have worked. She shouldn't have been able to break through."

I sigh. How could I not have seen it before? When I threatened the girls because they laughed, she took the punishment for them. Not only that, she gave them a day at the price of a night with no pain. She did it because she knew that she couldn't escape, so instead she took all of their pain and paid the price. All Alena has done since she has got here, was fought. The only time she hasn't fought was when…

"I know her weakness," I pronounce.

"What do you mean?" Will asks.

"Think about it, when she got here all she did was fight in the dining room right?"

"Not until you threatened her."

"I didn't threaten *her* specifically, I threatened other innocent lives. That's when she stopped. The only thing that made Alena not fight, when she was kidnapped, was that we threatened the entire neighborhood. When we left the dining room and I took her to her bedroom, I threatened Emily and Lilly with no food for today. Then she said she would pay for it all, and then gave them the day off the next day, and then she would pay for that too."

"Where are you leading with this, brother?" Will questions me.

"Her weakness is love."

Chapter 6

I wake up in my bedroom, but not on my bed like every other time. This time, I am lying on the floor in front of the fireplace. As I sit up and look down at myself, I find my arms have bruises, most likely from the strong guards holding me. I stand up to walk to my closet and am pushed back by an invisible force that I cannot see. I watch my doors open, and see James, Will, and David walk in. I glare at them and stand up. I do not care how I look as I stare at the brothers heading over towards me.

"I see that you figured out your new little home. How long you stay in there for, is your decision," Will says coming to stand in front of me.

"You can't just keep me here. Eventually, you're going to have to let me out," I say, stepping forward.

"I think that you will stay in here if you misbehave. Like Will said, your decision," James raises his voice.

My anger starts to rise, and my insides start to twist. I find myself gasping for air, clawing at my throat. I panic and the pain rises. I kneel down feeling dizzy.

"This is an emotion cell. Everything that you have an emotion for, it hurts you. For example; that anger you just had towards us, made you lose your breath. That panic you had, made you feel pain. Of course happiness and joy are things you won't enjoy so those won't hurt you. Basically the more bad energy you have towards us, the more it will hurt you. Easy concept to remember," Will pronounces, watching me sink to my knees.

I stand up as quick as I can and run at the wall. Slamming my fist into it as hard as I can, over and over again. I try to keep the pain down, but it feels as if my skin is ripping apart. I keep hitting and am thrown back.

"Will told you, emotions will hurt you. It's what makes this so perfect for you, your emotions are all you have left." James says, bending down to eye level with me.

"You're a prick," I stare down the bastard.

The man actually has the audacity to wink at me, "And you're an emotional brat."

"You're wrong. But, at least I have a heart. That is something you will never take away," I spit at him, and a little blood splatters on his jacket. He stands up with disgust and turns to leave, motioning for his brothers to join him.

"Have fun, Alena." James says as he turns to go.

As soon as the doors close, I run to the barrier keeping me here, and am thrown back as soon as I touch it. I try again and again; each time being thrown hard across the floor. Eventually, I cut myself, across a sharp edge, on the floor and start to bleed. I stop trying to break out and go to lie on one of the sofas next to the fireplace.

Blood, leaking from my side, soaks into the sofa. I laugh a little. Let his couch be ruined. At the very least it will bug him, and it will be a pain to get out. The emotional pain starts to fade when I laugh. I remember Will saying that happiness and joy won't affect me. I lie back and keep thinking about it, eventually I don't feel anything whatsoever.

I stand up and look at the invisible wall. If I was hurt when I was angry and sad, I wouldn't get hurt if I didn't feel those things. But if I feel nothing, I can't be hurt. I wonder if it was the same for the wall. I walk towards the invisible wall, guessing where it is, with curiosity.

If I could pass through, then I could go home. No one would expect that I would have gotten out, making it easy to escape.

I take a long breath and lift my hand to where I assume the barrier is. I reach out, trying to keep my emotions and feelings from sparking. If they spark and I touch the barrier, it could alert them that I was trying to get out, or just get me even more hurt than I already am. Both are bad for someone in my current situation. I relax my mind and think only of calmness, and start walking.

I remember a memory of my mom and me, I was around the age of 6, it was after I had gotten a shot at the doctors and I was crying. She felt bad for making me do it, but she knew that I would have regretted it later when I was sick.

Mom got me in the car, still balling my eyes out, and she brought me to Culver's right down the hill from the hospital. When we got in the parking lot she reached into the back seat where I was sitting and asked for her purse. I handed it to her, and she proceeded to rummage through the purse. She pulls out a free scoops coupon and goes through the drive-through and orders a chocolate ice cream with cookie dough. I smile when she hands it back to me. Only mom would know that my favorite topping on my ice cream is none other than Culver's cookie dough.

I open my eyes to me standing up with my hand out, halfway across the room. I push my hand out a little farther to see if I am still in the cell, but it doesn't stop. I breathe a sigh and look down at my side. I can't walk out with blood spilling everywhere, so I have to bandage it up.

I go to my bathroom. It is grand, with marble countertops and flooring. A huge bathtub sits in the right-hand corner and there's a walk-in shower in the other. The sink is on the left, right near the entrance to the bathroom and cabinets are behind the door, to the right. I look within the cabinets and find an assortment of many soaps and conditioners on the top shelf, feminine products on the second, towels and washcloths on the third.

I take a towel from the third shelf and go to the sink. I take off my bloody, pink shirt, and throw it to the ground. I turn to get a good look at my side in the mirror. The gash isn't major, but big enough to lose a lot of blood. I take the towel and turn on the water. I turn it on just barely so it can't be heard. I don't risk shutting the door, just in case it creaks. I place the towel underneath the softly streaming water. I run it underwater until it is completely soaked, and then I slowly turn off the water nozzle. I gently press the towel to my wound and hold it there, I clench my teeth in pain, so I don't yell. I clean it out as best I can without screaming and try to clean up the blood on the floor, but I give up when it only spreads everywhere. I accidentally make the bathroom look like a murder scene.

I walk out of the bathroom and to my closet. In the closet, I find an assortment of dresses in all the colors of the rainbow ranging from red to purple on one side, not to mention the silver, brown, and bronze at the end. The other side holds jeans, tunics, t-shirts, and everyday wear. Lost in the beauty of the clothes, I look at everything. Then I find at the very end, there sits a single golden dress that takes my breath away.

It sparkles with millions of what looks to be diamonds and actual gold flakes. I turn away from it quickly knowing it is just a scam to draw me in.

I look back at the rainbow row of dresses, and pick out a bright, cotton, orange gown and rip a long strip of fabric off. I am careful not to make a loud noise. I take the piece and tie it around my abdomen, securing the towel to my side to keep the blood from dripping. It may not be much, but it should hold until I am out of the castle.

I grab a t-shirt before continuing on my way. I leave the closet soundlessly and go to my window just to the left of my bed. I am careful not to get too close, in case anyone is patrolling outside. I see a couple of guards on the ground, but they are facing outwards. I figure my best bet is the only set of doors leading in and out of here.

I am putting the success of this whole plan on the guards being taken off duty at the doors, by James. His brothers and him probably think that the cell will hold up. They're foolish if they do.

I slowly, but steadily, open the right-side door and peek out. No guards. Thank God. For a kidnapper, especially one with brain control, he sucks at keeping his target locked up.

I shut the door quickly and look down each way. Going left would lead me to the dining room, and probably closer to James. Going right would lead me into unknown territory, unless that's the area where the study was and the place I was caught and took out those guards. But that is all on chance.

If this is an actual castle, most likely the king and queen who built this would put the dining room close to the entry. Allowing the guest to walk a short distance through the castle, hiding their secrets and treasure better.

The only problem is that it's closer to James, and there is sure to be a number of guards patrolling. I must choose between turning right into unknown territory, left toward the dining room, or going out my bedroom window. The window means a good chance of being seen and an even greater chance of me getting more hurt than I already am.

I decide to go left. I stick close to the wall, and crouch low on the stairwells, hoping that if someone comes, I can catch them by surprise and take them out. I may not be a soldier, but I know that if a life is on the line, I have some fire.

Luckily, my trip to the dining room is undisturbed by anyone. I peek into the room to see if anyone is eating, but no one is there. Glassware is set up, confirming my fear that someone soon would show up.

I look around and see two exits. One leads to what I guess is the kitchen for the maids on the right side, and the left side leads to what looks to be a hallway.

I walk towards the hallway. Going into the kitchen would have probably been a smarter choice considering that the maids are not closely guarded, but I don't want to risk any of the maids turning me in. Not to mention, if any Dawns are in there, they can send a direct message to Will and David that I am out of my cell, making my situation even worse.

I finally make it to the hallway and let out a sigh when I see huge, oak wood, heavy-duty, double doors. I look to the other side to see two stairwells curving upwards and an opening in the middle of the two; this is the main entrance to the castle. I don't notice anyone milling around, so I run for the doors and heave them open. I blot onto the rounded, cobblestone driveway. I continue running until I am out of the castle's shadow, and that's when I am seen.

Guards from their posts, surrounding the castle, scream at the top of their lungs to sound the alert. Even with the sheer size of the castle, almost the size of Hogwarts only slightly smaller, the alarm is passed around quickly.

I look behind me to see guards from inside the castle already spilling out of the two double doors I had just exited. I turn back around and see more guards surging toward me, and I bolt toward them. They may have more guards, but they are more spread out and they're blocking my closest route out toward the main road.

I take a sharp right toward the smaller group of soldiers, and weave in and out of them like a maze. All of them reach to grab me but are too slow. One even falls jumping for me. I make it through the guards and keep running, toward the safety of the tree line and, eventually, the road.

Like the guards I weave in between the trees, trying my hardest not to slow my pace. There isn't much ground to cover from where the treeline begins and where it meets the road. It doesn't take me long to clear the small forest.

I reach the edge of the road and I am shocked back. Another frickin' barrier. I look at the invisible wall at an angle, trying to see what it is. My mind briskly comes up with an electrical barrier, due to the shock and the electrical pulses barely seen in the air. I am about to run at it again when I realize that it'll hurt like a bitch, and instead run left along the barrier. Hopefully there is an opening for other reinforcements that I can use to my advantage.

That was a huge mistake because sure enough there was a reinforcement entrance, but it's being used by the guards spilling through it. I turn to go the other way, but there are guards coming from there too.

Then, I look straight back at the castle and I sprint for it. My plan is to get reinforcements away from the entryway and then I can turn around and go through it and onto the road. There has to be nearly fifty guards chasing me.

I am running so fast that I don't notice the rock before me, and I fall and hurt my ankle. I don't know if I sprained it or not, but my adrenaline forces me not to care.

I stand up and notice that my bandage is soaked through and I am bleeding heavily. I continue to run, though, and I turn right, hoping that the doorway is open to the road. I am met by guards hurling through the trees. I am quick to turn more toward the castle, costing me precious steps, but keeping me from being overtaken by the tens of guards on my tail. I turn a little more to the right, toward the doorway. I am so close to the road that I can hear cars driving nearby, but it's quickly drowned out by my heartbeat; I feel it pounding in my eyes. My body is stopped when I notice the doorway gone, replaced by faint lights in the open air. Well shit.

I turn around to see all the men and women chasing me start to slow, knowing that I have nowhere to go. They finally stop, making a semi-circle around me, caging me in on the wall. I see some in the back start to move and I get nervous. My mind is racing with all the punishments that this idea could have.

James and Will break through the crowd and look dead at me. David is nowhere in sight, and that scares me even more. I put my fists up and close my eyes, maybe trying to block everything in front of me, and I feel a blast, of what I don't know. I open my eyes, to see guards thrown back to the ground. I stare at the other guards surrounding the ones that have fallen and see them start to back away. I look at my hands in shock. Did I just do that?

"That's not possible," I hear Will say in shock.

"You cowards, move in," David orders to my left.

I finally see him at the edge of the line, in uniform, leading the soldiers. All the soldiers start to move in, but some stay back. It seems that they are more scared of me than of David's wrath. I step away and my back starts to heat up, I must be getting closer to the wall.

I put my fists up, too quickly for the others to find cover, and they are blown back. I stare at my hands, not with a likeness, but with fear of what I have done. The guards get back up and some start to pull out weapons. Then, without even thinking, I raise my hands up and feel a calming warmth in front of me. One soldier shoots and I hear a hard ping, but I don't feel it. I look down at my body to see if I was hit and I see no blood but the blood at my side.

"Stop! Do not shoot! We are not here to kill her," James yells out, placing his hands in the air and stepping more in the open to allow all of the guards to get a good look at him. He is careful not to put his back to me.

I look at Will and see his shocked face. His mouth hangs open and his eyes are wide. James looks at me and his features harden as he plants his feet, a big sign of standing his ground.

This angers me.

After everything, he can't even show that he is a little bit scared. I can show him what fear is, but I don't know how. Until the shield.

It peels off of my body, like a second skin. It shifts and alters its form, until it is a tall rectangle, bent at the sides slightly towards me. It sparkles like it is just air but shimmers as if a solid, like water does with the sun. The colors of gold and red move within it's outline, as if marking the space it requires to advance.

My shield shifts as if on command. It moves forward toward James, a hint of fear shows in his eyes, and he slowly backs away. I look to the right of him to see all the warriors are still stunned from before, and I dash toward them.

Every inch of me is burning with adrenaline as I run for the other side of the wall. I don't reach my destination for I am met by another group of soldiers; they just can't seem to let me go. I back up against the wall again, heat from the electricity running the length of my body.

I feel a warmth in my hand, whether it is the wall or me, I feel it growing bigger and brighter with each passing moment. I look back to where James and Will once were, but James is gone and Will is walking toward me. I feel my hand push through and I fall hard onto the pavement of the road. I shake my head at my confusion and sprint away from the wall. I bolt down the road toward the most noise, but screams overpower any sound that I dream of.

"Alena. I think you might want to come back here. Before anyone gets hurt," James says.

I turn around slowly and look to see him holding sweet Emily with one hand, and the other has a knife to her throat. I stop dead in my tracks. I thought she might still be in New York with her sister. If she is here, then where is Lilly? More importantly, what is happening to her?

"You will come back to this side of the boundary line Alena, or she dies," James says, trying to project his voice to everyone. He is using this as a power show. He knows I will come too. It's the reason he chose her.

My weakness is my love, and I have shown it outright for everyone to see as I walk closer to the barrier.

I feel the warmth again coming from inside, and I can't stop it from pulling me back. It is literally dragging me away from the barrier. I punch at nothing, and it lets me go. I look back at my hands, and they have this certain glow to them. I try to shake off whatever thing is using me. I feel it back off as soon as I enter the other side of the wall.

I look up at James hoping to see him let Emily go, but he pushes the knife all the way up to her throat. I put my hands up, trying to make it look like I have given up. He sees me and takes the knife off of her throat by inches.

"You would kill a child? What kind of man has the guts to do that, but a monster," I ask, trying to project my voice as he did, and it works. The soldiers know exactly what I am getting at. If he is willing to kill a little child, what's stopping him from killing his own men?

I see eyes start to turn towards me, but not in anger, rather in disbelief. They know that I am right, but they are still trying to deny it. Others turn as a defense for James and start to block him from any deserters that might try to hurt him, and the rest come for me. My hands are up, but I will not give up. I will fight to escape, if not for me, then for Emily and her sister.

I sprint for Emily, sprinting in the complete opposite direction of the castle, who somehow was let go, toward Lilly if I had to guess. If they catch up to either one of us, they will use the one to get to the other.

I am sprinting faster than ever, the girls should never have been dragged into this, I shouldn't have been dragged into this. All I think about now is trying to protect others. The girls in the Valley, my friends and family at home, and my maids. They're all my responsibility to keep safe.

I finally catch up to Emily and grab her wrist and pull her back. I put up another shield-barrier of my own for the soldiers running after me to crash into.

Some have the brains to stand back and watch, but eventually, they get tired of watching and pull out guns and knives. I don't expect them to shoot, but my mind is proved ever so wrong when I hear the pitter patter of bullets spraying off my invisible layer.

It isn't long until I start to lose focus and I feel pings on my body, like bullets, but they don't make any marks. At first it feels like safety pins being pushed against my skin but it grows to rocks being thrown at ten miles an hour. It hurts as I clutch my chest and claw at where the spots of pain are.

I pull an arm up to push Emily behind me. The pain was getting almost unbearable when I felt myself start to lose all sense of control. I try to hold on, but it is no use, I'm losing control, I can feel my grasp on the power pull away. My adrenaline melts away and as a result, I feel the old wound that I tried to patch up in my room, start to open.

"Stop! You will kill her!" Will screams coming up in the middle of the crowd.

As soon as I see Will running up, I shield Emily as much as I can, holding my wound as I let go of the last bit of remaining barrier and fall.

The guns had slowed before, but not fast enough. All I hear is a single shot ring through the air before I feel my abdomen explode.

I scream out and my whole body stops fighting and I fall back onto Emily, as she catches me and lowers me to the ground. I feel the hot blood exiting my body and soaking my shirt and the grass around me.

Emily comes around to my side in tears just as Will slides to my other side with amazing speed. I look at him with pain and fear, hoping that he will do something to stop the pain.

"Make it stop-pp. Make the pa-i-n go-oo awa-y," I force out, trying to hold on to consciousness. His idea of making the pain go away is not the same as my idea of it, as he plunges his hand into the bullet hole and starts to dig for the bullet. I start to see stars and I look at Emily, her beautiful face is wet with tears.

She is looking at the blood and is shocked to a frozen statue. I lift my arm up to turn her face away from what feels like a giant hole in my stomach to look at my face, as a result making four lines of blood along her cheek. I smile when her eyes meet mine. For someone so young, she is so strong. I am surprised she isn't running away yet, if only to not see the blood.

I feel Will's hand exit my stomach as he pulls out a sharp, metal bullet covered in metallic, red blood. I feel the tears burst from my eyes as he presses his hands onto the wound and pushes down. I understand he is trying to keep the blood in, but can't he be a bit more gentle?

As soon as that thought crosses my mind, I see James out of the corner of my eye, running up to us. Frantic, he shoves all the guards aside as he bends down next to my head.

I look back to Emily to find her backing away. I go to reach for her, but James is already there pulling her back over to me, showing her that he is not mad. She takes the hand that reached out for her, and holds it tight, but always looks at me to make sure it doesn't hurt me.

To be honest, the amount of pressure she is placing on my hand, hurts a lot. But I am careful not to show any pain. The stars return to my eyes as I reach for my side, where I tried to patch myself up. James notices and motions to Will.

"Holy shit! James you need to take off the old bandages and take off your shirt. I want you to place your shirt on it, and apply enough pressure to stop the bleeding," Will says nodding his head towards James' shirt.

James does as he is instructed, takes off his shirt, and applies pressure to my wound. I scream through my clenched teeth and squeeze Emily's hand. I know she doesn't mind when I do it, by the look on her face. I can hear the guards moving around, but I am not quite sure what they are doing.

"The blood won't stop spilling, what should I do?" James says. I can hear the panic in his voice, and that scares me.

If James of all people is scared, then I should be deathly afraid. I start to feel the pain more and more every second. Then, the warmth starts to come back. It gets closer and closer till I can't stop it.

"Move!" I scream, just as it blows them away from me. I start to scream even more. I can feel the blood pouring out of me. The sudden blast of power sends my nerves into a frenzy. I can feel my entire body tingling. Will and James are back to trying to hold the blood in.

I try to speak, "I am sorry, I don't know what's happening."

"I know. James, hold the wounds. It may hurt her, but hold them as hard as you can," Will says sadly smiling at me. That's when he moves to take my head, James takes over holding blood in from both openings, and starts to chant. I feel that warmth coming back, I try to fight it off.

"James. It is coming back," I force out, short of breath.

"I know. Stay strong. Emily come back over here, she needs you," James says, giving Emily a nervous smile.

She takes my hand again as I hear Will's chants getting louder. I try to fight the comforting warmth, and I start to question myself why I am fighting. All I can come up with is that it is hurting me.

I try to focus on slowing down my breaths, because right now I am panting like a dog in summer. I keep feeling the strange warmth fighting and fighting to come back out. I try over and over again to keep it at bay, I can feel it getting stronger. The more I fight, the more pain I put on myself. Not nearly as much as when the warmth comes out to attack Will and James, but enough to make it hurt.

"Start talking to her, James. Distract her," Will says, sensing my pain.

"Okay." James pauses, thinking of what to say. "Do you remember that time when you were at school and you were talking to a friend. That girl, Sapphire, came up and started making fun of your friend's outfit. And you turned to her and said, 'You may be beautiful on the outside, but no beauty shines more than that of a heart. Something you don't have.' You smiled as she walked away, and took your friend's hand and said to her, 'You will always be beautiful. Don't let anyone make you believe differently.' You and her laughed and smiled as you walked to class after that. You were so confident the rest of the day. At lunch, everyone stared at you. They had all heard what you did and were impressed. I don't think just anyone would do that. That's what I found so fascinating about you. Even if you hurt yourself by sticking up for your friend, you still decided to help."

I smile at that. I remember that day clearly. Ava was having a bad day, and Sapphire heard and had wanted to make it worse. Usually I never talk to Sapphire. There really is no use talking to her since she won't stop until she 'wins'. That time, I felt like I had to say something.

Ava had come to school with tears in her eyes. Her father, Brad, had come home early that morning, drunk and angry. He had lost his job and was taking it all out on Ava. Her mother, Jennifer, wasn't there to protect her like she often did. What her father did was too hard for her to talk about. All she had told me was that her father came home drunk again. It wasn't a huge surprise to me.

Her father was an alcoholic in rehab. He had been sober for a year, but that morning was when he broke. I guess my anger towards Brad had come out at Sapphire. Not that she didn't deserve it, but she certainly hadn't expected it. Sapphire was a brat, and she deserved what I told her.

Will's chanting brought me out of that distant memory. He just kept getting louder and louder and the strange, but comforting, warmth was growing more intense with each word that Will said. I felt like I was losing control, but maybe that was the result of the memory taking me out of focus.

I looked up at James, and for once, I saw him smile. Of course, I have seen him *smile* before, but not like that—not at me. Especially not *for* me. It is unusual, but it definitely calms me.

At least, before Will started squeezing my head harder than he had been before. That's when I wanted to fight back. I didn't like the pain of, first my side, then being shot, and now being squeezed on the head. I start to fight back, which makes James push down harder on my wounds, making me scream out in pain, and making Will start to lose his grip on my mind or whatever he was doing.

My head is spinning like crazy, and all I can hear in the back of my head is a voice saying *Let me through.* The pain is getting unbearable, and I can't take it any longer, so I listen and let the voice through.

The second I let it through, everyone is thrown back. I don't want Emily to be thrown back, but she isn't thrown as far as the others. Guards, soldiers, Will, and James are laying fifteen feet away from where they once stood.

The warmth is still pouring out of me, like a wave. It doesn't feel solid, or anything physical; more like something that you can't see, but you know is there. All I feel is this warmth, and it won't stop. All the while, I am thinking of my anger and how scared I am when Will and James are not being pushed away.

I could maybe ask the warmth to stay longer and run, but that's only if it stayed, not to mention the fact that I can barely keep conscious, let alone run. I feel the warmth pouring out of me start to slow, as my hope of escaping gives way.

I look at the sky before the warmth completely leaves and see a cloud that resembles my mother's face, floating in a sea of blue. My longing for her makes me smile.

Maybe this is God letting me see her, one last time. Out of the corner of my eyes I see everyone standing and running back to me. All this time I've been trying to stay awake, but I can't hold on, so I decide to let go. This way I won't feel the pain.

I am pushed back by a force I cannot see, only feel. It is powerful and strong. It holds me down with the strength of a thousand men. I barely have the strength to look at my brother and the soldiers lying scattered around me. My ears are ringing loudly, but her screams are louder.

I look at Alena; her back is arched, and she is screaming out in pain. I can hear her cries, I can see her blood on my hands, and I can feel her pain. Emily, lying a few feet away, looks at her with tears. She can't move either.

Whatever is holding all of us down is not only powerful and strong but is trying very hard to protect Alena. I almost think that it is trying to help her, but then why is it hurting her? Maybe it is the brunt force of it, but I think it is just trying to hurt us.

It seems as if Alena acts as a sort of gateway. Whatever Will was trying to spell away, certainly does not want to leave. I watch Alena and see blood pouring from her body. I see her wounds tear open a bit wider, allowing more and more blood to gush out.

Her cries of pain start to slow, as does the pressure keeping me down. I try to stand up, but the pressure is still too strong. I look back up as the pressure continues to lessen to see Alena's back start to straighten out as she lies flat back on the ground.

Eventually, the pressure completely stops, and I see her eyes open. She stares at the sky and smiles as tears roll down her face. I start to run to her, seeing the giant puddle of blood she now lies in.

As soon as I reach her, her eyes close and her body is limp. I sink to my knees and gather my strength as I place my fingers on her neck, just below the jaw line, and feel for a pulse. I breathe a sigh of relief as I sense one, but not a strong one.

I gather her up in my arms and stand to bring her back to the castle. All I can think about is getting her to the doctor.

Our doctor is a highly trained surgeon, doctor, and therapeutic. We had kidnapped him years ago when one of my men had been hurt badly. We haven't let him leave yet. After a while he requested to have his family with him, and now his immediate family stays here with him. The treatment that is given to them is better than any normal kidnappers would do. They have a big place to run around, and the work we give for them to do is like any other. Except, of course, all of it is illegal, but they really have no choice.

I feel my arms being soaked in her blood as I reach the doors of the castle, and the guards are quick to open it. The sight of me is probably horrendous. I can feel the blood on my hands, soaking my shirtless chest, and probably a little on my face. The anger and fear are probably being plainly shown as well.

I turn right to go up the stairs to the doctor's quarters. He lives in the East wing of the castle with his family.

I am running so quickly that I have to look down at my feet to make sure I don't trip and fall. I barely have time to stop as I almost walk right past the doctor's quarters. I yell at the guards to open the doors for me.

As soon as the doors open, I start yelling out for Joe, the doctor, to get out here. I see his two children come out of the living room and run back in to get their father. I see him walk out in a faded green t-shirt and blue jeans.

He takes one look at Alena and immediately bolts for his closet, and changes into his scrubs. Joe then walks back out and motions for me to follow him out the door. He takes us to an operating room just down the hall.

I remember I had bought the equipment years ago for him to use when my men got hurt. I had forgotten it was still here.

He motions for me to place Alena on the operation table. I was thinking that he would just put some stitches in and call it good, but when I start to place her down to get a closer look, I realize how wrong I was. Her injuries were much worse than I originally thought.

"What happened?" Joe asks as he scurries around the operating room, grabbing materials.

"She has a cut on her side, from what, I don't know. She has a gunshot in her abdomen. My brother took the bullet out, but we were not able to stop the bleeding," I say, carefully lying her down onto the table.

Joe finally comes to the operating table and takes a look at her wounds.

"That bullet hole is bigger than an average one."

"Something was happening that tore her wounds open bigger. I don't know what it was," I say, looking at Alena's face. The color is draining from it fast. Her lips have turned a light purplish-blue.

"Blood lost?" Joe asks, picking up sears and ripping apart her blood soaked shirt. Her skin on her middle is the same as her face, pale, and the only color on it is the blood plastered to her stomach, and the white bone showing at her side from who knows what.

"I don't know how much, two to three pints, maybe more," I respond.

"Before she passed out, was there any abnormal behavior? Any rapid breathing, sweaty skin, confusion?" Joe asks as he reaches for alcohol and surgical pads.

"Rapid breathing, she did have some confusion about something right before she passed out. She had sweaty palms, and she is obviously pale," I say gesturing toward her skin.

He nods and gets to work. He starts by taking a syringe with a fluid in it and injects it into her. I look on with concern.

"It is a sedative, just in case she wakes up. This will keep her from being in any pain, making her still, so I may do my work with no interruptions," Joe says sensing my unease.

"Sorry I don't mean how to tell you how to do your job—just nervous," I say, looking back to Alena's face. Her paleness and blood aside, she looks peaceful. I don't know why, but I feel overprotective.

I shouldn't care about what happens to her, after what her family has done to mine. For some reason, I have this giant urge to protect her.

Joe moves to cleaning the wounds, pouring alcohol onto the sterile pads and gently dabbing them on her wounds. He goes through four pads, all full of blood, before he continues on to stitching up her bullet wound. It takes six stitches until he finally closes it up with a knot. He moves around the table to her side. Before he goes onto stitching up the side, he examines her wound closely. He looks at it with such curiosity and then moves to get a camera, sitting on a table to the left of him. He takes a picture of her side. After he sets the camera back to its original place, he turns to me.

"She is bleeding internally, but I can fix it up no problem. I need to be sure that I am allowed to do this, and my family will not be hurt for it," Joe says to me.

All I say is, "Do what you must."

"I need your blood," Joe states.

"Why?"

Joe sighs his annoyance at my question but answers anyway, "You have the blood type of O- which makes you a universal donor. Judging by the shallowness of her breathing and the blood loss that you described, she wouldn't make it through surgery. Either she gets blood or she dies. You pick."

I yank up my sleeve with severity, exposing my veins to the doctor, already holding a transfusion needle in his hand. I look away from the needle, but not before I see the length of it. I absolutely despise needles. I look back to the scene when I feel the tape secure the needle in place, blood already flowing from my veins to hers.

After a minute has passed, Joe goes and cuts open the side wound even more, making a straight line with the wound in the middle. He makes quick work of closing the wound, stitching up the internal bleeding, and cleaning up the blood. I am now grateful that Joe put her to sleep. I can't imagine what this would feel like. Joe throws the stitching needle onto the surgical tray, along with the bloody cloths used to clean up the blood.

It takes double the amount of stitches than it did for the bullet hole. Not only does that scare me, but his sudden interest in the wound does as well.

He finishes sewing up the wounds leaking blood, and moves to cleaning up the blood plastered to her stomach and face. He finishes just as Will walks in.

"Do not throw away that blood yet. I want it. Put it in a testing tube and keep it cool. Don't let anything come into contact with it until I come back tomorrow to test it," He says coming up to stand beside me.

"Of course, sir. I will be on that right after I finish up with her," Joe says, not skipping a beat or looking up from removing the needle in my arm, and placing a cotton ball with tape over the opening.

"What is the blood for Will?" I ask.

He looks more closely at her face as he says, "I have a feeling our family and hers goes back further than our parents. Allow her to rest, and don't give her any grief about what happened. Act as if it wasn't her fault. If you have to make it sound like it was you that pushed her over, do it. Whatever you do, do not make her feel scared. Just trust me."

"Of course, brother."

Joe finishes cleaning up everything and starts to harvest her blood in testing tubes, exactly as Will instructed.

"She is free to go. The wounds are still tender, and the stitches are able to tear easily. Don't let her move too fast or too far. She is going to be in a lot of pain so," he hands me some pills. "Give her these if you find she needs any. Call me when she wakes. Just a simple checkup and that's all."

"Sounds good. I will call you when she does."

I pick her up, and gently carry her to her bedroom. As soon as the doors open, I see Emily crying on the couch. She quickly stands up and wipes her tears away. I nod my head toward the bed, and she goes to pull the covers back so I can set Alena down. Emily covers her with blankets and sits on the bed and grabs her hand.

"Is she alright? Will she be ok?" Emily asks, rapidly firing off questions.

"Emily, relax. She is fine. A few stitches. Doctor said to keep her calm. No shouting at her. Just make sure she doesn't move too much. Act as if everything was not her fault. Keep her in the dark as much as possible. We just need to let her rest. Go get your sister and take the rest of the time off. When she wakes up you will be one of the first I call. I will watch over her, make sure she is okay."

"Thank you, James. I appreciate it," she kisses Alena's pale, pasty forehead and leaves.

I sit on the bed beside Alena. I go to hold the same hand that Emily had just let go. Pulling back the blankets, I look at her bandages, just to be sure she hasn't bled through them. I reach up to push back a piece of hair that was out of place.

"For one so fragile, you are an immense handful."

Chapter 7

I open my eyes and find I'm back in my bedroom, and James is sitting beside my bed in a chair, holding my hand.

Noticing my eyes opening he says, "Hey, how are you feeling? Are you in any pain?"

He drops my hand immediately and struggles to find something to do with them. He settles on running his hands through his mess of hair.

"What happened?" I rasp, trying to sit up. I quickly figure out what a mistake that is. My head instantly starts spinning, and pain spikes in my stomach and side. James gently lies me back down, making sure to push on my shoulders and not my stomach.

I notice the move of him as he stops me, exhaustion clearly estranging him. I notice the bags under his eyes and a cotton ball over the front of his elbow.

"I wouldn't do that. You lost a lot of blood, and you have had quite a bit of stitches put in. You're going to have to take it easy for a couple of weeks," James says as he finishes making sure I won't move. "What do you remember?"

"Not much. I remember running, and then fighting with soldiers and you and your brothers. Then I remember being on the road and turning around to see Emily and you. I remember walking back and running again. The entire time feeling this… warmth I guess is the only way to describe it. Then, oh my gosh, I was shot! How am I alive?" I say, reaching for my stomach to feel the bullet wound. It is bigger than I imagined. Then again, the amount of fabric covering it is probably exaggerating how big the hole actually is.

Noticing me reaching for my wounds, James takes my hand, that is feeling over the wound, and brings it toward himself.

"I promise everything is fine. Do you remember anything else?" James asks with interest.

"Um, I remember the warmth coming back, and then I remember everyone being thrown back. The pain was unbearable. It felt like every part of my body was electrified, almost as if it was on fire. It felt like it went on forever, and then I remember thinking that I wasn't going to be able to hold on any longer. Then the pain stopped, and I was looking up at the clouds and saw my mother's face. Other than that, all I remember is blacking out. Did anything happen after that beside the stitches?" I ask with concern, my eyes flickering to the cotton ball on his arm.

A flush races across his cheeks, "I just had to give you some blood."

"Oh," my own cheeks heat up.

He finishes answering my question, "No, nothing that was major other than the blood clean up and yelling at the person that shot you."

He turns to the doors, "Boys! Can you please fetch Joe, Will, Emily and Lilly? Be sure to keep Lilly out for the first bit. I want to make sure Alena is alright first."

Afterwards I hear the scurrying of feet. I look to the bathroom to see if there are any remnants of the blood from my first injury, but see nothing from my point of view.

"How long have I been asleep for?"

"Not long. Only a day, and that is a very short amount considering you lost over thirty percent of your blood. Not to worry, love, you just need to rest, and it will come back." James says, right as a man with a doctor's jacket strides right toward the bed and James moves aside, letting go of my hand in the process.

The doctor, Joe, is a tall and slim man with dirty blonde hair and a goatee. He looks to be around fifty, and he has one of those 'everything is okay' smiles. I look up at him with worry—whatever he is here for can't be good. He notices my unease and puts his bare hands up, showing he has nothing to hide or anything of danger on him.

"Relax. I got nothing on me. I am just here to make sure you're not in any pain and to check to see if you have bled through your bandages yet."

He turns his words to James, while rummaging in his medical bag that he brought with, "Have you noticed anything unusual since she woke up?"

"Not much. Only that she gets short of breath and can't move more than a few inches. Her usual instincts still seem to be intact," James says, filling the doctor in on everything.

"Are you in any pain, dear? Anything seem off? Are you in any discomfort?" Firing off questions, Joe turns to me.

"I am really sore, and I have some pain. Not in any discomfort. But I can't seem to remember much from yesterday. Like how everything started and what happened in between. The only thing I clearly remember is the pain," I state, answering his questions.

"Okay. The missing memory may or may not come back, depending on how much blood you had in your system then. Your body is still in a little bit of shock, so I think that is playing a part as well. Your pain may worsen, so don't be afraid to ask for some pain meds. Obviously, we are not going to give you too many." He turns to his bag and finally pulls out a little flashlight. "I am going to shine this in your eyes to see your reflexes."

With that he does what he explained. The light is really bright and the first time it hits my eyes I flinch away. Joe gently holds my eyelids open so I don't move. After he finishes with that he turns back to his bag and puts his flashlight away.

"I am just going to put a little bit of pressure around your wounds, you tell me right away if you feel any pain."

He goes to press down right above my bullet wound. Will walks in as Joe begins to move more toward the wound.

"How is she?" Will asks.

"Fine. In a lot of pain but that's normal. Waiting to see what else," James answers.

I grind my teeth as he places his fingers right on the edge of the bandages, only a few inches from the hole.

"Right there. That hurts," I grind out.

"Alright, I am going onto your side."

Joe moves his fingers closer to my side wound. I continue to hear Will and James murmur things to each other about my mental and physical health, as Joe continues to move closer to me putting me in even more pain.

I can't quite hear what those two are saying, but as soon as I start to hear them talk a little louder I say, "Okay, we are done here. That is really pushing my pain level too high."

He is a couple of inches away from where I will be crying. Joe immediately backs off at my version of stopping him. Will and James turn back around, from where they were facing the door, to see what had happened. Once they come to the conclusion that everything is fine, they don't turn around and continue to listen in for the rest of the check-up with the doctor.

"Alright. I am done with the pain measurements. Now, my last question is, how did you get that wound on your side?" Joe asks, pointing to my side.

To be honest, my memory is a little blurry, but I can still remember bits and pieces of what happened.

"I don't remember all of the details, but what I do know is I was trying to get out of the *thing* by hitting the wall repeatedly. So much that I kept being thrown back, and then there was something sharp on the floor that tore open my side. I also remember lying on the couch and trying to relax. Then I started laughing about how much of a pain it would be to get the blood out of the fabric. I thought that even if I was in there, I could still manage to annoy James," I finish the last part off and look over to see James walking towards the couch.

Obviously, they didn't see the blood. James inspects the couch for a little bit and then looks back at me and frowns. However much blood I allowed to leak into the couch, it definitely did some damage, and from his shrunken shape, the couch must have been expensive.

"That is 3,000 down the drain. Thank you, Alena! When you are healed, we are going to have a repeat of your first night," James says, walking up to my side again with an annoyed frown on his face.

And just like that the warmth in his eyes, that I woke up to, is gone.

"I am kind of sorry, looking back on it. When I first sat on it, I just wanted to rest, but when I noticed the blood was leaking, I was going to move. The pain was worse when I started to move so I just stayed. I only thought of making you mad after a few minutes had passed," I say to him.

All of it was true, my only regret is that I didn't let more blood seep into the velvet couch. It's not that I want to be mean, it's just that I feel like I got a little payback after everything he has done to me. Not to mention, everything he will do to me. The cold of his stare settles back into my bones.

Joe takes out a clipboard and then turns to James and says, "Sorry about the couch, but I am finished with everything. Her pain levels are high, which is normal with that amount of blood loss, but whatever opened up her wounds more did some serious damage. Her reflexes are exceedingly slow, which is also the result of that blood loss. Her side wound is not as serious as the bullet wound, but the side wound made up 20% of the blood loss. Her memories are still a little fuzzy and they may come back in time, they may not. Her body is going to feel very lethargic and sore, so I am going to give her some blood bags for a day or two and some fluids—just some water, nothing major. If she has any pain, of course, give her that pain medication, but if it gets to the point where it is unbearable, then call me down. I do suggest that someone is always in here. She should not be yelling but make sure she is exercising her voice. Other than that, she is fine. I will go and get the blood and water."

Joe turns back at me with a smile after telling James my status, then heads to his room.

After Joe closes the door I ask, "Is the blood really necessary?"

"If you want to get better sooner, then yes," James says, coming back to sit next to me, frustration lacing his movements.

"Well what if I don't want to get better?" The longer I stay in bed, the less time he can hurt me.

"Alena, James can hurt you whenever, but don't think that he is not hurting you for one second, because you *are* hurt. He just knows that it was not your fault. You were not yourself and you had no control," Will says, clearly invading my privacy.

"Thanks for that, Will," I growl at the infiltration, but I change my mood. "It's just that the thought of other people needing the blood more than me, and giving it to me, seems wasteful."

"It's not wasteful, and besides it is for people in this estate only. We have a secret stash," James states, just as the doors are thrown in and Emily comes barreling through the room.

"Emily..." James tries to stop her, but she comes right for me and embraces me in a hug.

"Hey! Look I am fine, I am alright," I try to give her a reason to relax, but that just makes her hug even harder.

"I am so glad you are okay! I got so nervous, there was so much blood, and you were so pale. And you were screaming and—"

"Emily! Look at me! I am *fine*," I exaggerate the *fine* part a lot to get the point across.

She releases me from the air-killing hug, and goes on, "Lilly is outside waiting for you. I didn't tell her much other than you got hurt. She was worried a great deal too. She wasn't crying too much at least. But she really wants to see you!"

"Alright well let her come in then. There is no point in making her wait outside," I say, letting my arms fly around for emphasis.

As soon as Lilly hears this, she sprints through the doors and crushes my stomach. I try not to yelp out in pain, but Emily pulls her off before I do.

"Remember what I told you! She got hurt on the stomach, you are not to touch there," Emily says, scolding her sister.

Lilly just comes right back to hugging my head this time. She gets uncomfortable and moves to sit on the pillow above my head and continues to hug my head.

"Is this okay?" She asks Emily.

Emily shrugs her shoulders in defeat. Lilly can always find a loophole in any command. James, to his credit, is still holding in yelling at Lilly, even with red growing in his face, he's clearly vexed.

"How are you feeling, Alena? Emily said that you got in an accident and that you were hurt! I was so scared for you!" Lilly says loudly. Clearly, she wasn't told that my ears were okay.

"I told you that she was hurt on the stomach, that doesn't mean the ears, Lilly," Emily says with a bit of laughter in her eyes. I don't blame her. I may have been the one with the actual pain, but I can't imagine what it was like watching me.

"I am alright, Lilly. Just a little sore." That wasn't all of the truth.

But I am not going to tell a 9-year-old that I am in so much pain that I want to crawl out of my own skin. No, I will let her believe that it was nothing more than a simple accident that will heal in a week's time.

To be honest, I don't even know how long it will take to heal, but I know it won't take just a week, not even to cover the wounds. Unless the brothers have some magical potion that will magically heal me in a day—not gonna happen. The only thing that I know can do that is something I will not do.

James's blood may heal, but it makes invisible scars of pain and disappointment, and not in him, but in myself for allowing such a thing to happen. I want to fight, but if I couldn't do it before, how could I now? I can't use the girls; I shouldn't put them in danger. If I could just make some allies…

"Will, I want you to release your Dawns," I blurt out, my words finishing my thoughts for me.

Will and James look at me, astonished, "Why in the world would I allow that?"

"Because clearly you want to have people watching me, if only so what has happened doesn't happen again. James is the one who said that I am not going to be able to get out of bed for a while, and I am sure the girls would appreciate you more for it," I finish trying to think out the rest of my plan.

"That is a lot of people to just let go, and how do you know about them anyway?"

"Girls, why don't you go downstairs to the kitchen and get something to eat for yourselves. Will, Alena, and I need to have a grownup talk," James says, trying to make sure Emily and Lilly won't try to figure out what this all means.

Lilly probably won't, but Emily certainly will. She is smart and knows what to do and when to do it.

The girls close the doors, and Will walks towards me. The face that I thought would be filled with rage, turns out to be filled with curiosity. Then again, I can never really tell with Will what his emotions will be until he lets me know. I try to block off my mind so he can't see my plan. If this works, my promise to them would be fulfilled. Although it may not be entirely fulfilled, at least I have half of the work done.

"I will ask again: how do you know of my Dawns?"

"I saw them in the "Valley". That is what they call it. Julianna, Nora, Olivia, Megan, Lucy, Isabella, Hannah, and Katia. Along with all of David's as well, and of course none of James', but then again, they said I was his first and that you have been talking about me for awhile. I guess I should be flattered to be talked about. Lovely girls too, beautiful, even with the dried blood on their skin and hair and their torn clothes. Though I can't say anything about their hands, too much blood, dirt and cuts to tell what they may have looked like," I stop talking, realizing that I am babbling. I always babble when I am trying to hide something.

"And they told you all of this?" Will asked.

"Don't see why they wouldn't. I was—*am*—just as innocent as them. Not to mention, I haven't given them any reason not to trust me. They are alone and hurt. The only thing that I think keeps them sane is each other. Me showing up just helped them more so, but that doesn't mean you should put more in," I make sure to get my point across as I finish.

Will doesn't respond immediately. I watch his face as the calculations and scenarios run through his head. I even now cannot tell whether or not he is angered by this. After a few minutes the tensions give way.

"Fine. But I need to keep Nora though, I need her for her studies," Will says, finding nothing wrong with my request. "Although, I am not letting them all have their own rooms."

"That's okay, they can stay here. They would probably prefer that anyway," I say, fixing the one problem that he came up with.

"Why do you want them in here?" James asks, coming up from behind Will.

"Because I made a promise, and I intend to keep it. Not to mention, I am sure you have better things to do than sit in here and babysit me. The girls can, and I am certainly not moving so you don't have to worry about me running again, and I prefer not to be shot again. It is extremely painful, let me tell you," I finish, seeing both of them look satisfied and curious as to what type of promise I made, even though the promise is relatively easy to guess.

"I will send the girls in then. Remember, if any of them even think about running or trying to get you out, I will turn them back into Dawns forever, and you won't be able to make another deal to break that. Understood, Alena?" Wills yells over his shoulder as he turns to go.

"Yes!" I reply, right as Will shuts the door behind him.

"You are in a rather odd mood. Waking up with no attitude and now trying to make my life easier on me. What is fabricating up in that mind of yours, I wonder?" James goes on, coming to sit next to my side again. The coldness in his eyes lessen with no one here, but the kindness from before doesn't fully return.

"Nothing. Like I said, I am just keeping a promise. Besides, I know you don't want to sit here with me anyways," I say, breathing a sigh.

"Just because you *think* that I don't want to sit here, doesn't mean I don't want to, love. Watching you sleep and whine about how you can't move is entertaining."

"That's another reason why you should go." I continue, "I need to think about what I am missing at home and how I will make up for it when I get back."

"If you ever go back," changing his expression, James looks at me with concern and interest.

"What now?" I ask, wanting to know what he is thinking.

"I find it interesting that you still have it. By now I would think that you would have given up," he goes on.

"What do you think I should have lost?" I ask, still trying to place his look.

"Hope."

She lies among the many blankets I had brought in for her. Alena's expression when she woke up was warming, and inviting.

Her confusion at first might have been it, but she seemed quite afraid of something. That's when I realized that she actually didn't want to hurt my troops or me. She didn't know or have any control. That must be what's clouding her hatred for me, her fear of herself.

To be honest, I am not sure what to believe anymore. Will said to keep acting like she had done nothing wrong, but hadn't she? She had run before whatever took over her, or had it already been inside of her? The other problem was that she was smart, too smart for her own good. Eventually it was going to get her in trouble. I mean she is already sitting in bed with a bullet hole in her stomach.

In all honesty, I am surprised that she isn't dead yet. From the amount of blood loss, and how close the bullet came to vital organs, she should be dead. Not to mention, she had some internal bleeding as well. Yet, no matter how crazy and carefree she is, she still has a way of floating right on through, but not without consequences.

Somehow, I feel like I have known her all my life, or maybe that is just my yearning side. To be her friend. When I was younger, I was all over the place. I could never sit still, and I loved playing tag with the few friends that I had. Though, I never had the same friend for longer than two months.

Father always had new friends filing in and out, and most of those friends had children that I would play with, when I wasn't being taught by my private tutors. As soon as I got close to any of the kids, they would be taken away, because father's friends always left.

The only close friends that I was able to hold onto were my brothers. Even then, my father kept my brothers busy so we wouldn't spend too much time together. Will, he kept him studying, and David he kept training for his own personal army. Me? He trained me to run the company, and he twisted me up inside. All my life he made me like him, cruel and merciless.

My mother, on the other hand, was kind and loving. My brothers and I would always try to spend time with her. Mother never was involved in clan business, which was part of her innocence.

The month prior to their deaths, father started training mother into the family business. She trained to fight and took on the role of learning the ways of the clan; all of the secrets, even the ones that father didn't tell me. She became a hard woman, but she always tried to be the best for us.

Despite her efforts, my brothers and I could tell she had changed. Mother was loyal to my father, too loyal for her own good. It's what led her to fight by Edward's side, and what led her to die by his side.

I never much cared for Edward, my father. He beat me constantly, but I miss my mother day in and day out. Mother's love is what kept me sane throughout all the beatings and teachings.

I always wondered how my parents ended up together—they were polar opposites. Father was cruel, and Mother was kind. Maybe that made them the perfect contrast, but I have no idea how they survived with each other.

I think that is partly why I envy Alena. She adores both of her parents, and she was loved by both her parents. At least, until her father died. The announcement of her father's death came shortly after the announcement of my own parent's death.

My clan rejoiced. The person who killed my parents had died and his debt repaid with his life. At first, I had pitied Alena, but then I remembered that you are bound and are a part of your family's actions no matter how innocent you are.

The saying that you are bound by blood is true. Alena might not have seen or helped her mother in any way when she killed my parents, but it's her mother. No matter how far you run, everything your family does defines you.

That's why all of the other clans are scared of my own, my father made a legacy that frightens everyone. The face of his brutality and cruelness is the face of the clan. Just as Alena's mother is a murderer, it makes Alena a murderer. She can choose to either use it to her advantage or drown in it. After everything her mother has done, I am surprised that she still has that hope. Or, maybe, she doesn't have any idea of what kind of person her mother is.

Her compassion is unbearable at times, but that is also another thing that I envy about her. Alena's undying compassion is suffocating me so much that I just want to give up and take it, drown in it. It makes me angry that I haven't broken her yet, but if I continue to do what I have been, I can manipulate her into what I want. Will was right, the more I try to control her, the more she is retaliating.

"I find it interesting that you still have it. By now I would think that you would have given up," I go on.

"What do you think I should have lost?" She asks with curiosity.

"Hope."

"It's hard to give up hope, when I know that it is always there," Alena says with perfect calm, no sense of hurt or retaliation in her voice.

"Well as much as I would like to keep talking about this, I am afraid that it's time for the blood and water," James says, standing as the doors open to reveal Joe, with bags of red and almost clear liquid.

She looks at me with irritation, "Are you sure this is necessary?"

"If you don't want to be in bed for the next month then yes," Joe answers for me.

Along with him, Joe brought a holder for the fluids, a needle, clean bandages and medical tape. He goes into the kitchen and returns with two of the 10 bags he had before. Joe goes and hangs up the bag on the hanger that he had left beside Alena's bed, and takes out the needle and medical tape.

"I hate needles. Something you should know if you really learned that much about me," Alena looks at me.

"Yes, but I am sure you will thank me later," I reply to her with a smirk. "It won't hurt that much. Just think of the ice cream you would get."

"If I get ice cream, I won't struggle," she says with a pointed smile.

"Nice try, I am not your mother and you are almost an adult. Besides, if you really want to struggle, I will just bring in those guards again," I reply with an equal smile.

"You mean those guards that I took out earlier and almost escaped?"

"Yes. Those guards that I have running laps around the castle. I am sure that they would be happy to return the favor that you so graciously gave."

She just smiles at that.

Alena stays still as Joe places the needle into her arm. The only show of pain is her face scrunching up. As soon as the needle is in place, he secures it with the medical tape, and connects a tube to the needle. The tube is small and has a little hole at the end in which Joe inserts a syringe that he pulled from his pocket.

"This is going to taste a bit metallic, but it is just a cleaning for the tube," Joe says, already knowing that Alena was going to object.

She relaxes as Joe pushes down on the end of the syringe and the liquid goes through the syringe. Afterward, he plugs together the tube connected to her arm and the tube connected to the water. He turns a nozzle up where the bag connects to the tube, and the water trickles down into her body. Joe turns to me and motions for me to go to Alena's kitchen and dining area.

"I just need to show him where the blood and water is being stored," Joe says to Alena before we enter the dining area.

As soon as we are out of ear shot he takes out a black box from his jacket. The box has a mini padlock on it and looks just like any other medical box, except this one looks more secure.

"I realize that Alena is someone who fights. If, in any case, she gets out of hand, asks too many questions, or tries to run, take out one of these syringes and just shoot her with it. It doesn't matter where you hit her, as long as you allow the liquid to enter her body, she will be out in a few seconds. I will try to bring in more, but just be cautious about how much you use. Also, when you are injecting it, make sure someone is there to catch her so that she doesn't open up her wounds again. If you do use one of the syringes, I will bring in a bag of the sedative to keep her down. Otherwise, she is all set," Joe says, making sure to keep his voice low.

"Thank you, Joe. I appreciate it."

"Don't mention it."

With that, Joe goes back into the bedroom, says goodbye to Alena, and takes his leave.

I walk back into the bedroom and go to Alena.

"I have to go, but the girls should be here soon. I will be posting more guards outside your door, so don't even think about trying to escape with them." Making sure Alena understood that she wasn't going anywhere.

"That worked out so well last time." She comes back with another insult.

"You can't keep using that against me because I am fixing that problem that should never have happened. Not to mention, you can barely sit up, let alone stand, and you definitely can't fight," I say, matching her insult with my own. "I would love to stick around here and watch you complain, but alas I have things to do."

"Here I was thinking that you would love to sit here and stare at me all day. It doesn't matter, the girls will keep me company," she says, her face turning into a sheepish smile.

"Have a good rest of your day, Alena," I say, returning her look.

"Goodbye James," she says as I go out the doors.

James left 20 minutes ago, in which time I sat there thinking about him. James was so concerned for me and wanted to make sure I was well cared for. Not to mention, his funny and kind demeanor that made me feel a little less worried.

I know I shouldn't be feeling this way, especially since he is the one that got me in this mess in the first place. As hard as it is for me to admit it, I feel drawn to James. I don't know why or how but I just do. Other than the fact that he did kidnap me, he seems to be a nice fluffy bear underneath all that heavy iron armor.

All of Will's Dawns, except for Nora, arrive in my room. They all come in sprinting for my bed. When I yell out in pain, they back off and that is when I see the tears in their eyes.

To my relief, the tears are of joy. They all start speaking at once. The girls tell me how Will had called them all together in the same study that I had woken up in after I had broken out of the "valley," and he had released them all. They continue to go on to say that they didn't have to break through the mirror like I did. Instead, the mirror turned into a portal. They jumped through it, returning them to their bodies in the real world. They also tell me that Will instructed them to take care of me and obviously had threats set out if they didn't comply.

Katia and Hannah later told me that after I had broken free of the "valley," all the other girls had tried to break through their own mirrors, but had failed. Their guess was that they had been there for so long that their "opposites" had too strong of a hold on them.

They all took their positions sitting on the bed, trying their best not to squish me too much, all the while keeping me a part of their circle. We talk about every experience we had, and so much more. It starts with everyone just being happy to have their bodies back, to being disgusted so much that they want to shower just to feel even a little clean.

While each one takes their turns, the others keep me company, telling me more about their lives before. Some girls had terrible home lives, but admit that they would give anything to go back. Also, adding their thanks for getting them out with each passing minute. After all of the girls finish showering, and I have Emily and Lilly come in to get them clothes from my closet, everyone sits down, including Emily and Lilly, as I tell the story of the events.

I start from the play, to breaking free, to being shot, to Joe and his weird conversation with James. The whole time, everyone listens intently, crying, laughing and talking about how I had to go back to the part regarding me beating the guards.

Our conversations last long into the night, and when the guards come in to give them pillows and blankets, the girls turn away most of the blankets except a few. Most of the girls end up sleeping with me on the massive bed, and because I can't fit them all, the rest sleep on the floor.

In the end, they all could have slept on the bed, but all of them wanted to make sure to not get too close, that way they couldn't hit or kick me in the middle of the night. Even though the girls have been in that prison for years, they still have the decency in their hearts to be kind. The girls, even through everything, are laughing and still trying to find the best out of life. I have to admire them for every effort they make to try to forget.

To be honest, I don't think they will ever forget that place that held them away from their parents and their own bodies. Just the idea or thought of that is sickening, to the point where I want to throw up. These brothers could've used their tricks to help people, instead they use it to hurt.

Despite what Will and David have done, I still can't help but feel somewhat connected to them, drawn even. I want more than anything to go home, but I know I can't. Though they may be threatening the girls to stay for my sake, the true threat is if I run, they die. James would never do anything to kill me, nor Will. David will never care for me, not in a way that is to protect me at least.

Everything that has happened since I have been here has been because of them, because of James's obsession to use me to get revenge on my mother. Will and David would do anything for their brother, just as I would do anything for mine. James is all they have left, and my mother and brother are all I have. They may be doing this with the right heart, but they are still monsters.

"Alena? Are you still awake?" Isabella whispers beside me.

"Yeah. Sorry did I wake you?" I whisper back.

She turns fully to look at me, "No, not at all. I just woke up because of a bad dream that's all. Why are you still awake?"

"Just thinking,"

"What about?"

"Nothing to worry about, you should get some more sleep. Heaven only knows how much we will try to do tomorrow," I whisper trying to make it sound like I wasn't just thinking about how terrible my life is becoming.

"Why don't I believe you then?"

"I can't answer that for you."

She turns onto her back and murmurs, "Well just so you know, you can always talk to me. Goodnight Alena."

"Goodnight Isabella."

Chapter 8

I wake up and find the girls all up and moving. Isabella is sitting beside me on the bed reading a book from the expansive bookshelf against the wall.

There is still a lot that I do not know about the girls, however, I feel the closest to Isabella. Compared to the rest, she and I connect on a deeper level. When the others are lost in the thoughts of their past, Isabella sits with me, confides in me about hers.

Her family abandoned her as a kid, forcing her to provide for herself on the streets. At first Will was just a random man buying her food, until she woke up in the castle like I did. The way she talks about how Will put her in the valley, almost as if she is sorry for him. Her words paint him as someone trying to help, even while her memories haunt her.

From what I gather, Isabella was never truly loved by her family, not as a child should be. It breaks my heart, the lack of love from her parents. We talk about the loss of our fathers, mine by death, hers by abuse. It connects us in a way.

Hannah had gone with the guards to get breakfast. Apparently, they were supposed to go and eat breakfast in the Grand Hall, or what I call a giant dining room. The girls had refused since I wasn't going to be with them and asked if they could eat here in the bedroom or in my own personal dining room with me. My dining room could easily fit 10 people, four on each side, and 1 on each end. The girls said if they needed to, they could just eat in there. However, when the food did arrive, they decided to eat on the ground beside my bed.

I smile all during the meal. I may have let the girls out all because of a promise, but I am so happy I did, for the girls have shown me a kindness that I had been longing for every day since I arrived here.

James stops by after the meal to check in on me, and to give orders to the girls to change out my bags of water and blood. He has to leave shortly afterwards for another meeting. Not that I mind, it felt weird with the girls and James in the same room. James may not have put the girls in the valley, but he was still associated with the ones who did. Not only that, but he had knowledge about Will's dawning and did nothing to stop it, rather he encouraged it.

Hannah doesn't have to say anything to tell us that she is very uneasy around him. Not that I blame her, she had been stuck in that valley for five years. Who knows how long she was stuck in there for alone? I can't imagine how scared and chilling that would be. Being stuck in a place you don't know, with no one knowing where you are and being all alone, I know many people would just try to die at that point. When people said there are worse things than death, I never agreed, but now I do.

Throughout the day, the girls and I talk nonstop. When I need to go to the bathroom, they always help me to walk to and from. They always scold me when I try to get up on my own throughout the whole time playing games and joking around. They change my bags of blood and water and help me eat.

Each day it is the same: breakfast, bathroom break, talk, blood and water change out, lunch, bathroom break, James's visits, more talk and some games, dinner, the begging of dessert, bathroom, water and blood change, then bed. For two weeks it is the same process over and over again.

The girls never waver helping me, and throughout it all, I notice the color and light come back into each of their eyes, one by one. The joy coming from me makes them even happier as I watch them keep growing into what they would've become, with a few extra scars.

After a few weeks, Joe comes in to check on my stitches, and to possibly take them out. James and Will are present, David is not, which doesn't surprise me because I get the sense that he doesn't like me very much. Which is odd because he seemed to like me just fine at dinner when I was roasting his brother. He also seemed fine when I was sitting on the couch with James. Then again, that was my opposite too.

After Joe finishes checking out my stitches, he concludes that he wants to see me walk before he takes them out. He has me stand, with my shirt off so he can watch how the stitches hold. It's weird having my shirt off in front of James. He looks a little shy, but Will just looks at me like a concerned medical person.

The girls are also sitting off to the side watching. They try to stay as far away from Will as they can, not that I wouldn't do the same.

I pull back the blankets and turn so my feet can touch the floor when I come off the bed. I'm hesitant at first as I place my feet on the ground, using the bed to steady myself. I take one step, and I start to stumble and almost fall, but Isabella runs to me from where she stood. She holds onto me tightly as I straighten myself out. I look up to see James a few feet from where he once stood.

"Are you alright?" James asks with concern.

"Yes, I am fine. Thank you Isabella," I turn to the girl helping me to stand.

Joe looks up from focusing on my stitches to me, "Continue."

I continue to walk, as instructed, Isabella holding me up all the way. When I am near the wall, I am able to almost walk on my own.

"Alright, walk back to the bed," Joe commands.

By the time I get back to bed, Joe is already done checking out my stitches.

Joe turns to the brothers and says, "Her stitches just need a couple of more days to do their job. What day is it? Monday?" the girls nod their heads yes. "Well then in two days, I will come back in to take them out, so expect me on Wednesday around this time."

"Thanks doc. We appreciate it," James steps forward.

"Actually, before we let you go, I need to talk to the both of you out in the hall," Will says, gesturing to James and Joe.

Will leads the doctor and kidnapper out of the room and leaves Isabella to help me back into bed. Whatever they are talking about is definitely about me. Or it is about the girls going back, in which case I am going to have to fight to keep them out of that Valley for as long as possible.

I only hope that I can save them all.

Chapter 9

"A royal! Are you sure?" I yell out, then quiet down after knowing that I just spoke very loudly.

"I tested her blood over and over again, it matches with the last Queen's blood," Will tells me. "I want to do some tests to see if she has any magic, but between the DNA match and the blast of power before she was shot, it matches up."

"How is that even possible?" I ask. "The last Queen died over 100 years ago!"

None of this could be true. The last Queen was murdered before she could have her child. The legends of the child being alive were just fairy tales because everyone knew that she had never conceived. If another Royal were to be put on the throne, the balance that all the clans have tried to have would be ruined.

"Maybe the Queen had a child in secret before she was murdered. Perhaps she put her child in another mother, maybe to try to hide the child. There were spells that can do that you know," Will lists off all the possibilities of the child being real. "Joe, when she was on the table, did her wounds have abnormal healing?"

Joe has no emotion on his face as he responds, "Yes. Only partial healing but yes, it was there."

I keep trying to deny it.

"You know as well as I that the Cunningham's made sure of it."

"Yes, they left her bleeding out on the floor of her bedroom! That's enough time to conceive if someone came in time to help or spell the baby to another mother! The Cunningham's didn't wait until they were dead!"

"Okay, but what are the chances of Alena being the next heir? Especially finding out here!"

"Slim to none, but maybe it was fate."

"Fate isn't real! If it was, then mom and dad would be here and would tell us what to do!"

"Fate doesn't work like that! You can't control what happens!" Will shouts.

"Well if fate is so powerful, then maybe it should've kept mom and dad from being murdered too!" I storm off before Will can say anymore.

Despite what he says, fate isn't real. If this so-called *fate* had the power to keep an entire royal bloodline alive then it should have the power to keep my parents alive.

Father may not have been the best person, but he certainly didn't deserve death. Nor did mother. She never did anything to anyone.

I walk through the castle halls and remember running through them when I was very little, playing tag with David and Will. I miss those times dearly. I would go back, if only to get away from this mess.

If Alena is a royal, I will be charged with treason. Not only that but trying to Dawn a royal has worse outcomes than death.

If a royal were to be turned into a Dawn, the person that turned them into one could control them. It is forbidden to force a royal to do your bidding while on the throne. The same outcome of blackmailing as well. It is against all laws that if the current ruler is to be controlled by another person, that all decisions made during the time of corruption, would be overruled. Added to that the person would then be put to death by the royal that was taken over.

The traditional way is to be chained to the floor, flanked by two guards. Before that, they torture the traitor and put them in as much pain as they can. The royal takes the Sword of Guidance and plunges it into their chest, cuts out their heart, throws it to the ground, and then takes the blood on their fingers and writes an ancient symbol on their forehead. The mark means "traitor" or "mutiny" to forever mark the person as a traitor to the crown. Not only to the crown, but also to the kingdom and his family as a whole. The body is burned in the Royal's fire and thrown into a random body of water, to forever be lost.

Stargaze Palace was where the Royal Family ruled, lived, and partied. Despite what the punishment is for controlling a ruler, the family was the nicest you would ever meet. Unlike other cartel families, the Royal Family did not enjoy killing. They didn't even enjoy killing to protect their own family. Of course, when it came down to it, if anyone was a threat to their kingdom, they would take them out without batting an eye.

I must have been walking for an hour because by the time I am pulled out of my thoughts, it's dark outside and I am standing in the castle gardens.

This castle actually came from one of the dukes that was on the Royal Family's council. The duke was part of a very powerful cartel, one that my family destroyed to get this castle as a base for our own cartel.

The castle's original family, the Raindalls, was given the castle as a gift from the Royals. The Raindalls were a wonderful family that were always nice to everyone, which also led to their downfall. They were too trusting, but of course not as trusting as the Royal Family.

The King tried his best to be kinglike, but the Queen could never put aside her gentleness and compassion for others. Although in other cultures the King was most powerful, in this one, it is the Queen.

Where France and Great Britain want their first born to be boys so that they can be heirs, we want the first born to be a girl. If in any case a boy is born first, then the King and Queen must keep trying until a girl is born. Even if there are ten boys in front of the girl, the girl is still going to be Queen.

There were, of course, cases when the Queen was not able to conceive or no girl was born before their cycles were up, then the family would adopt. At one time the family tried to keep it from the kingdom, but eventually they made it a law that the heir can be adopted, if any of these cases should happen, but not without a cost first.

If the heir is adopted, they cannot continue the line without Starfire blood. As soon as the heir is adopted, they must start being taught to be a ruler immediately. The first step includes the blood extraction. The process is more painful than many let on, because in order to do so, you have to use magic.

Starfire blood is pure magic, so in order to place blood in the heir, they must drain some first. By some I mean *most* of the body. The process of draining is hurtful because many things can go wrong, but as soon as Starfire is transferred, the body is healed completely. Because Starfire blood is pure magic, the pure light makes it a healing blood.

It's rare—mostly only found in Royals—but there are some occasions where healing blood has been found. A family with a healing blood child is considered sacred. Which is why the blood transfusion is so necessary for the royal family to have.

Of course, all Royals are considered sacred, but the reason that this certain Royal Family is kept so secret, is because of their blood. You see, our King and Queen were well known by all the other Royals across the world, but whenever our kingdom's rulers were invited to a party by the rest, they would always decline.

Despite how caring and friendly they were, they would not risk the safety of their children or the kingdom by accidently showing their powers to the other Royals. The Starfires learned long ago that it was not safe to trust anyone outside their inner circle.

I stop in front of a fountain in the middle of the garden. The fountain always gave me an eerie feel, like it was watching me. It has the head of a Panther with a crown on top. The panther has a silky black coat with gold eyes. The crown looks exactly like the Royal's crown that was lost long ago. No matter how many times I try, I always wind up coming back here to look at the Panther.

Despite the water coming out if it's mouth, the teeth are still sharp, even after the many years of wear against them. The fountain is huge, so huge in fact, it could even be a small pool if it was deeper. I continue to gaze at the golden eyes that are staring into my soul, losing a staring contest. As I turn to go back into the castle, I swear I see the eyes turn to look following me.

I walk back to the castle at a brisk pace. As I near it, I can see Alena and the girls from the window in her bedroom.

During the initial stages of planning, David and Will agreed that she should have floor-to-ceiling windows. Not that they knew what the real reason was for her, at the time, but their ideas still came in handy. Will's reason was that it would bring her more peace. David's being that guards would be able to make her more accessible.

Suddenly, I am glad that I went along with it, able to now be able to clearly see her. She giggles with the girls and has this contagious smile, sending all the girls into a laugh attack. Even from here, I can see the light in her eyes sparkle and glow a little brighter. Eventually they all run out of breath and go to sit on the couches in her living room.

I continue to walk into the castle. The guards bow to me as usual, and I go to find Will. My outburst at him earlier was unnecessary and uncharacterized. He didn't deserve it, but whenever I hear him talk about stuff like that, I immediately think about how that could have saved mom and dad.

Alena's father may be dead, but she still has her mother. At least she had a parental unit there for her. I had no one, but a giant cartel for me to run, only using what I had managed to learn from my father.

It was hard at first, as if having to deal with both my parents' deaths wasn't enough, but the entire cartel looked to me for support; to lead them in a new direction, where they could know that my parents death was not in vain.

Soon word would get out that her mother was missing her daughter, and all blame would go to me. My cartel loves what I did, but at what cost will it be for doing such a thing? Sure, her mother did wrong and that goes to Alena, by being born, but some might not think the same way I do.

The first place I check for Will is in the library. He isn't there. My outburst about the whole fate thing not saving mom and dad was a little out of line. I thought that after all of this time, I would've gotten over the fact that they were gone. I'm now realizing that that's not the case. Will couldn't have known that I would've said that, unless he looked into my mind as he does constantly with Alena.

Will had only just been learning how to look into people's minds weeks before father left to his death. Tutors from all over the world flew in to teach him. Those tutors stayed only a few weeks after my parents were murdered. By the time the tutors left, Will had a good understanding of mind control, but not enough to do what the cartel had always needed: find answers.

Digging through a person's mind, especially a guarded mind, was hard enough as it is for a beginner. Will spent months learning and practicing how to control a person's mind.

There was a time that Will never left his study for weeks and had to make maids go up and give him food. Eventually the maids started coming back and always asking me what I wanted them to do. Every time I gave them a task and they finished it, they would always find me, no matter how hard I tried to hide. I had to deal with them until I finally got to the point where I went to Will's study myself and told him to stop. The week following that day he had mastered brain control.

Every time that we brought in traitors, he was able to get the information that I wanted without breaking a sweat. No matter how hard they tried to block him out, Will always got in.

After a while of serving me and David being gone fighting, Will left in search of something to do in his spare time of torturing people. He spent a long time searching, while we kept bringing in traitors and finding our own ways of getting the information out of it.

When I am done eating my dinner, I go straight up to my room. The maids are already in there, cleaning my room as always. I dismiss them with a wave of my hands, they bow and scatter within a moment's notice.

I usually wait until they are done, but exhaustion is nagging at me. I do not even remember the last time that I had a full night's rest.

Ever since Alena was shot, I haven't been able to sleep. I always wake up in the middle of the night, my clothes soaked in sweat, her screams still ringing in my ears. I am never able to fall back asleep afterward. I just get up, build a fire, sit there and watch the flames crackle. I drown in my thoughts about my nightmares that have woken me up every night for weeks.

While she has been recovering, I have been dying. I haven't eaten in days. I can't even bring myself to look in the mirror to see how bad I look. Alena didn't seem to notice today, meaning that she doesn't suspect anything is wrong. If Will's findings are actually true, it's going to be a long time 'til I ever have a full night's sleep again.

I don't even make it to my closet as I lie down on my bed and drift off into a much-needed sleep.

Chapter 10

Yesterday was weird. Joe came to check on how I was healing, but both Will and James showed up too. They watched intently as Joe made me go through a series of tests. During one of the tests, Joe had me take off my shirt so that he could watch my stitches.

Even a day afterward, I can't stop thinking about the way James looked at me, or the concerned look he gave me when Isabella caught me from falling flat on my face.

A few minutes after the three men left, I heard shouting and my name being mentioned. It quieted down as soon as I tried to hear but I continued to attempt to hear anything before giving up.

The girls were tense through most of the night, jumping at every creak and sound that they heard. It took hours after Will left for them to completely calm down. Not that I blame them. After what he did to those girls, I don't think they will ever be the same.

Soon after the men left, the guards brought up food for dinner. There was roast beef, mashed potatoes, green beans, and juice. No wine like the first night I was here. James had the chef only give me juices and water. Not even coffee! I really got mad when I asked for coffee a few weeks ago and the guards told me that I wasn't allowed to have any ever since I was shot.

Apparently, caffeine doesn't help the body heal itself, but juice does. Water, that makes sense, I mean most of our bodies are made up of it. But juice? I don't think so. Orange juice sure, but grape, apple, pineapple, mango? They can't all help the body.

Not only that, but I haven't even been allowed to leave my room. Every few days, the girls are allowed to go outside. It took me three tries to convince them to go, but even then, only some of them went while others stayed to keep me company.

As promised, there has been no talk about how we can escape. The only things we discuss related to the outside world are what our lives were like and what we would do if we ever got out. Most of us just talk about our dream jobs. Many of them, after this experience, want to help find kids that go missing.

That's partly why I absolutely love the girls. There is no dark side to any of them. Of course, other than the desire to get revenge.

Everyone has a dark spot. If someone didn't, I wouldn't trust them. Don't get me wrong, I don't trust people who do, especially James, but I think it is scarier if you are not able to see someone's full potential. My mom clearly has hidden her's well. That is, only if what James says is real.

I don't want to believe him, but all the secrets, it makes sense. Like why we live in such a big house. Why every month, there are people that come in for a couple of hours and talk in my mother's private study. I was never allowed in there, but my brother was—only a few times of course. My mom promised that when I was older, I would be able to join in.

There was once a time that I believe her. That was after my brother was acting weird when he was done with this first meeting. My mother made him keep whatever secrets he had heard. They kept me in the dark after that and found excuses to get me out of the house every time the other people came over. They sent me to Ava's house, family friend's house, and even one time mother sent me to stay at a hotel for a night.

My brother started keeping secrets from me. We never kept secrets from each other. He drew away from me, with all his secrets and lies. We promised each other, the day that dad died, that we would never hide from each other. At least, he made one to me.

I was a baby when my father died. I never really got to know him, but I have a few pictures painted for me by my family. Sometimes we would just sit in the living room and tell stories about my father. They would tell me how brave he was. Of course, he was brave if he tried to save a person from being killed at a bank robbery.

They described him as the most handsome guy you had ever seen. My mom used to tell me how his green eyes would spark whenever he was about to start trouble, she said that is where I got my troublesome side from. Jeremy used to tell me how father would hoist him up on his shoulders, his arms like boulders. Everyone else that met him, would comment on how alike we look. I got my red-brown hair, and my green eyes from him.

Mostly, people just say how unique and honest a man, how rare of a find he was. Even with this image in my head, I still feel lost because I never got to see for myself.

All the girls stared at him when he walked into a room. That's why my mom always thought she was so lucky that father picked her over all the other girls that were drooling over him.

Mom never said one bad memory about dad, nor did Jeremy. That made me believe that he was literally the picture of perfection. My father was nothing short of a hero. Not only was he a hero, but he was someone that everyone adored and loved.

If anyone had the best life, it would be him. An amazing wife and kids who adored him. From the few memories that I remember as a child, he was always smiling, always happy.

These girls need someone like that; someone who will protect them, is never negative. They need someone who will give them the attention they require. I am no parent, but I am trying my best to make sure that they are happy. It's hard to watch them all go through each day like it is any other. Forgetting what their parents look like, their home that was their sanctuary, their friends at school who probably think that they are all dead.

I can't even begin to imagine what that is like. I have a feeling that soon I might, but I also have a feeling that my family will never believe that I am dead until they see my body in front of them not breathing, cold, and eyes closed, never to be opened again.

It's my own hope and theirs that makes me believe that there is going to be a day that I can be in their arms again too. I just hope that is the same for these girls. I hope that Lilly and Emily are able to find a family that will care for them too. Where they can travel to all the places that they want. Three meals a day, plus dessert just to put a smile on their face.

All the people in this castle deserve to go home and be happy—even Joe and his wife and kids. Those three brothers—Will, James, and David—have destroyed them all, making their lives unlivable. It's not even living anymore, it's just surviving. That's all it has been since I have gotten here: surviving. I would think the same for everyone else if I wasn't staring out the window at all the girls playing in the garden.

I finally convinced all of them to go out without me. So, I am just standing at the window watching them run through the mazes of roses and tulips. Vines grow on the hedges as tall as a bus. There are fountains that spill water like a goddess gives life, gracefully and never stopping.

There is one fountain, in the shape of a Panther, that is the most beautiful. Even from here I can see its golden eyes and the jet black, metal coat. The mouth is set in a growl as water spills like whispers of the life it looks as if it once lived. The secrets of all it has witnessed locked away in the solid, black, iron head. I swear I see it move its eyes to look at me, but before I can look back, James walks into my room.

He looks at me with…awe? It is so hard to tell what he is thinking, just like it always is with Will. Although I kind of expected that with Will the moment that I found out he was a mind reader. I bet Will wouldn't be so high and mighty if he wasn't able to keep his mind locked.

At least with James I can usually tell what he is feeling, but not this time. I think he is trying to hide it, and he is doing an okay job. We just stand there and stare at each other.

"I thought you were supposed to be resting?"

"I wanted to see what the girls were doing out in the garden," I say. I know I should be resting but I can't relax.

"Can't sit still you mean?"

"I have been sitting in my bed for weeks now. It is hard to sit still."

He winces on my first sentence, and then says, "Then you wouldn't mind taking a walk with me?"

"I thought I was supposed to be resting?"

What is he up to?

"Well you clearly are not going to so you might as well move around a bit. If you start to feel tired or can't walk much, we will just come back here. Besides, you haven't seen much of the castle."

"I have seen some of it." It wasn't a lie.

He huffs out a laugh, "Right, when you tried to escape those two times. Come on, the girls won't even know you were gone."

"Alright only for a couple of minutes."

"We can come back whenever you want," he says gesturing to the doors.

I walk slowly to the exit. If I fall, I don't think that my stitches will come out this week, or at the very least I won't be able to walk around as I please.

I also find it weird that James even wants to be around me. I have not seen him all that often, only when he came to threaten me about running away again. Apparently his guards were going to be ready for any challenge I posed. James did inform me that they were trained so hard that they wouldn't feel a bullet, but I have a pretty good idea that they will fall down when I attack them again, if I ever get the chance.

I usually would feel bad and maybe even a little disappointed, but fighting those guards was actually exhilarating. Not only that but also life-fulfilling. For whatever my future may hold, I am uncertain, but it definitely was fulfilling when I took out bad guys.

In movies there are always the bad guys and the good guys. But movies are not real life, even though they may feel like it at times. If this was a movie, then I would be able to call for help from a phone that is hidden in a wall. I'd see a police officer walking by and call out to him for help. This is no movie; this is a nightmare. An absolute nightmare.

When people watch about other people being kidnapped on TV, they don't really think about what it is like. They think that if you are by a police station that you should be able to just run to them and they will save you. It's not like that at all. What if the police officer doesn't believe you and sends you back to your kidnapper? They would probably kill you after pulling something like that.

Being here, kidnapped, I understand fully now. I kind of did before, but now I do more than ever. The thing is, I don't think that they would kill me if I did run to the police. The brothers are smart enough that they could probably talk their way out of the police and still keep me.

I honestly thought they were crazy before, still kind of are, but I in a way envy their cleverness, especially James. He has control over everyone. He convinced his brothers to do his bidding. He runs an entire cartel. It's absolutely insane how much control he has. Which scares me more than I care to admit. If he can do that to that many people, I can only imagine what he could possibly do to me.

Which is why this walk scares me so much, why I hesitated. What if he says something that could possibly convince me to trust him? Or worse, work for him? Doing everything he says? I can't even begin to fathom what it is like for Joe to work for him. Joe had to drop his entire life, leaving his family behind, and convincing the world he was dead, along with his children and wife.

"Are you alright?" James asks, gently grabbing my arm to stop me from walking further.

"Yes, of course!" I reply quickly.

"Your mind seems…absent."

"Just thinking, that's all."

We continue walking again, "What are you thinking about?"

"Just my family, and how good it is to be not in my room."

The family part isn't all lies, nor is the room. I have been wanting to get out of it for a long time. And my family is constantly on my mind, even when I try to shut them out so I don't have to deal with the pain.

"What about your family?"

"My mother is probably frantic, but I am guessing you already know that," I say, turning my head to face him from my position of staring at the stairwell ahead.

"Yes, you are right. I know that your mother is quite worried about you, but I also know that your brother now shares the same fate as her."

I can feel the tension start to fill the hallway. Even the guards at the doors hold their breath as if a battle was about to begin, and they might be smart in doing so.

"What fate is that?" My own breath catches in my throat as fear starts to bubble.

"A lifetime of torture." Not even blinking, he says it as if you were saying hi in the hallways.

I stop dead and turn to him with the most hatred that I have ever had in my eyes.

"What did you just say?"

"Your brother will have a lifetime of torture, along with your mother for conspiring against my family and me."

James and everyone else within 10 feet of me don't have the time to cover themselves as fire erupts from my hands, and the corridor turns to ash.

I hear it before I feel it; the unbearable, burning fire that sears my arm closest to Alena. If that wasn't enough, I'm thrown back, just like when she was shot, and I don't have to be held down because the pain is enough. My eyes burn when I try to open them. Smoke is everywhere mixing with the dust from the walls and ceiling being shook so violently.

When the smoke and dust start to clear, what I witness isn't any better. Guards are on the floor everywhere, legs stuck underneath fallen stone or unconscious from impact, blood running down their heads. Those who are able to move come to me. As their cartel leader, it is their duty to keep me safe at all times.

They crowd around me as other guards from all over the castle crowd into the fallen corridor. While some try to tend to the wounded, and others to me, some try to go for Alena to try to eliminate the threat.

When I hear their curses, I take my eyes off of the people around me to the sprawled body across from me. People crowd around her, trying to get in, but not succeeding.

Fire surrounds Alena, but not like the dying fire around us. No, this fire won't go out, as if it has its own heartbeat. It rises and falls in a steady rhythm, never wavering even as water is thrown on it. Jackets slap at its red, hot core, desperately trying to suffocate it.

Guards all over are slowing their clean up work as they see what is happening. As some get closer to the fire surrounding the reason for the injuries that surrounds them, they hold in their breaths. When Will comes in, he does as well. He doesn't tear his gaze from the girl as he bends down to help me stand up from where I am sitting.

"What are you all staring at?" I ask as I am pulled to a standing position and limp closer to Alena. No one responds to explain, because what I see is explanation enough. Alena is surrounded by not a ring of fire, but fire shaped in a star. The star is surrounded by five blazing points, rising and falling with the fire that guards the unconscious girl. The shape is no ordinary star…it is the *royal family seal*.

"Well that answers the question then," Will breathes out.

I reply, short of breath, "I wish it didn't."

The guards and everyone step back as David bursts through to see what everyone else witnessed. That an heir to a throne, that has long since been destroyed, was just brought into one of her subjects' homes, unwilling. Treason that is dealt with by death. As Will bends down to look at the living fire, I take a step away from the girl who can destroy me and everything I stand for.

"It is her heartbeat," Will says standing.

"What do you mean, 'it is her heartbeat'?" David asks.

"We cannot get to her because the fire is not actual fire," Will explains. "It is a living part of Alena. The only way to get in is by having her let it go,"

"I have a better idea; why don't we just kill her?" David takes a handgun from a holster at the side of the soldier next to him and aims at the girl who cannot defend herself. Before anyone can object, he shoots, but doesn't make it.

"What the hell are you doing!?" Will exclaims, while the guards around David turn to him in disbelief.

Not responding, David continues to try to kill the young heir, the bullets never making their mark. Again and again he shoots until his barrel is empty, the fire surrounding Alena melts the bullets before they get within three feet of her.

"Enough, David. She is just a girl, and a helpless one at that. Not only would that have been a cowardice murder, but treason to the crown," I command to him.

David's face turns red from his anger, "Treason to a crown that doesn't exist. Murder of a problem that could destroy us all!"

"Detain him and lock him in his study. I don't want to see him for the rest of the night," I demand. It's better than me coming over to rip out his throat for not only disobeying but disagreeing with me.

"James, come over here please."

"What is it?" I walk to Will knelt before the fire.

"I need you to walk through her fire."

"Are you crazy? I would burn up in a second! Did you see what happened to those bullets?"

"That only happened because that was supposed to kill her," Will gestures to Alena. "You are clearly not intent on killing her so it should let you through."

"Quit looking through my mind. And if I can walk through, why don't you?" I am not going to risk myself because he is too scared.

"Alena is your dawn," Will says, standing. "Therefore, you and you alone can control her. The fire is keeping me from reading her mind, but you can do that. It's a risk, but unless you want to have her wake up and know how to control this power, then I suggest you help me get through."

"Well I am not walking through fire, so how do you expect me to do that?"

The guards around start to gather closer.

"If you won't do it then I need you to go and get someone that is a part of her old life. Someone that she dearly trusts, but not someone who could possibly get out. Not her mother, or her brother, they are probably trained to fight."

"Like a best friend?" My eyes say all the devilish part of me that it needs, as Will smiles big.

"Exactly like a best friend."

Chapter 11

The trip to Alena's neighborhood was long and dreary from the rain that never seemed to stop, as it hasn't for the past 12 hours we have been here. As soon as we landed, there were puddles everywhere we stepped. At least the hotel in town is dry and warm, and the perfect place to get information about an innocent girl who was friends with the daughter of a monster. It isn't that hard because apparently Alena's best friend Ava has come in every week since Alena's disappearance to ask if they have heard anything about her.

In the month and a half she has been gone, I was sure everyone would have moved on with their lives, but every week there is some search party going out to look for the missing girl. They even held her own special little prom and graduation. This town may be small, but it definitely is not small enough for everyone to know her. Not unless she personally went out of her way every day to meet someone new.

The girl I have locked up in that castle of mine is more important than I initially realized. The guards, I know, are feeling the tension too. Ever since they found out that Alena is a royal, they have been on edge. When we checked into the hotel, the innkeeper made them even more nervous than they were before they stepped foot in the hotel.

The worst part was when he said, "Sorry that the town seems so dull, it usually is pretty bright and lively. But ever since that young girl went missing, everyone is on the verge of breaking. We were all really close to her you see, she would always make sure that we were all having a good day. Sometimes she would even bring by some donuts when she knew I was too busy to make any."

That really got my guards into a state of unease. Usually they are always on guard, as they should be, but it's getting to the point where some of them can't even sleep. But my two closest soldiers, Hunter and Jack, are sleeping fine. They were the ones that beat Alena up that first night in her room. They don't seem to be distracted from the mission.

My team is lucky too. We came the night before Ava usually comes to the hotel to check up on Alena. The owner said that she always comes around noon, since school got over a week ago, and sits in the cafe until someone can come tell her an update, which is always nothing. The night Alena was taken, I took extreme measures to make sure no one saw us or looked too long in the right direction.

So, the next day I sit at the table right next to Ava's usual, and Alena's old one for that matter, and wait until she shows up. As if on command, the doors to the restaurant open to show a chestnut brown haired, deep blue eyed girl stride it.

In the few reports that I heard and saw of her when we were watching Alena, I heard of how confident Ava was, the light in her eyes that brightened up every room.

Of course, I was only focused on her friend at the time, but I can see now how she has fallen apart without her closest companion. She walks to her usual table and as soon as she sits down she fidgets relentlessly. Her eyes constantly dash back and forth, toes curling and uncurling, picking at her broken nails, tying her hair in knots. Ava is an absolute mess without Alena.

From the short time that I have had with Alena there is one thing that will never change about her and it's her love and loyalty to her loved ones and the people that respect her. As I said before, I envy that, but not entirely.

You see, there is one major problem with love—it's a ginormous weakness. One that I am going to use to destroy yet another life.

"Hey, are you okay?" I ask, trying to sound as concerned and gentle as possible.

"Yeah, I am just waiting for the sheriff to come and talk to me, that's all," she gingerly wipes away her tears streaming down her face.

Before I ask her any more questions, I make sure my group is set up correctly. Five guards are dispersed throughout the cafe in case anyone starts trouble, three wait outside to grab her, and two sit in the getaway car down the street. Having been put together so quickly, it is quite a smoothly moving plan.

As soon as I am done checking I ask, "Are you that girl who just lost her best friend?"

Ava chokes on the water she had started to drink. Her eyes glance down and gloss over, like she is remembering a painful memory.

"Yeah, her name is Alena. She was taken a month and a half ago. How do you know who I am?"

"Well you are the buzz of the town, you and your friend Alena. I am sure she is very lucky to have you as such a loyal friend," I say, trying to keep my smile from reaching my lips or eyes.

"Thanks. I am Ava by the way," she reaches her hand out to greet me. "And you are?"

"James. James Anderson," I shake her hand firmly.

Such a big mistake on her part for letting me do such a thing. I only shake her hand to get a feel for how strong she is, so I know how many need to take her, if hand to hand combat becomes necessary. Ava is definitely stronger than I thought. I put up four fingers discreetly behind my back to my guards in wait. That's how many I need to grab her. With three already waiting outside, only one goes out to see them. Four in total, lying in wait for the snatch.

Her eyes brighten a little bit at the pleasantries, but quickly fade as the owner comes up to her table, along with the sheriff. This is not good.

She quickly stands, "Have you found anything yet? Any whispers of where she might have been taken? Any leads to who?"

"Ava, I am sorry but no we haven't. Just dead-end leads, and no one saw anything," the owner answers.

"Well, maybe we need to check the dead-end leads again, maybe there is something you missed. A clue, she would've left behind a clue. Dragged feet, broken branches, maybe even a circle drawn in the dirt. Alena wouldn't go without a fight!"

"Calm down. We have checked the woods in the back of her house for a few miles. There was nothing but some footprints that were messed around so you couldn't track an exact place. I am sorry Ava, but we have done everything we can to find Alena. I think it is time that we start looking at what has become of her. It's been long enough for her—" Ava cuts him off before he can finish.

"Don't you ever say what you were just about to say to me. Don't imply it, don't mention it, and don't even think about it when I am around. Alena is alive, I would know if she were… gone. You may be Sheriff, but I know I can find her with or without your help," Ava shuts down any room for debate.

"I don't mean to be rude Sheriff, but that is something that we shouldn't even put in the picture. She is probably out there fighting hard to get back here. We should keep searching, just for the hope of finding her," I chirp in.

"And who are you exactly?" The sheriff asks with suspicion.

"He is a guest here at the hotel," the innkeeper says trustingly.

"James Anderson, at your service. I am just on my way through to visit my family a few towns over. When I saw all the ruckus, I thought I would stick around to see what the noise is all about. I wish it wasn't this," I say with my best respectful voice.

"Sorry that we couldn't have met on better terms Mr. Anderson. Regarding the missing young lady, she will be found but I can't promise anything for you Ava," the sheriff turns back to the young girl with tears in her eyes, suspicions of me cleared by the innkeeper's tone.

Ava pushes through the owner and the sheriff to get out of the restaurant. Her tears glitter in the setting sunlight.

She runs to the left, the exact opposite direction of her and Alena's street. Right in the direction that I have no guards lying in wait for her. The car is in the wrong spot, and the plan is all ruined.

It all depended on her going home! Why do these girls always have to ruin my kidnapping plans? It is so unfair!

I motion for my guards to trail her to wherever the sorrowful child ran off to. I bid the sheriff and owner goodbye and say that I am exhausted and going to retire to my room.

The two old gentlemen are too deep in conversation to see me slip out of the back entrance, walking hastily in the direction of the car that is speeding to me. When I reach the end of the alleyway, I am flanked by my two most trusted guards.

"Go and find out where she went. I want to be on the plane tonight heading back to the castle. Alena is probably already trying to wake up and I am sure it is getting hard for Will to keep her asleep," I order in a low, growl like voice.

Hunter and Jack slip off like shadows in the night, silently and stealthily. I walk swiftly to the getaway car and hop in the back seat.

"Follow behind slowly and far enough back that we don't draw attention to ourselves."

The driver does as I instruct him to do, and soon enough we are sitting at the base of a mountain. It's actually more of a glorified hill, but it is tall, and it has a valley below. It must be beautiful at the top. You can probably see the entire town from atop.

I get out of the car and climb to the top swiftly, trying not to make too much noise. The sun is setting as I climb. It's been almost 24 hours since I left Will with Alena. He is currently trying to keep her asleep in the position she is in. It's quite hard considering that he can't touch her, but he said he knows a way. Will said to hurry back because it was going to take a lot out of him.

I also instructed the guards that were going to watch the two of them that when it looked like Will was struggling too much, to just tranquilize her. I don't know how well that is working considering she has a massive barrier protecting her. I am confident that together they'll be able to keep her down.

David, in the meantime, is protecting the palace. After I gave him a long talking to, I sent him out on duty to make sure every inch of the castle grounds and the castle itself was secure from anyone getting in. Or out. I also gave him the task of making sure that Will's dawns were being locked away in Alena's rooms.

Despite her breakout, we decided that she probably didn't have any control over the power, so we let the girls off of the hook. They listened, for the most part. When Alena turned that hallway into a death place, a large boom sounded throughout the castle and its grounds. The girls hurried in as fast as they could from the other side of the castle. When they arrived, I immediately sent them back to her rooms and locked them in there ever since.

I break through the tree line just as the sun finishes setting. I find Ava sitting on a smooth rock in the shape of a throne. Her legs are drawn up to her chest, and her waist-length hair falls around her head, covering her face from being seen. I walk closer, and despite trying hard to be quiet, Ava whips her head around to face me.

"Who's there?" Her voice cracks, like one does after a hard emotion hits.

"It's me, James," I answer back, slowly motioning for Jack and Hunter to move in before I step into the setting sunlight for her to see me.

"What are you doing here? How did you find me?"

"I followed you. Sorry you seemed upset at the restaurant, I just thought that you could use a friend," I flip my hands so my palms are up, showing her I am unarmed.

"I don't need a friend. I have a friend that is going to come back for me, and I will not replace her. Once I find her, I am never letting go."

"You are that loyal to Alena?"

"Why shouldn't I be?"

"And you would do anything to see her again?"

"I need to see her again, whatever it takes," Ava's voice sharpens and becomes distant.

"Well then it is your lucky day," I motion to the Hunter not two feet from Ava. He grabs her by the neck and injects her with a sedative in a syringe. "Because I am taking you to her."

Her eyes start to droop, and her body falls limp in the Hunter's arms.

She sleeps the entire plane ride to the castle and sleeps a little while longer as I place her in the bedroom next to Alena's. It isn't until the next afternoon that she awakes and screams loud enough to wake an entire city.

Her screams are in my dreams, my thoughts. And I just can't seem to get them out of my head; my dad, Ava, mom, Jeremy—they are all here with me.

Our once amazing family picnics in the park, the usual sub sandwiches from Subway, Sunchips, sour cream and onion, and of course Doritos, pops for everyone, and a big, cozy, red checkered blanket that everyone sits on.

It was the usual conversation about how school was going and the new boy crushes. They were all really just lies. Ava, I knew, always made up one to hide her feelings for my brother. And I just make up one so that they don't have to ask all the questions of why I don't have one.

We were in the middle of our sandwiches when her screams shakes me from my fantasy into a nightmare. The sky turns black and giant birdlike figures fill the skies. Cries like dinosaurs coming from the air. When I look back down for my family, all I see is Ava, her mouth set in a scream. The rest of my family is nowhere to be seen, and the food for the picnic is toppled over.

"Ava? Ava, what's wrong?" I ask crawling over to her.

She doesn't answer.

My nerves crackle as I sense something behind me. I whip my head around to find a demon-like bird, crouched and looking at me. I close my eyes, and shake my head, willing it to go away. When I reopen them, the sky is back to normal. When I look back around at Ava, her face is wet with tears and her eyes are full of sorrow.

"Ava?" I ask as tenderly as possible.

"Alena? Alena! What did you do to her?" she screams out at me.

Before I can ask anymore, her figure disappears. Where did she go? What is going on?

I get up and run through the park to try to find her, if only so I am not alone.

I don't succeed. Before I get up a small slope, two black figures emerge from the sky above. They don't shoot straight for me, instead they bank to my right into a cluster of tall oak trees.

For a moment I try to think that maybe they were just birds—very large birds. The thought is gone from my mind the moment I see two large, *human* figures emerge from the blackness of the trees.

The closer they get the more I realize that whatever *they* are, it is definitely not human. At first, I assumed that the darkness around them was just the shade of the trees. In actuality, it was them, the two things that walk like humans, the darkness seems to swirl around them. It was as if the darkness was them, growing and moving to their will. The closer the *things* got, the more of a stench I could smell. If pain had a scent, it would be that, along with fire, crackling and burning bodies.

Whatever these things are they are certainly not from around here, and I have no intention of finding out where they are from. I dash up the rest of the hill to find a growing field in front of me. I look to see that the figures are only a mile away and running. I suck in a large breath and sprint for the safety of the wild grass.

In what feels like seconds, I have crossed a mile and a half of ground and have safely made it to the wild grass. I bend over to catch my breath. That's when I realize something is wrong.

Very wrong.

I whip my head around to find the black figures three yards from where the hill meets the meadow. The field looks as if it could go on forever, nowhere safe in sight. I have no idea where to go. I cannot hide, I stick out too much in the grass with the blood-red of my shirt. I can't run with no destination, and I most certainly cannot fight. Whatever those things are, whatever they give off, feels wrong in every way. But I have no choice.

Even if I did run, I would run out of energy and that's if they don't catch me. So, I turn fully to the two figures, and plant my feet firmly on the ground.

"I don't know what or who you two are, but you need to leave me alone," I try and succeed in sounding tough.

The only response I get is a low and dark chuckle. Well at least they are somewhat human—and I don't use somewhat loosely.

"Who are you?"

"You cannot speak our name in your common tongue," in unison they answer.

Now I know that they are not a part of this world.

"Shut up you stupid, stupid girl," I yank Ava back by the hair.

"What have you done to her?" She whirls around to face me as best she can.

"I did nothing. And this," I gesture to the fire. "This is all her. Alena did this to herself. Now shut up so my brother can speak."

"This would have never happened if you had just left her at home where she belongs. Left us both alone! I was nice to you! This is how you repay me?" The tears running down her face dry up for she is so close to the fire.

After I heard her screaming, I had guards go and fetch her. And as soon as she saw Alena lying in the middle of the fire star, she screamed and kicked and tried to get out of my guards' grip. She's definitely not as strong as Alena, nor as intelligent for that matter. She never thought to have an actual fighting technique. Then again, Alena was not dragged here and actually decided to fight the guards.

"Ava, if you want to see and talk to Alena again and get her out of that fire, you are going to listen very closely to me."

"Why don't you just throw water on it?" She asks, clearly impatient.

I chuckle annoyingly, god this girl is naive, "Because this is no normal fire. It is hard to explain. Now please listen."

She does as she is told and shuts up.

"I need you to walk up as close as you can to the ring of fire surrounding her. You need to call out her name, and then start walking through the fire. You cannot be scared, nor angry. If you are either, it will burn you and you will never see your friend again. Do you understand?" Will asks, trying to get the point across and be as gentle as possible.

"It will burn me," She says, staring at the fire.

"No, it won't. If Alena is truly your friend, then the fire will let you pass."

"Of course she is my friend! She's my best friend, which is much more than I can say for either of you," Ava storms off to the fire wall.

She definitely has the fire that Alena has—figuratively of course. She has the sass, and the way that she walks, it grabs Will's attention, at least for a moment.

Ava reaches the edge of the fire. Even from this distance, I can see the sorrow in her eyes as she looks at her unconscious friend.

"Alena? Alena if you can hear me, let me in please." She raises her hand to the fire. "I just want to talk to you again. Please, let me in."

Before Ava can take a step, the fire parts just enough for her to walk through. Ava sprints through to her friend and holds onto Alena's body tightly.

"Alena, please, please come back to me. I am nothing without you."

Nothing.

Then Ava's body shakes, and her eyes turn into the back of her head, white.

"Alena? Where are you? Alena!" Ava screams from across the park, question in her voice.

My heart jumps at the sound of her, and I race in the direction of the sound. She sounds different than when she was at the picnic, more realistic. Despite the two figures that are undoubtedly tracking me, my need to see my best friend overwhelms me.

I make it out of the weeds back to the top of the hill, and that's when I see her.

"Ava? Is that you?" I hurry my pace, in her direction.

"Oh my god, Alena! You're alright!" Ava starts running my way.

It is not only her voice that is different, her body is too. She's more naturalistic, which gives me another thought. Ava may be real, but that causes a whole bunch of other issues.

I pull her into a tight embrace and ask, "How are you here? It isn't possible. I made sure that you were safe. I did everything that they asked."

"I thought that I would never see you again! Wait... what do you mean that you made sure I was safe? Alena, what happened to you?" Her face of happiness quickly turns to concern and fear.

"I..." my voice breaks. "I had to protect you all."

"Protect us? From who? James?"

Well that proves my belief.

"You have met him? Ava you have to listen to me, you cannot trust him, not for anything. If he tries to strike any deal with you, no matter how good it is, do not agree. Ava do you understand me?" My anger rises.

"Alena, he brought me here because he wasn't able to reach you. Outside this *place*, you are unconscious, and your body is surrounded by fire in the shape of a star. They said that the only way for you to come back is for you to trust someone. Someone that you would let in. So they took me and told me to walk through the fire to you. I got through and then I touched your hand and I... I came here." Ava tells the story like words firing from a gun. Hurried and rushed.

"I did everything they asked! You should be home, where you will be safe," I straighten and turn away from my dearest friend.

"You should not have to protect us, least of all sacrifice for us. It was just by chance that he took you. Not to mention that the town is much more on guard now. No one can be taken again."

"Like you were not able to be taken?" My tone is sharper than I mean it.

"As fate would have it, yes I was taken, but only because some greater force needed me to come and find you."

"You shouldn't be here."

"Too bad, I am here. Now tell me what you need so I can get you home."

I take a long breath and look at the closest thing I have to a sister. Feeling her realness, I realize that this is all in my head. Which means, I know how to get out, but I need to be careful.

"You need to tell me who is all in the room that I lay in. Don't leave out anyone."

So, Ava told me every man and woman in the room. Where I lie, where the fire is, and where the corridor has fallen to pieces, in which places the soldiers are, and how many, and lastly the position of where Will and James stand.

"Well, what do we do now?" Ava asks when she finishes the layout.

"There is only one thing to do. I need to go back. I need to face them."

"You? You mean us? If you think that you can leave me in this place alone so that you can go and face James alone, you have another thing coming."

"Ava, it is too dangerous. I can't risk you getting hurt. We will go back together, but you stay behind me. You do not try to fight or do anything without me. Ava, do you understand?"

"Yes," she plainly states.

"Good, then grab my hand and hold on tight."

Chapter 12

When I wake up, the extra guards that were added while Ava was asleep ruin the chances of me getting my best friend home safely, and possibly me too. I sit up, just as Ava opens her eyes from the dream world. I help Ava to stand up, and just as I look forward, I see what I never imagined.

Just as Ava foretold, the Star of Fire. It is bright as it rises and falls in rhythm. As my heart races, the fire rises and falls faster than before. The star has five points to it, Ava and I in the middle and there are five dash like marks surrounding the star, also on fire. As my eyes fall on the faces in front of me, James and Will, my anger rises. As a result, the fire gives off waves of heat that make those closest to the fire sweat.

My fire. If I had heard a month ago that I had magic, I would've laughed. Just like everyone else in the world believed, magic did not exist. The only thing that was real in our world was science. Now, if you asked me if magic existed, I would most likely agree. Of course, a part of me has always wanted powers, but that part of me died when

I turned into a teenager. Now that I actually have magic, I don't know what to think.

David walks through the soldiers and raises his left hand, and on command the guards raise their guns. I can feel Ava cower behind me, and I knew then that me fighting my way out was never going to happen.

"Why would you put up your guns if I haven't moved a step?"

"You must believe that we are idiots if you think that we didn't feel the room's temperature rise. Yes, you are right you haven't moved, but you also are the one that caused this mess," James gestures to the ashy corridor.

At that moment I officially realized what I had actually done. I cannot even fathom who I could have hurt.

"I... did I hurt anyone?" my voice cracks.

"If you mean killed, no. But injure, you bet you did," he snaps.

"Alena come out of the star before things become worse," Will coaxes me.

"Make things worse? You kidnapped my friend, even after you promised not to hurt them if I listened to you! Who really made things worse?" The heat in the room once again rises, and tears start to reach my eyes.

"You were knocked out and you wouldn't let us in," David says. "I think if anything you should be thanking James, because if it wasn't for him, you would be at the bottom of a river."

Ava tries to lunge for him, but I grab her by the arm and pull her back. Before I can let go, Ava wrenches her arm from my grasp.

"*OUCH*! Alena, your hands are freezing!"

Before I look at her, I start to see ice grow underneath my feet. I feel the fear of everyone, and Ava backing up a single step. *What is this?*

"Ava, let me see your arm please," Will asks in front of me.

She lifts her arm out so Will can see, but she doesn't walk too close. In the light of the fire, I can see her arm is all black and blue, the skin around it is red.

"I don't know what happened, I just…" the ice continues to grow as the color of the fire deepens.

"Alena, relax. She is fine, but she will not be if you don't calm down."

My breathing becomes uneven, and I can feel the tension in the room is so thick that I could cut it with a knife.

"Alena, *relax!*" Will yells at me, as I see Ava's eyes turn to fear.

"I don't know how to calm down!"

"Oh for Christ sake, put her in an emotion cage, let this end," David, clearly annoyed with waiting, suggests.

Even though he meant it as a joke, I take it seriously. I attempt to push down my emotions, think of only good. I can sense Will there, searching to find a way to help, but nothing is going to work. The situation starts to overwhelm me again and I lose my concentration.

"Ava come out here to me. If she can't calm down, you are going to get hurt."

"No! You know what will happen once he has you. Do you think that him trying to help you will not cost you something? You cannot trust any one of them. Ava please don't go," I reach out my hand to her.

"I have helped you for the past month to heal! What have I done that is losing your trust?" Ava just stands in a crossfire, as James steps up.

"Are you serious right now? First off, you literally took me from my home, and you beat me on the first night for trying to give food to girls that you were going to let starve. You locked me in my own mind, giving me a front row seat to watching my body moving without my control. You turned my emotions and used them against me. But you are right, you have helped me to heal after I was *shot* by one of *your* men!" I exaggerate shot at him because I am pissed off to no end.

"You did what?" Ava's eyes go wide when she hears me say 'shot' and she turns from Will to James.

"It's not like it was my fault! I tried to call it off," James says.

"It doesn't matter, I was still shot. And let me tell you, if Joe wasn't here, I would be dead," I say, lifting up my shirt to show the bandages across my stomach.

Showing my stomach to everyone, Ava comes over to me, and the guards' guns go down, remembering that day. Then something that I didn't expect happens.

A guard lays down her gun fully on the ground, kicks it six feet from her and says, "I will not threaten a royal, let alone a child. I can't believe that you have known this whole time and yet you still treat her like a prisoner."

"What did you just say?" James turns feral as he spins to the woman, someone that seems familiar.

"I *said* that you have abused this child that we should actually be serving."

Then my mind clicks, it is the same woman who was with me on the night I was taken. She is the one that gave me the water bottle to drink. I guess my sorrow didn't work then, but it must be working now.

James jerks his chin towards the woman that spoke up, and two guards come in and try to guide the woman out.

"Stop! What did you just say about me?" I shout. She is lying, she has to be.

James turns back to me, "Nothing, do not worry about it."

Guards quickly try to escort the woman out, keeping whatever secret James is hiding hidden.

But not before she gets the last say.

"You are a royal, and these brothers are using you to get to your mother," the woman yells to me from the archway leading to the rest of the castle.

"What is all this talk about my mother? You all seem so fixated on my mother, so why in the world am I being brought into all of this? And how in the name of god am I a *royal?*" My curiosity turns into anger quickly.

The entire time that I have been here, all I have heard about is my mother. Not only does it annoy me, but it hurts to know that my mother did this to me. Whatever she did, it was something bad enough to send this entire clan on a killing spree.

"Whatever one family member did, they all did," James's tone is harsh and cruel.

"How can you say that when you would be considered a killer? A monster? Because let us all be honest here, your father was the definition of the devil. Kill me for saying such things, but you know it in your heart that he was only using you to become more powerful. He even dragged your sweet, innocent mother to her death," the woman, who is still being dragged away, asks.

"You will not speak of your former leader like that. You will also learn to bite your tongue around your current leader," James snaps, saying nothing about his mother, and the woman disappears from our sight.

"What is she talking about James?" I whisper, still trying to get a direct answer.

"Nothing that you need concern yourself with. Now, you are going to come out here and surrender Ava to me if you want to see her live," James replies, quickly changing the subject.

"You can't actually expect me to just surrender my friend," I say. James's expressionless face says it all. "You cannot be serious. Especially after you have not told me a single thing about my heritage or why I am being punished because of my mother's... I don't even know... actions?"

"I actually do expect you to obey and listen. On another note, I don't listen to a petty girl who doesn't even care for herself and gives away everything she has to protect people that don't deserve it!" James shouts, gesturing to all the people that have now been gathering in the small corridor.

"How would you know if they deserve it or not? You haven't lived a day in their lives! You have not even experienced anything like the valley or not being able to enjoy your childhood because if you try to you go hungry! And now you want me to turn over my friend's freedom and basically life? The entire time I have been here I have been trying to survive!

"It is not my fault that my mother made a mistake that I don't even know of! It is not my fault that my family made a mistake. But you know what is my fault: trying to give a small break to the lives of people that have been broken and hurt over and over again by a man that has so much power that he knows not of what he wants! I will not hand over my friend to be tortured by you and I will not just give away my right to be happy that easily." The fire rises as if on command to my anger that rolls off of me.

"Alright enough of this," David demands, as James' eyes blaze with rage. "Guards, take them both. Put the friend in the dungeon while I decide her fate, and Alena in her room. How much Alena struggles is how much closer Ava comes to her death. Oh, and when you take her to her room, have a harder repeat of the fight night she had here," David's grin turns wicked, as James fires off commands.

"And anyone who think that they should be loyal to a *dead* bloodline, you can join Ava in the cells below," David spits the word dead like a poison when some guards hesitate."

The guards advance as James starts to retreat back to his side of the castle. Watching him walk I can see how badly I hurt him, he limps on his right leg and his right arm hangs loosely. Good. I am glad I hurt that monster.

Guards move in fast, guns rising against me once again. As soon as they are all on the edge of the star, I give a warning flare.

"Leave us alone! You can't do this. Most of you were just going to protect me. If what that guard said was true, then that means that I am a royal. I am pretty sure that if I am that one day, I could possibly rule over you. Do you really want to do this to a future queen? Your queen?"

As the guards start to falter, David butts in, "You will all do well to remember what I said."

As much as I try to persuade them, it will not work with so many threats on their lives, not that I will ever be upset at them for it.

When I first met David, I thought that he actually liked me because I was being rude to James. Now I see how much David actually hates me. I don't even know why he hates me. I have done nothing to David to make him do such a thing.

The closer they get, the more scared I am. Not for myself, but for Ava. If she is taken, and if I try to save her and fail, she'll die. I have suffered much, but I can take more than I think she can. It feels like it's my job to protect her and that's exactly what I will do.

The decision that I promised myself that I would never make, I run through my head. All the aspects of what must happen, and the payment in return for it all.

My heart aches as I step forward.

"James, I'll go. Whatever you want, I will follow and obey, just like you want. All I ask is that you leave everyone I love and care about out of it. Ava, my mother, Jeremy, my town, even the Dawns and Emily and Lilly. You let them all go home. I am not going to try to hide a weakness that you already know about. Please, just take me and leave them. Make me your Dawn, experiment, even your own slave but you leave them alone." Tears fall rapidly down my face.

Will's eyes go wide.

"Alena, no! Are you crazy? I cannot let you give yourself up again," Ava tugs on my arm.

"You expect me to believe that you will just do and say what I want?" James asks. "I have a hard time believing you will just give up your freedom," James turns his back around to see me raising my hands in defeat.

"My freedom has been gone for a month and a half now, I will not give up theirs for a shred of hope for my own."

"How noble of you Alena. Alright. Prove it then. Do what you have always sworn to never do. Bow to me," James says, coming up to the star. "Let the fire be smothered, the ice disappear, and bow to me."

"I will. But you have to promise to let her go as soon as I do," My heart skips a beat.

Ava takes both of my hands, forcing me to face her, "Alena, please, we can fight. If you really are controlling those flames, then burn them. Make a pathway out, lined by fire. Please! I won't lose you a second time."

"That's the thing Ava, I can't control it! I have tried, but I just can't. And I most certainly will not risk your life in the process of me trying to be free. It is not worth it."

"You need to trust me and yourself. Alena, please."

"And what if we get out? How long will we live running away? I won't do it," I say.

Ava's tears fall swiftly.

"Do me a favor when you get home?"

"Don't. Alena don't say that. You will be there when I get home."

"You know as well as I do that will not happen."

"Alena, please, please, come with me! Fight!"

I ignore her pleas, "Say hi to everyone. Say that they let you go because I made a deal. Don't say anything that you know of the deal, or the magic for that matter. Not to my mother, no one. You will keep everyone safe and you will not come looking for me. No matter how much it hurts, you will forget about me.

"Live your life like you wanted. You are such a talented singer. Go live that dream. I will be with you every time you sing. Just be happy, okay?"

I reach up to wipe her tears away.

"Be strong. Be smart. Be brave. And don't forget that I will never stop thinking about you. I love you my friend, and I always will," I cup her face, and drop my arm as I embrace her in a giant hug.

"I can't lose you again," Ava breaths into my shoulder.

I whisper back into her soft, blonde hair, "You can never lose me. I will always be with you."

I release her and walk to the edge of the fire, in front of James, my eyes trying to burn holes into his head.

"Will, tell me how to put the fire wall down," I ask, my voice fraying under the pressure of trying not to show any emotion.

Despite my tears falling down my face and me giving up my entire life, I feel happy, satisfied almost. There were times of me being here that I thought I would never get out. This deal just confirms it, except this time I am not surrendering because I am weak, not in the way that most would think.

Whatever James thinks about my supposed 'weakness' about loving my family, this is a strength. It will be them that keeps me from breaking. So even as Will explains how to put out my ice, and my last defense of bright fire, and as I sink to my knees, I realize how I will never have my first kiss or get married.

I'll never teach my kids the importance of kindness and love in the world. I won't be there when my brother gets his first girlfriend, to teach him what girls like and don't like. I will never see my family or friends again. I will never be able to say goodbye to my mother on her deathbed. I will never be able to inspire the world to change for the better as I have always wanted to.

I will never celebrate another birthday or Christmas again. I will never see the stars shine brightly in the night sky. I will never dance in the spring stream next to my house. I will never get my first real job as an adult. Never be able to be alive and not have to look over my shoulder. And I will never ever live again, I will always be trying to survive.

As soon as my knees hit the floor, and the fire starts to fade to embers, I realize now why James is so intrigued by me. I remember him telling me that he could never do what I did. I sacrificed my life for my neighborhood, for the girls in the valley, and even for my maids that should be only children.

I would sometimes ask myself during my days of lying in bed what the difference between him and I was. I came up with plenty of differences, but not many similarities. The only thing that I could think of at the time was that we were both human. We both come from twisted families.

I have now found what it is that we actually have in common. We will do anything to both avenge and save our families, no matter the cost. He is trying to avenge his parents, to make sure his brothers are happy, and to protect them. With me, I am trying to protect my town, which has been my family ever since my father died.

They took me in and always checked in to see how I was faring, and I took over my father's job of always caring for the townsfolk. I guess that's why I feel so obligated to do this, because my father would have done the same.

Before I bow my head, I look up to see all the people that I will forever be chained to. David's smile says everything I knew I would get, and how I will live out the rest of my life. But when I look to Will, I see something that I never thought I would see.

There are tears in his eyes. How do two brothers smile and love the fact that they have a woman to hurt over and over again, and the other brother can barely stand watching a girl bow to his own kin? I don't understand why he's being so soft-hearted until I notice the presence in the back of my mind. It's almost as if I can see him standing in front of me. He was reading all of my regrets and all my reasons for doing this.

I take one last glance at everyone before I look down at the last embers of my flame, before they turn to ash.

"Take Ava back home. Stay there for a while and make sure she doesn't speak of this to anyone. A word about this and Alena pays. Understand Ava?" James instructs the guards closest to my friend and to Ava.

"Take me instead of her please. I am sure she is too much to handle anyway," I can feel Ava step forward behind me.

I turn around as I say, "Ava, no. You can't do this. You—"

James cuts me off, "Alena shut up. You are not allowed to talk without my permission. Understood?"

"Yes," I lower my eyes away from Ava and to the ground.

"Yes, what?" I can feel James bend down behind me and grab my chin so that I turn around to his direction once again. Lifting my head to look him in the eyes, James smiles a mischievous smile.

"Yes, James." Disappointment shows as I say that.

"No, not James. You don't have the right to call me James. I am your kidnapper, yes, but this lovely deal of yours makes me something else," James looks at Ava. "I am sadly going to decline your wonderful offer. Although new people to hurt is fun, Alena is more valuable than you can even imagine."

"Please just let her go. I'll do anything," Ava pleads.

"No. Alena I am your master now. You will address me as such. Nothing less, nothing more because that will *never* change. Is that understood?"

"Yes… master," I choke on the words as if there is a poison in my throat, still staring at that cruel face.

"I am glad we agree, darling. Guards do as I asked and take this one to the cells down below. And as for you," I watch as James looks at Ava. "You will go home as the deal was set. Listen to your friend, Ava. I thought that I wouldn't say this, but Alena was smart, for once, in making this agreement."

I watch as guards in front of me surge toward my innocent friend behind me with the biggest heart I know. I stay on the ground, fighting my own self to not run to my friend. Just like Ava, guards come to grab me as well. As my body is lifted without me trying, I keep my eyes glued to the floor. I know that if I lift my eyes to see my oldest friend being dragged away, I won't be able to keep the hurricane of tears back.

No matter how hard I try to keep looking at the ground, I can't fight when James grabs my chin again and lifts my eyes to face him. That is when, out of the corner of my eyes, I see four guards fighting against Ava to move. They are not moving very fast, and I have never seen so much fight in her. It is so hard not to look at Ava's face straining at the fight, and I turn my eyes to her.

"No you look at me, you don't serve her," my eyes fall back on James as he turns my head. "For obeying without question, you can give her a blanket for the night."

"Stop struggling you dumb girl! She made her choice you need to deal with it," a guard snaps at Ava as she continues to brawl.

I keep my eyes on James as I was instructed, at least until Ava gets out of the castle. I am no longer holding back the wall of tears. I close my eyes before I make a decision that I might regret. That is before I hear a resounding slap that makes my eyes fly open just in time to see Ava on the ground, holding her cheek closest to the guard that was yelling at her before.

The guards holding me are not holding onto me very tight until I try to run to Ava. My feet don't move fast enough because the guards pull me back before I can get to her.

"Alena, we had a deal. You need to honor that deal and obey," standing in front of my line of sight to Ava, James commands.

"You are right, we did have a deal. A deal that kept everyone unharmed. One of your guards just *harmed* my friend, breaking that," I twist to see Ava.

"Zach stand down, you are to honor my deal," James turns to look at the guard standing over Ava.

I continue to twist and pull against the guards. Even though James commands Zach to stop, Zach does not step back from Ava. Instead he leans down closer to her. I struggle harder against the dumb people who think it is okay to keep me from helping.

"Stop! Leave her alone you asshole! You have no right to hurt a person who cannot defend themselves, let alone a girl. If you were a man you would understand that. Not to mention that you are to obey your leader," I yell at the man who I most certainly want to beat to a pulp.

"Shut up, Alena. I am handling it," James says over his shoulder.

"Sure, looks like you're handling it. So why don't *you* shut up and let her go home without being all cut and bruised," I yell at a turned back.

That certainly ticks off James, as he whips his head around and strides over to me. Just until he is within reach of me. I see the guard bend down far enough in Ava's ear, soft enough that I cannot hear, but bold enough to make the color drain from her beautiful face.

"I said it once and I will say it, One. Last. Time. Shut that mouth of yours before I shut it for you," his hot breath hits my face.

Threats are strong, but not as much as my fiery, and I have enough of it to do something that I am definitely going to regret. Before James starts to turn back around, I use the one thing that the guards haven't held onto yet, and it kicks right up into the place that takes a while for men to recover from.

That gives me enough distraction from the guards to throw my head from side to side and kick wildly at the guards holding me. As soon as their grips loosen enough, I run for Ava, not checking from behind to see all that I had done. It was close to ten feet between where the guards lay, and where my friend is staring at me with wide eyes.

I am within an arm's length of my friend as a hand grabs me by the hair and yanks me back.

Before I can fight, the same hand wraps around my throat and propels me to the floor. My head is still spinning from using it to get away from the guards before, but now I can see stars in my eyes as my head hits the floor, hard. My vision swirls with black spots, and my eyes dart back and forth. I can only make out shapes until I feel James lean down closer, his body pressed against mine. It takes a while but eventually I can make out the face of the man that just threw me to the ground.

Although I want to yell at him, not only does my head spinning make it difficult, but the breath was knocked out of me. As I try to suck in the air I lost, James's hand tightens around my throat. I claw, trying to rip his hand off my airway. Try as I might, his grip is firm.

"Alena struggle all you want, but I am stronger than you. I would like to keep this wonderful deal of yours, but only if we clear this slate. Ava will go home as promised, not to be harmed on the way and for the rest of her life, along with the rest of your family. You will do anything and everything I ask, and you will listen to me. Do you understand?"

How much it would delight me to make him mad by not answering, Ava was still in the room. It did, however, take a lot of effort to push out, "...yes master."

"You will take her home as I promised, Zach. You will not touch her in any harmful way. Disobey me, and I will make your life a living hell," James turns to the man standing over my friend.

"Yes sir," Zach responds, backing away from Ava.

"And as for you Alena, you will spend your days in a cell, until I think you are worthy of my company. You yell, you will be punished. The punishment... well, depends on how loudly you scream." The smirk on James's face twists my insides as he stands and I gasp for breath. "Oh, and about that blanket... you should conserve your body heat, I hear that it is pretty cold down there."

Chapter 13

I watch as Alena bows down to the man before her. Next to him, Will starts to cry. Alena doesn't even look up as the brother walks away in tears, and as James tells the guards to take me home. I try to ask him to take me, but all James wants is Alena. Not only her, but her suffering. That's why when James secretly signaled to a guard next to me, and I was slapped to the ground. I understand how far they are willing to go to make her hurt.

When Alena fights and then runs for me, I understand why he did it. James wants her to suffer, and the only way he can do that is by making her play into his hand. I watch as Alena is thrown to the ground and forced to obey once again. The same guard that put me down, pulls me up again and forces me to watch as Alena is taken off the floor as well. James walks away as she is restrained. I can't run to her, knowing the men's grips are too strong, so I do the only thing that I can think of.

"Alena, you once said to me that the world would eventually get better; that it doesn't always have to be someone sacrificing. Prove to me that you were right."

I am met with silence.

"We can find a way around this! Just fight a little longer!"

I am angry when she doesn't answer me right away. I have been searching for this girl for months, praying to whatever gods out there that she would come home. I spent nights printing missing posters, going door to door. I had to listen to people whisper behind my back that she was gone for god sake.

Now she's here, not ten feet in front of me, and she won't respond to me. I don't care what she's been through, I deserve better than this. We deserve better than this.

She turns to me with anger and tears in her eyes, "You don't understand! This is the only way to protect you! Why can't you see that?"

To hell with trying to protect us! Does she not see the need for her to be home? Does she not see how broken and dead I am? That conversation all that time ago rings in my ears, a time when things were simple and black and white. But Alena lives in a world of grey, where life has taken the very best of her. I just hope that even though she is not the same girl that left me, she can still fight to come back to me. To herself.

"I do understand! I understand that you are only a child. You should not be the one to bear this burden. Show the world what it should be! What could happen if you were the one that led them the right way. You can protect your family by talking to the world. So do it. Fight Alena! Fight!"

A few seconds of nothing, and then...

Alena's responding grating scream brightens my heart as she thrashes against the two guards that hold her. With most of the soldiers having left with James and Will, there are not many people to help hold Alena down. She kicks and pushes and pulls at the guards' arms pinning her in place. She screams as she fights—screams that could curdle milk. The screams and her thrashing did, however, bring in James once again.

"What is going on here?" his voice booms with authority.

"She is resisting sir," the soldier on the right side of Alena says to his commander.

I start to pull on my own guards, as I watch the guard speaking to his boss become distracted, giving Alena the perfect opportunity to strike the guard to her right in the face with her elbow, and slip free of the left one's grasp. I watch in fear and disbelief as she whirls with non-human speed, knocking them both to the ground.

As Alena runs for me, I feel my guards start to pull me back. Although I want to go home, I can't bear the thought of leaving Alena all alone here.

That's when I realize that the guards are not pulling me to the exit where I came in. In fact, they are pulling me in the complete opposite direction. It makes sense when I see that the only way for me to get out of here is going past Alena, and these guards are not going to risk that.

Even when a literal wall of living guards starts to form, blocking Alena from running to me, slowing her down, it never stops her. If the fire in her eyes isn't enough to make me guess, then the way that she cuts through the guards is.

Proving what James says holds true, something non-human runs through Alena's veins. It makes me scared out of my wits. It's not the fact that it is not of my species, but because this is something that I truly cannot help my friend with or understand.

When more guards try to run for her, the more they are blasted back. I keep on trying to fight my guards that are still pulling me away from my furious friend. I smile at the damage that Alena is causing James. At least if she is caught, then it will be a pain to keep her at bay. The more I fight, the more Alena fights.

Until a voice threatens.

"Alena turn around and look at me," James says from his position behind his own wall of guards.

Regardless of the wall of people protecting the monster, I can clearly see James and the people next to him. I see what the devilish man holds before Alena does: the gun that he holds to a girl's head. She has to be no older than 17. I stop fighting, fearing that my resistance could result in the death of the innocent girl.

As I stand there just staring, so do the guards that have a hold on me. James's wall of guards disperses as Alena turns away from her fight. Her body goes rigid as she sees the girl on her knees, gun to her head.

"Isabella?" Alena's voice cracks.

"I am sorry Alena. I heard you scream, I thought you were hurt," the girl's own voice breaks.

"Shut up Isabella!" James yanks at the girl's hair.

Apparently, this guy has a thing for yanking on girls' hair to make them listen.

"You should've stayed in the room, Isabella. I can't keep putting you in situations like this where you can get hurt."

The guards that Alena knocked to the ground now starts to stand back up and come for her.

"This seems familiar. Doesn't it, Alena?"

Even from here I can see her eyes are downcast.

"Except, this time your power cannot help both your friends."

With a jerk of his chin, I have a knife to my throat.

As quickly as it started, it ends with a choice that, if chosen incorrectly, could result in two souls leaving this earth forever. Alena doesn't even resist as the guards take her arms, knock the air out of her lungs with a blow to the stomach, and kick her legs out beneath her. She doesn't even struggle, just watches the girl, Isabella, softly crying.

I want to tell her to fight, but I know what that would do to Alena right now. She is stuck between doing what is right for me and what is right for this girl. Some part of me wants her to choose herself over both, but the way that she looks at Isabella, tells me that something between them happened that was very painful. The bond between them is strong.

That is something that Alena and I will never share. We may have grown up together, but we have never before been in a situation that has threatened our lives.

"Because I am feeling quite generous today, I am giving *you* the punishment," James says to Alena. "I would love to kill Isabella, but that means that I would have to put up with Will's whining and I don't feel up for that right now. But then again, I could kill Ava. She did start all of this, I am told. I think that would be too merciful for you. No, I think you should have it. You have worked hard for it after all," James' merciless smile says everything before he even opens his mouth.

Positioned on the floor, curling around her stomach, she looks up at the man stalking toward her.

"Do your worst," Alena spits out.

James' grin is wild as he says, "Gladly."

The moment he says gladly, I immediately regret it. Not because I know it will hurt, but because Ava *and* Isabella are going to watch.

Trying to stand up was not going to happen thanks to the guards pushing me back on my knees. Whatever James whispers to the guards standing next to him is something I figure will hurt because they smile and laugh.

These are guards that probably had no problem killing babies and can sleep like monkeys full of bananas. I have no idea what is coming, but while I wait, I think of all the reasons why I am doing this. My family, my friends and my town.

I scold myself for regretting my decision when I see what the guards have gone to get. My breath catches in my throat when I behold the long, leather, wicked whip being handed to James.

"Get her up," James orders the guards at my sides.

If I am being completely honest, I am sick and tired of being pushed around. Then I remember the agreement I made, obeying him in exchange for everyone's safety, and now have broken twice. My thoughts shift to the girls in front and behind me. I can tell they are trying to find a way out of their holds, but I know the only way they will get out of that is either by being let go or killed for trying to run.

Another jerk of his chin and my shirt is torn in two. Revealing my back to him made me feel sick to my stomach.

"We normally only use this lovely thing here to get our animals to run or slaves to walk. I am sure we can make an exception for you, darling," James says, hand gliding along the whip, like he's petting a prized horse's mane.

I look at the two guards holding my friend. One with a knife, and the second who took over for James, with a gun. Both killers since birth if I had to guess. Both willing to kill now, and not shedding a single tear.

"Now, let's see how much you can use that loud mouth of yours," James steps closer to me.

"You won't be getting anything from me," I shout at him.

"I guess we'll see about that. Funny how not even two months ago we were talking about how if you give slaves too many whippings they lose their sense of feeling. I suppose today we get to find out if that is true." He hands the whip to the man next to him.

"Let her go!" Isabella screams from behind James.

"Please! We will do anything!" Ava echoes.

"As I said before, no, but it is quite a lovely offer. Why don't we make this even more interesting? Every time that you don't scream, you will receive extra lashings. How does that sound Alena?"

The man with the whip comes around to my backside.

"Go to hell!" I yelled in his face.

"Go ahead Avid," James commands to the man behind me.

I smirk to myself as I land a blow before one lands on me, "If you had balls, you'd do it yourself."

The man, Avid, uncurls the whip. It's so long that I can hear it hit the floor. Amusement shines in David's eyes as he comes up beside James to watch, giving James the strength to ignore my insult. They both share a smile of pure evil.

I will not scream. I will not cry. I will never give in. I will take each lashing, as a reminder of what I was protecting. I don't care how many lashes he adds; I will prove to him and everyone else, and myself, that I will not be easy to break. I will not show pain in front of my friends. I will be strong.

Unbreakable.

An intake of breath as the whip raises.

Brave.

I grit my teeth as I growl through my pain when the first lash hits, hot searing pain goes through me.

Iron-willed.

The second lash sends sparks of pain all the way to my hands, my body attempting to numb itself.

"Again," is James' only order.

The third lash makes me close my eyes to hide my pain.

Unyielding.

"Harder."

The fourth sends blood flowing down my back. Ava and Isabella scream.

Stubborn.

My own screams become synchronized with my friends', as the fifth lash lands harder than before.

Resolute.

Sixth lands as I lose my footing and fall, only being held by the guards' arms.

Unbreaking.

David's inhuman smile brightens at the seventh.

Shatterproof.

Eighth.

Resistant.

Ninth.

Armored.

Tenth.

My hot blood pools around my knees.

Indestructible.

Eleventh.

I go limp in the guards' arms.

Everlasting.

James walks up to me as the guards pull on my hair so I look at him.

"You are quite resilient Alena; more than I thought you were. The first one I expected no screams, but four straight lashes with only a few grunts. Even your friends were screaming before you."

I continue to hear the cries and pleas from the girls, my labored breathing quieting their pleas.

I want to go to them more than anything, but I can't feel my legs. It feels like my whole body is on fire. I am still not able to stand up or even sit up for that matter.

"I guess it's in my blood," I rasp out.

"I guess it is. I wouldn't be too proud of that though, Alena. Four lashes without screaming equals forty extra lashings. Of course, we could finish it here, but we wouldn't want you to be broken now would we *Princess*," he pushes out the last word like a joke.

What if I was actually a Royal? If I was an actual *Princess*? That is like something out of a fairytale. And my life is anything but a fairytale. Only, James is too blind and idiotic to see that.

"You love to hear yourself talk, don't you?" I chuckle out.

That really gets him.

"Throw her in the cell. I will send for her when I am ready to put up with her bullshit attitude."

The guards heave me up into a semi-standing position.

I grunt at the weight put on my back by the movement, which earns a smile by David which had only disappeared moments before. The next time that this happens, when my friends are not here, I am gonna whoop his ass.

The look on the girls' faces makes me forget about all the pain I just endured. Pale, sorrowful, tear-streaked faces make me sink into a hole inside my soul. I look away from the sight that is too painful to watch, as I am dragged from the room.

Room after room, corridor after corridor, stair after stair we go, sinking deeper into my own personal prison. Filled with passing people who stare, some with fear, some with anger, and some with sorrow. I can feel the trail of blood that follows behind me.

When we reach a set of doors that has two guards posted outside, much like my own doors except more enforced, the guards open it up immediately. If they know of me, they certainly don't show it. As soon as we pass through the doors the stench and reek of bodily fluids hits my senses like a wave.

As we pass the cells that line each side, I see men and women, bloodied, bruised, and broken in cells. A few are chained to the wall or floor, some huddled in the corner, others curled up against the cell bars. Most of the cells contain old blood stains on the floor and walls, a moldy bed, finished food trays at the cell doors, vomit and urine in the corners. If the stench wasn't overwhelming enough, the sight certainly is.

We pass through another set of doors, the guards dragging me with my feet being ripped apart by every sharp crevice in the floor, and down another flight of stairs. This one goes deep enough that only some sunlight peeks through the barred window cells, high above. These cells hold less people than the last ones, but the layout of everything is the same, except hay litters the floor where beds should be.

We pass through yet another set of doors, this time the guards are wearing all black. The soldier to the right hands a ring of keys to my guard on the left. As we wait for these doors to open, I try to stand up and walk, but the soldiers just yank me forward, causing me to lose my footing again. They just laugh as they continue to drag my bloody body down the set of stairs.

These cells are so disgusting that I take one look and think that I might vomit myself. Moldy hay litters the floor everywhere, and there is no need for windows because we are so far down that no light reaches here, save for the light pouring from the stairwell that we had just exited.

The many cells all consist of chains that adorn each wall or floor. I only pass two men as I reach a cell that I am to guess is mine. As a guard to my left takes out the keys given to him before and opens the door, I take a quick peek back to the stairs. I want to remember what the sunlight looks like before I sleep in the dark for who knows how long.

With aggression, the guards heave me into the cold, small cell interior. I find it funny as they chain me to the floor. James must think that I am dangerous if he thinks that it is necessary for my escort of guards to chain me to the floor. The metal bites at my skin as I hiss at the cold.

The cell is simple, but it looks like it was just cleaned, almost as if this particular cell has been waiting for me. New, clean hay is spread out in the back right hand corner. Nothing but chains, hay and a few pebbles decorate the cell.

The guards and I struggle to get the chains on, my limbs unmoving, forcing our bodies to entangle. They stand, smirking down at me before they pull me onto my feet. As I am pushed into the wall, I yank on the chains that somehow had wrapped around the tallest of the two guard's leg, causing him to fall face first into the cold stone.

"You little bitch!" the tall man on the floor bellows at me.

As the man scrambles to his feet and saunters over to me the other guard intervenes.

"James said not to touch her. You will obey your Master as she soon will," the wiser one says to the man just a few feet from my breathing space.

"Yeah I know what Master said, but he only said that thinking that she wouldn't fight," he turns to his comrade.

"You are all complete idiots if you think that I am not going to fight back," I burst out.

"Mason let's just go. Don't waste your time on a petty child."

With that they both walk out of the cell, but not without a promise from Mason.

"You will pay for that, pig."

"I am sure I will," I joke.

Within minutes, both men have disappeared up the flight of stairs we had just come from, leaving me alone with only my thoughts and a set of chains to accompany me.

As my legs once again tire of the pain and weight, I sit down against the wall and hiss against the cold that bites at my new wounds. The cell is so small that I can go to every corner and the chains still reach. Only a single stream of light comes through a crack in the ceiling.

I guess it is a gift from God, telling me that it was going to be there for me when I pushed everyone else away. I tell myself that they will be safe, if only because of my sacrifice. I guess that all those years ago when Ava and I had the conversation about how the world needed to change, Ava was right when she said someone would have to sacrifice themselves to save it. At least, my world would have to have one.

I stare into the dark abyss of my cell wall, where faint scratch marks and carvings adorn the wall. During those brief moments of sitting, all of my adrenaline sinks away adding to my levels of pain from the numerous injuries I've amassed in the last 24 hours.

But those injuries are not even the worst pain. It's my heart aching, thinking of everything and everyone that I will never see again.

The only sound in my cell is the pitter patter of water droplets hitting stone nearby. I look from my ripped and bloody feet to my chained wrists. If this is what I will endure, maybe I should just let infection set into my open cuts. That way, maybe I can go by sickness rather than pain at the hands of those monsters. At least then I would be at peace.

As tears start to fall down my face, I watch as the single strand of light coming into my cell disappears as the sun goes out of range. I hug my knees to my chest and hum a lullaby quietly to myself. The lullaby is one that my mother used to sing for me, that would always comfort me when I was sad.

Hush little Firestar, don't you worry

Allura is watching over your crown

May darkness run from your bright light

During the night

May Panthers protect you

Your people guild you

And your heart ever love

May The Fire Star guide your way home

The tears flow freely as I sing the verses of my childhood lullaby over and over again. When crying starts to take away energy, I lie face down on the hay, careful not to get any straws of hay on my back. I continue to hum the tune until my eyes flutter closed and I drift off into a fitful sleep.

Chapter 14

As soon as Alena is dragged out, I turn to the two girls that have made this a lot easier than it would have been. The whimpers from the girls become louder as servants come in to clean up the puddle of blood from the lashings on Alena's back. I watch as the girls are brought to their feet, weapons put away, no threats. It looks quite hard to pull them up because the men had to literally pick up the girls.

"Come on girls, just get up already," I complain as they try to sit back down on the floor.

"How could you do that? Alena has never done anything to hurt anyone!" Ava bolts up from the floor and tries to come for me, but is pulled back by the men.

"You know as well as I that she had it coming for her when she made that deal. Sure, she hasn't hurt anyone on purpose, but she said I could do anything that I wanted. She disobeyed, so she gets punished. It is as simple as that," I state in absolute disbelief.

I don't know what is wrong with me. As soon as David started threatening the soldiers about not attacking an heir, I knew I had to agree. If I showed everyone how broken our family was, that is a sign of weakness that we could possibly die for. I tried to put on the best act that I could, showing that threatening Alena and her friend was okay to do.

I tried to get out of there as quickly as I could, but then I heard her scream. And my lord, can that girl fight. If her mother really didn't teach her anything about the clans or about fighting, that was the most impressive thing that I have ever seen, even if she was trained.

My soldiers have been drilled since birth to protect their leaders, to never break under interrogation, and to never lose a fight. I never understood before how those men were taken out by a 17-year-old, but that non-human speed made me understand.

I didn't want to admit it, but I think Will was right; Alena really is heir to a long-lost throne. A kingdom that has long since turned to ruin and rivalry.

If my parents knew about Alena's family... No, no that is not possible. They would have left clues or told us if there was that big of a threat. If a future Queen was indeed still alive, I know of many clans that would fight for her. They'd destroy, ruin, and kill everything in their path, even if that meant my entire clan would be wiped out. I swore an oath that I'd protect them, and I certainly don't plan on breaking it. Which means that I need to have a sit down with Alena's mother to ensure that she will keep her mouth shut if she wants to save her daughter.

"Ava, you can go on home. But I swear on my life that if you tell a soul of what you saw here today, I don't care what promise I made, I will make your life a living hell. Understood?"

"What of Mrs. Nightglade? She should know about her daughter. You talk about her so much, doesn't she know who you are?" Ava asks.

"Yes, Mrs. Nightglade knows of me. I am actually glad you brought her up. I want you to set up a meeting with her for me. Tell her to meet me in the park south of the town, right by the waterfall. If she decides not to, her daughter will die. Don't disappoint me Ava," I turn around to Isabella.

"When I first saw you two in the same room, I actually thought you cared for her. This just reminded me of how you and your family don't have any love in their hearts for that," Isabella glares at me. Her tone is empty of any emotion.

"You can go home with Ava as well," I say to the lifeless girl.

Her face hardens as she says, "No, I am staying here with Alena. You can't hurt me because I am still Will's dawn. My life is his to control, not yours."

"Go find my brother then, and tell him I need to have a talk in the lab. Afterwards, you can go into Alena's room and stay there with the rest of the girls until I have decided what to do with you." My demands grow weary on my soul, "Take Ava home, then stakeout at the meeting place until tomorrow."

With my orders given, I turn around and head to my part of the castle. As I walk I try to forget all the events that just unfolded. Maybe I pushed Alena too hard when I told her about her family's fate. Maybe it was a bad idea to bring her out of her room, maybe that was my mistake.

Even with the corridors filled with nothing but the sound of my footsteps reverberating off the walls, I can still hear the screams of all three girls. Alena's echo loudly over the others.

Part of me wishes I listened to that voice in my head telling me not to hurt her. I wish that those who stood up for Alena would have broken through to me. I have respect for all of those who stood up for the young heir, to stand against me is like signing their own death warrants.

From the multiple fights, to the threats, to the pleas, I was so taken aback by their undying loyalty, especially Isabella and Ava. Maybe the loyalty from Isabella came from hating my family, and Ava's from growing up with Alena.

I am so confused as to why it took so much effort to keep Alena and her temper at bay. I mean, I have had enemies fight like hell, sometimes doing so much to kill everyone in their path, but this was much different. She had no technique, no strategy, no end game, except to get to Ava.

Even afterward, she put up such a fight when she was whipped. Over and over again defying. Not against the guards, but against her own body showing fear and pain—weaknesses, both of them. Yet, the restraint that she had was so amazing that they almost seemed like strengths.

As I walk past my study, then my bedroom, I realize that I don't know where to go. I need to get out—some place where I can't hear her screams, feel her pain or her love. And most of all her forgiveness. A place that no one will disturb me.

I don't want to see David, not after all the pain he has caused me, and Will... I can't stand to look at his sorrow filled face when my heart is full of so much on its own. I need to figure out why I feel so obligated to take care of her and keep her safe. If anything, I should be enjoying her pain, relishing in it actually. Maybe it is the bind of dawning, if that is even possible.

Never have I heard of the Dawn Masters having the same personality traits as the Dawn Slaves. Then again, the dawning process has only been used by my family ever since magic disappeared.

During that process, many books containing the history of magic were burned or hidden away from the rogue cartels that wanted to wipe out magic for good. They succeeded with all of us, although the royals' powers were only lessened. They couldn't conjure a storm anymore or control the minds of people as they once were able to. They could only do the simple stuff: move water, make the wind blow, and start fires with their hands. As for everyone else, well, the only thing they could do was imagine and feel the lick of power left in their veins.

As the years have passed, people have lost track of their magical traits, and when children are born no one ever knows of the true power that they may possess. Whoever Alena's father was, he was powerful. Even without knowing what magic I possess, I can still feel hers pouring off her in waves; and if that star is any indication, she is a royal.

With no sister, Alena could be a queen if people figured out her existence, causing a big mess for me and my clan. Not only would she rule my clan, but every clan and cartel in the world. Almost every city has at least one clan or cartel. The larger cities usually have a major clan, then smaller cartels.

There are only two ways for clans or cartels to be official. One way for you to become a major clan is to once have served the last Queen closely. The other, you could be like the cartel that took out the Queen and kill all those that disobey, earning your spot amongst the clans by using fear.

My father did so by serving that same clan, Embroke, but eventually broke ties with them after learning what had happened with the last of the Royals.

My father never explained fully what he learned, only that the way the last Queen died, was the same technique now used on everyone that defied Embroke. My father was an asshole, so him being turned off by a killing technique surprised me. Ever since my father left, we have been hunted by the Embroke Clan.

The Embroke Clan was the brains behind killing the last Queen. That basically made them the worst of the worst when the kingdom fell apart.

Although they have slowed, the clans that had once served the former rulers started going after them for revenge. Those clans have slowed too, looking for their Queen's heir that was supposedly not found with the body of his or her mother.

There is no clear answer to how the last Queen was murdered, or how the plan was executed. It is clear that it was an inside job, and that a Jumper was involved, easy then to get inside the castle walls.

I have been walking in such deep thought that I almost walk straight into a wall, although I stop before I get a bloody nose. I am at the end of the castle. This part is ancient and not many people explore this area. Many rumors have claimed that the ghosts of the previous owners still haunt this part of the home. I still call it nonsense, all of it. I don't believe in ghosts, but then again, I didn't believe magic still existed up until the day Alena was shot.

Deciding that I have nothing to get back to anytime soon I choose to turn left, and walk down the dark, damp corridor. As I go, I realize that the light dims here, ancient torches hang on the wall, unlit. With no lighter or match I continue on in darkness, using only my phone's flashlight setting.

Despite this castle being my family home, I've never ventured this far from the main area. My mother always warned me against it, telling my brothers and I horror stories to keep us out. Back then I listened to my mom enough to listen.

Although being a little kid, my curiosity did get the best of me once, and I disobeyed. My father never cared where I went in the castle, but my mother did. She stopped me before I even got past the darkness here.

As I continue to walk down the corridor everything becomes black, save for the light coming from my phone. The ancient walls here are covered in ancient, worn and faded tapestries. No rugs adorn the floors. Chills creep down my spine as I start to hear whispers in my ear. I shake my head, trying to block out the sound, my mind already full of my own thoughts.

The further I walk, the more I realize that this was a bad idea. Fewer and fewer doors appear. Each one I try to open, but they are all locked, as if someone wanted to keep some secrets hidden. A window must be open somewhere because it is freezing here. Cold, brief gusts of wind pass by me every now and then.

I continue down the cold corridor until I come upon an open wooden door. From the crack comes an eerie, twilight colored light. Like the others, this door one is worn with age, still hiding secrets of the past. It is old and carved with odd symbols and phrases in another language.

As I come closer, I feel the cold gusts of wind I had noticed earlier were coming from the room behind the open door. Curious, I reach my hand out and push ever so slightly on the handle and slip inside. I shiver from the icy air adding to the chill already running up my spine.

The room is old, made obvious by the cobwebs adorning the walls, dust coating the few wooden shelves, and the ancient books piled everywhere. A bed sits to the left of the room, in between a door to the bathing chamber, and a bedside to the left of it closest to a shut door. On the complete opposite side of the room is a giant oakwood desk, also covered with books and a thick layer of dust. But that isn't what catches my eye.

Directly in front of the entrance, lies yet another set of doors, but these lead outside. The doors are agape letting the chilly air inside.

As soon as I pass onto the cool stones, I freeze at the sight that lies before me. Even with the late sun setting, the sky is jet black, painted with white dots everywhere.

Often as I am looking at the stars, I try to look for the constellation Starfire, which points to the once great city of the royals. Where people walked around freely, went to bed with food in their bellies, and had magic protecting them from every which angle.

Most nights it takes me a while to find it, but tonight is not one of those nights. Directly in front of me lies Starfire, the symbol of our people, and our rulers. It is sacred and untouched by anyone that is corrupt, being reserved only for the holy and pure; Innocent children with great destinies, or young adults with a pure-hearted reason can wish upon the constellation.

People nowadays don't believe in the myths and legends of its holy power to bestow people with glorious power. Claiming that no one can touch a star, few know that there is a hidden place that many venture to find. Only the ones that return are pure. Those that do not are never heard from again. Only few have ever tried, fewer live to use their wishes. Most of them are recorded in our history, whether it tells of a great battle that was mysteriously won overnight, or a mother that was infected by an incurable sickness that later ran around the town. Though everyone knows of the very first person to whom a wish was gifted: Gianna Starfire, the first of the royals.

She was gifted with the power of healing in blood, elemental fire, and the power of shifting to a form of choice. A form that was once chosen can never be changed again. Gianna chose a Panther for its cunning and fast movements and changed the fur from typical black to white with golden eyes instead of green.

In choosing so, she got the animal's heightened senses and abilities, as did every future generation of the Starfire line.

After the wish was granted for Gianna, the Wishing Goddess Allura granted a final gift for her first descendant: A sword of Guidance, a throne of Fire and a crown of living Stars. Of those three she became a Queen. People worshipped her power, her wisdom, and her leadership.

Those that worshipped Gianna were ordered to worship Allura, Goddess of Wishes, for it was she that gave the power. The first few that worshipped her were gifted with special powers, portions of what Gianna had, but also powers of opposites.

Elementals: Blazers, Torrents, Zephyres and Terrens. They have the typical elements that humans see everyday, only they can create more intricate and imaginative objects with their power.

Healers. Shifters. Seers. These three were often found on the outskirts of civilization. These groups wished to be near nature, either because humans overwhelmed them, or nature granted a great access to their magic.

Supernatural creatures: witches, vampires, werewolves, familiars. The ones you read in books are the same in real life. They always separated themselves from the group of magically gifted people, apart from familiars. Familiars often attached themselves to elementals, and on rare occasions, the last group of gifted individuals.

Silencers. Readers. Champions. Jumpers. Teleis. Ironers. Blooders. Considered some of the most dangerous and out of the ordinary powers. They had the ability to bend things other than the elements to their will. Whether it was blood, the mind, iron, space and time, or even other gifts. Champions were always the odd ones out, with skill sets of fighting like never seen before.

Each is dangerous in their own way. As time went on and powers were combined and passed from generation to generation, some of the people became out of control.

Those that tried to strike against the monarchy were cut down. The Starfire Royals created an inner circle of the most powerful of gifts. Over time, the ones that became too powerful were hunted by others to almost extinction. As royals rushed to save them, people started to revolt and kill. When it was clear that the monarchy could not handle all of the powers by themselves, they created the clans and cartels. Each possessed a separate gift and belief.

For a time, the leaders were in control and people were safe and peaceful. The supernaturals kept together in their own worlds, followed the Queen's rule with peace and justice. The gifted separated into two different sides. Most elementals stayed with the Healers, Shifters, Champions, Seers, Silencers and Readers, called the Adels. Of those were some of the hunted, ones that the royals saved and protected. Thanking them, the Adels protected the Queen and all of her family and bound themselves in blood to the Queen herself. The rest of the gifted, they fought the sovereign and built their own empire, the Vipers.

It stayed that way for lifetimes—each generation being taught to fight and protect each side. Children were caught up in a war that was waged until the Vipers murdered the current Queen and her heir. It was done by a group of gifted: Blooder, Jumper, and rogue Silencer. While a battle waged outside, the three slaughtered the mother and child. With the father dead and the guards killed, no one was left to save the young ruler who bled out on her bedroom floor.

No one ever saw a descendant of Gianna again. When the Inner Circle realized what had happened, they killed the remaining rebel army with their rage, and took the artifacts of the royals. Fleeing to the safety of their own walls, they ruled for the Queen from their homes, allowing the Vipers to take control of the castle and the Queen's Capital, Feka. They laid the city to ruins, leaving buildings as nothing but rubble, streets as burial sites, and the people as slaves, with magic no longer protecting them.

For years the remaining members of the Queen's Circle tried to get the slaves out but failed again and again, losing more men than they were saving. They eventually slowed but never fully stopped.

Looking at the constellation reminds me of the stories about the bloodshed and the lost heir to a mighty throne. Seers had before told of a downfall of a great empire, and a mighty powerful heir coming back to rebuild it bigger and better than before, not only with more power, but obedience from all clans and cartels.

Much too deep in my thought, I don't notice a mysterious figure walk up behind me until it taps me on my shoulder. I whip around, gun out, pointed at the intruder. What I saw was beyond anything that I could ever describe.

There in the entryway of the doors stood a woman. She was grey with age, dressed in a rich velvet cloth, but not fully human. Her features were lit by an eerie blue glow. There were no feet holding her up.

My breath caught in my throat at the sight. I never believed in ghosts, yet here one appears before me.

"Why do you come here, James Ashburn?" The lady asks.

"How is this even possible?" I reply, still in awe.

"You believe in magic, but not ghosts? We go hand in hand."

"I'm dreaming." I close my eyes tightly for a few seconds, trying to get back to reality, but when I open them nothing has changed.

"Think what you would like, but you are most positively awake."

Her smile makes the blue aura around her glow brighter.

"Good thing too, because we have much to talk about."

"Such as?" I question.

"Why you locked up the rightful Heir to the throne of Astraea."

"She is no one," I state, my shock subsiding.

"Alena of the Starfire is not no one. She is a Queen and a very powerful one from the looks of it."

"Why do you care? You're dead."

"I was blood bound to the Last Queen. My vows still stand, even after death."

"That means nothing."

"How disappointed your mother is in you for saying such things," despair and sorrow shine in those cool blue eyes.

"My mother?" I choke on the word.

"Yes, your mother. She is here with me now. She misses you, you know."

A statement, not a question.

"Can I see her?"

"No. You lost that privilege when you disgraced her family's home with the sacred blood of a Starfire."

"I did not know Alena was a Starfire! Or even close to being in the same family!"

"Lies," The ghost spits, displeasure written all over her face.

She takes a step toward me, "Do you know what is most sad about what you did, James? You didn't even want to do it, yet you did, just to show there were no fractures between the *Great Ashburn* family."

"Do not dishonor my family name like that." I grow increasingly angrier.

"Ashburn's are no longer honorable, not like they used to be all that time ago," She says, with no hint of a lie in her features.

"What do you mean by 'used to be'?"

"You need to look into your family history, son."

"What does my mother wish for me to do?"

Her face softens at my meek voice

"She wishes that you follow your heart. Do what you wish to do, not what Edward taught you to do."

"If I do not honor my name, then let it be my mother."

I start to turn to go back inside, but the ghost stops me.

"I hope that you realize not what she is, but *who* she is to you."

It isn't until I am out of the forgotten part of the castle, that I realize the woman did not mean my mother.

Chapter 15

I wake up to the scuffling of feet. My eyes flutter open to find the same unforgiving, scratched up wall that I fell asleep to. I try to think of how long I may have been asleep. I wouldn't be surprised if it was for a few days.

I try to move my arms, but I am met by a searing pain in my back and the rustling sound of chains. It is hard to breathe with the mustiness of the air. I shut my eyes and reopen them to make sure that this nightmare is real. Indeed it is.

"I'm sorry," a voice sounds.

I am startled at the sudden noise made from outside my cell wall. I look to my right and find James leaning against the cell bars. His arms and feet are crossed, giving him a very muscular and powerful look.

"Have you come to toy with my emotions or to gloat?" I ask, sitting back up against the wall.

"Neither."

"Why don't I believe you then?"

"Because what I did was horrendous, and no human with honor would do such a thing. And a human with no honor is not worthy of belief," James says. He pushes off of the cell bars and moves to stand to the right of my body, on the opposite side of the bars.

"Now he gets honorable," I say sarcastically.

"Who says I am honorable?"

I guess no one said it outright.

My silence must have been enough because he continues, "I am not quite sure where I was going with that."

"Sometimes the mind leads us places that we need to be without us even realizing it."

"That is beautiful."

I revert back to sarcasm, "Yes, well, I have much more time to think up more for you."

James blew out a long breath, "I wanted to..."

"You are not even sure."

"I can't say I am," he says, his eyes starting to soften.

"Why are you sorry?"

"Who says I am?" James quickly puts the invisible wall back up.

"If you saying sorry in the beginning isn't enough, I can see right through your shell."

"If you can, then what am I thinking about?"

I put it simply, "You are fearful of something you have just uncovered. Confused even. You are not sure what path you are to follow."

"That is creepy."

"There are many things that are creepy in this world, James. What I said is not one of them."

His expression lightens, "When did you become so wise?"

"Maybe I was wise all along. You just happened to not notice it."

"I don't even understand why I did it."

"I do. I understood it when I saw your brother with the guards."

"David is just doing his job. Just like I am," James quickly defends his brother.

"No. It isn't a job, it's a lifestyle. One that has been forced onto you your entire life."

James' confusion deepens his features, "I don't understand."

"I put it together when I heard that woman talk about your mother and how your father dragged her to her death."

He flinches at the mention of his mother.

"If I am wrong, correct me, but your mother was never fully a part of what your father did. She loved you, but your father was the cruel one. He beat you into his perfect image, his perfect successor. He beat your brothers to follow your lead."

"I am not broken."

"We are all broken in some way or another. Some just recognize it better than others."

"In what way are you broken then?"

I think for a while before answering, "I am not, but I think that I may be soon."

Too far, I said too much.

"You are starting to lose hope," a statement, not a question.

"I lose a bit more each time darkness descends. And I cannot see the stars. So yes, I am losing a bit of hope."

"I am guessing that has to do with me. I am sorry for the whipping. For the threats."

At first I don't believe him, it seems too easy, too quick. It seems like he hasn't had enough time to put thought into it. If he really is apologizing, then I want the pain of what he did to hurt him. I almost snap back at him, with the thought of pain in mind, until fragments of conversations remind me of what monsters are. Broken human beings.

"I don't blame you, so don't apologize."

"But I made the order," James' confused face confesses.

"'Let me ask you this: if your father wasn't the monster he was, would you be acting the way you did however long ago?"

Another silence. Then, "No, at least I don't think so."

"Then I am not mad at you."

"I whipped you like an animal, like a slave," James' eyes deepen with disbelief.

I turn my body as fully as I can to him, "And I am guessing that you got that idea from when you misbehaved as a child?"

"What?"

"When you were… hurting me, Will was there in my mind. He didn't know that I knew, but I was able to access a memory of his. One where he watched you get whipped. Where you vowed to never leave him."

"You saw them?"

"I wish I didn't, but at the same time I am glad I did. It helped me to remember that no one is born a monster, but they are made. And that they can still be saved."

"How can you have so much understanding? After everything that has happened to you, you should want to punish me."

"I did. And I hate myself for it."

James wipes something away from his face and takes a step back.

"I need to go."

I stay silent as I wait for what he has been wanting to say, but it never comes. He shakes his head against the idea and starts to walk off.

"James," I stop him. "Follow your heart, do what makes you happy. Do not do what you were taught to do."

With that, James walks away. I can't see his face, but I know I said something that hit him hard. Finally, since however long I have been down here, my heart and mind finally feel free.

I carefully move my body back up against the wall and drift off to sleep with a clear conscience.

Chapter 16

I quickly get out of the bottom level of the dungeons to the second floor. It's still really quiet down here compared to during the daytime. I shut the door to the sublevel below and breathe out a long sigh. I am still not even sure why I decided to go down to see her, but part of me is glad I did. Seeing Alena in such a state, I can't believe I allowed such a thing to happen.

Maybe she was right, maybe my father did twist me up. I wonder what it would be like if I grew up like Alena, in a safe home, with a parent that encouraged me and loved me. And maybe my father did love me, in his own twisted way.

I let my mind wander, thinking about the ifs and maybes, until I fall totally in love with the idea of being a different person. Of not being a leader who is driven by hatred, who doesn't give chances, and who revels in the idea of pain. Maybe I could be kind. Maybe I could even possibly love without hurting people.

I am at the door of my room by the time my thoughts stop flowing. I push open the heavy oak doors with exhausted arms. Shutting the doors behind me, I walk to my changing room.

Suits adorn the right side of my wall, displaying a number of different colors. Mostly black and grey, but some splashes of color or white appear here and there. On the left side of my dressing room, any type of outfit that fits my mood hangs: leather jackets, some grey t-shirts, and others are mission suits. All are built for fighting, all built for the show of power.

I reach into one of my many drawers that sit below the hanging clothes and grab a pair of pajama shorts and a tank top. I change out of my current leather jacket and jeans into my sleepwear.

I trudge out of my dressing room and into the bathroom. The large chamber holds a steam shower, newly installed, a bath that looks more like a pool, and a sink fit for two, but I only ever use the left one.

A closet for towels sits in between the shower and the tub on the right wall, and the sink vanity takes up the left wall.

I go to the closet and pull out a grey washcloth. I move to the sink, dip the washcloth under the streaming water, and wipe the day's events off of my face. Continuing cleaning my face, I try to forget the conversation that had taken place only moments ago. I'm glad that Will isn't here so he doesn't look at me with a sad face like he does when I am lost.

Too lazy to hang it up to dry, I drop the washcloth in the sink, and drag my feet to my bed. I flop on the bed face first, exhausted. Slowly, I haul myself underneath the covers, and fall into a restless sleep.

A single light beam streams through my cell ceiling. Chains rustle as I try to sit up straight. Shooting pains run up my back, sending moans filled with anguish out of my mouth. Even with all the pain, it is the first time in a long time that I have felt so clear.

The previous night's events come back to me in waves. The conversation with James, his abrupt visit, not knowing his reason for coming down, his tears that fell down his face. I tried not to show it, but his actions were weird and had me concerned.

In all my time here, I have never seen James look so lost, or scared even. I never thought in a million years that a guy like James would ever say sorry to anyone, especially me.

With my days unable to be filled with laughter and friends any longer, I sit here and think about my childhood. I think about my family before everything happened, my mom and brother. I wished I would have known my father, but I guess some things just cannot happen.

I sit uncomfortably in my cell, hay tickling my back, rocks sticking to my dried blood on my feet. My pain is dull, but it flickers every so often when I shift in position. When I try to sit all the way up, I yelp in agony.

"Are you alright?" A hoarse voice asks from the cell next to mine.

When I don't answer I hear a scuffling of movement, and the clang of a body against bars.

"You know, just because I am in a cell, doesn't mean that I did anything bad," the voice of a man retries.

Guilt spreads through my body, "I never said that you were."

"You didn't need to, you didn't respond."

"You're assuming that I thought such a thing." Annoyance laces my words.

"I suppose I am, aren't I? Are you Alena?" Curiosity tickles his voice.

"Who's asking?" my fear replaces my annoyance.

A chuckle, "I'll take that as a yes-"

"I didn't say yes."

"I may be underground, but that doesn't mean that I don't hear things. Such as, a royal—a girl—has been discovered." The man clicks his tongue.

"Whatever you heard, I haven't the slightest idea what it means."

"Sure you do. Your mother is still alive, she must have told you."

"Stop. My heritage is no one's business except my own," anger boils.

"It seems that it is everyone else's but your own," he says. "Tell me, did you always know, or are you just figuring it out?"

"I am not a royal."

"Yes, you are. You can deny it, but you most certainly are."

Now it's my turn to be curious, "What do you know of my heritage?"

I can almost see the smile as he says, "My my, where do I begin?"

Chapter 17

I wake up to David loudly pounding at my door. When I go to open it, he is wearing his business uniform: black dress pants, black t-shirt, hair pushed out of his face and his army boots are replaced by simple dress shoes.

"Why are you waking me up?" I ask. My eyes still droop from lack of sleep.

"Did you forget what we are doing today?"

I roll my eyes and turn to go back inside my room, "Obviously."

"We are meeting Alena's mother."

I stop dead in my tracks, "Is that today?"

"You made the order yesterday. Or have you forgotten yourself?"

I snap around to my brother, "Clearly *you* have forgotten yourself, seeing as I am your boss. *Not* the other way around."

"I didn't mean to-"

"You didn't mean to what? Correct your boss on how to live his life or run his business?"

"I apologize, brother," David's eyes soften as he remembers his place.

My rage flares, "Get out of my sight."

When David shuts the doors behind him my rage dissipates, and I go into my dressing room to get ready.

All of the events that have happened over the past 24 hours made me forget about the meeting that I had set up with Mrs. Nightglade. I suppose I should use the name *Starfire* if we are being morally correct.

I still hate the idea of Alena being a royal, a queen. Even with all of my information on her and her family, I hadn't the slightest clue that they had any ties to a long-lost bloodline. I knew everything about her: her name, her address, her friends, her markings...

Wait.

Markings. As in birthmarks.

With all of the history on the Starfire line, there was one more thing that Allura decided to give Gianna. When Gianna was a girl, she was cast out from her family for an odd marking on the palm of her left hand. It was a star with five points—the symbol of the royal family. Allura gave every descendant the same birthmark in the same place. That was a main way to show if anyone was a Starfire. If that is true, then...

I burst into a sprint out of my room, down the hall, and into Will's office. Astonished by the sudden disruption, Will's eyes widen with shock. I must look like a maniac because Will's eyes quickly turn from shock to concern.

"James, are you alright?"

I ignore his question, "The legends about the Starfire birthmark, are they true?"

"I don't see why they wouldn't be. Why are you ask—" Will stands up from his chair. "You think that Alena has the mark."

"If the family was trying to hide, they would cloak it; probably why we never noticed it. And when Alena used her powers—"

"—it would have uncovered the mark." He finishes for me.

"We have to check," I say. "It's the only way to prove it."

With a nod of his head, Will leads the way to the first level floor. When guards see us in a hurry, they walk along as I explain our findings. It's probably not the best idea to tell them, but if I'm right, and Alena is truly heir to our throne, it could change everything.

The man next door starts to relay the supposed legend of Allura and Gianna—of the Wishing Goddess and her gifts to Gianna's bloodline. We are soon interrupted, however, by the stomping of feet coming from the floor above.

Only a minute later, the door to the sublevel dungeon swings open, accompanied by male voices. I make out James and Will as they near my cell.

"Open it," Will sounds through the bars.

A guard obeys and unlocks my cell door.

"What's going on?" I ask as I see James's terrified face.

I am met by silence as James, Will and all five other guards file into my cramped cell. Will reaches for my left hand and yanks it toward his chest. I yelp in pain.

"I'm sorry, Alena! I must check something."

Will cups my hand, as James bends down. Will's hands are soft, worn down from books. He pries open my fingers to reveal my palm. I had been staring at James until I heard him gasp, his eyes drifting to my open palm. I follow everyone's gazes to my exposed hand.

Printed on my hand is a star with five points. It's the exact star I woke up to, except this one is not on fire, but looks like a birthmark. Something that has never been there before.

"What is that?" My voice is hoarse from my lack of water and talking.

"Nothing has ever been here before?" James's gaze comes back to my own.

"No. What is it?"

"It's your mark," Will says, eyes not moving from my hand.

"What?"

James stands up, "Unchain her. I want her prepped and ready to go in 30 minutes."

A nod of their heads, and the soldiers swarm me. Two of them unchain my wrists and the other three help me to my feet. Part of me feels sorry for them when I scream out in pain, but the other part feels like they deserve it.

When they hear my cries, James and Will both look at me with concern. I didn't realize how hurt I was until I find that I can barely stand. My body starts to tingle and I fall into the guards' arms. Even they look sorry for what happened. I feel bad that I thought that they had no souls. It reminds me once again that no one is born evil.

Will comes up to my side, "Can you walk?"

When I try to say yes, all that comes out is pained breaths and no response. I realize that if I can't even speak, I am definitely not walking. Will must have understood because he takes over for the guard on my right side. I try to look up at his face to see what he is thinking, but I can't seem to lift my head. Although, I can see James looking hesitant to do the same. Whether it is because of what I told him last night, or he just wants to follow his brother's lead, James comes and takes my left side.

With both of them holding me, they lead me out of my cell, past the cell with the man, down the hall, and up the stairs to the next level. They continue to lead me, up, up, up until we reach my vacant bedroom. Or not as vacant as I thought.

Inside I hear whispers—hushed and nervous. They are quick to stop when they hear one of the guards knocking on the door.

"Who is it?" a voice calls from inside, Isabella.

"Isa-Isabella?" I gasp out.

Pairs of running feet answer my call, and when the doors open I am shrouded with screams and tears. All of Will's Dawns, my friends, come rushing out to greet me. But before they can, James tells them to move aside with a wave of his hand and continues to drag me into the room.

I don't think that drag is the right word to use, more like carrying. When they lie me down on the bed, belly up, I grunt at the sudden pressure put onto my body.

"Sorry," James and Will say in unison.

When I am on the bed, all the girls crowd around me, practically pushing Will and James out of the way. Millions of questions are being fired at me, all of them have some correlation with if I am hurt. I just lie there, hoping that they will see the face of absolute patience. When they do finally stop talking, I just mutter my thanks for their concern and that I want to take a bath.

When the boys hear that, they leave the room and the girls start to help me sit up. The pain in my back is still excruciating, but I clench my teeth and keep my eyes closed. Once my bloodied shirt is off, and my pants are stripped, with the help of Isabella and Emily, I walk to the bathroom.

The water is already filling the bathtub. Someone must have put something into the water, because it smells like water lilies and is a pale yellow color. Though it doesn't look pleasing, it feels amazing as I attempt to lower myself in, the girls again helping me. A moan escapes my lips when the warm water laps at my back.

Hannah comes in with her arms full of a variety of soaps and sponges. I shake my head no at the sponges. If the fabric of my ripped shirt was too much to handle, then the material of that sponge will kill me for sure.

Instead, the girls take a wet washcloth, which is not much better, and start to carefully clean my back. I cannot imagine the sight. With eleven lashings, some of them splitting skin, it must look like I was dragged through a bed of nails.

I watch each of them work on getting my body primed and cleaned to absolute perfection. Their faces are tight with concern and what seems like guilt. Maybe they feel guilty for what happened, but what could they have done? They would've only been caught in the crossfire, which would not help.

They finish cleaning my body, and I feel raw, exposed, and wonderfully clean. After I get out of the bath, extra careful not to let my back touch the hard surface of the tub, I am moved to my changing room. Nothing has changed since the last time I was in here, save for the orange dress that I ripped apart being replaced by a blood-orange sleeveless dress.

It looks quite scandalous. And if James really knows all these things about me, then he should know that I would never wear something that is so exposing.

Instead of the revealing dress, Emily puts me in black pants and a light blue tunic. It's a little old-fashioned, but the design of swirls on the shirt enhances its stunning blue shade. The girls help me slip on black combat boots that reach up to my knees.

I'm definitely keeping the shoes.

Walking around seems foreign, even though it has only been a day since I was put in the cell. It hurts, but after a few minutes of hanging on the girls, I am able to walk slowly by myself.

Moments later, two escorts come to get me. The girls are quick to pull me away, but with a little bit of effort, not too much, I walk through their wall of protection to the escorts.

Even with the painkillers that Joe had given me earlier, and the very stabilizing shoes, every step I take is agonizing. Not only physically, but emotionally too. We walk from my room on the second floor, past the ashy corridor, to the top of the grand staircase that leads to the exit outside. I stand at the top of the stairs and take in the sight that waits for me below.

James, David, Will, and a literal army of guards wait for me at the bottom. Each man and woman wear a black suit of armor, with some holding guns and wicked knives. Others carry long bows and arrows or hold medieval looking swords.

Descending the stairs, I take extra care of keeping my footing. Whoever made these shoes is quite skilled in their craftsmanship. They help me hold my balance exceptionally well.

James flicks his finger toward me, and four more escorts come to my aid at the end of the stairs. Having safely descended, everyone turns to walk out the doors to three waiting vans. Each can hold around ten people and a trunk for luggage—or in our case, weapons. I get into the second van, behind Will's, and my guards follow me in. At the very last moment though, James jumps into my van with me.

I look at him with disbelief, "What are you doing?"

"What does it look like I'm doing?"

"Something that is not normal," I say, and he knows it too.

"Well let's make it normal."

"Why would you do that?"

"Because it is something other than what I have been taught," James says. A wicked smile spreads across his face.

My stony exterior breaks and, after a while, I smile too, "Alright, fine."

The entire way to the airport, James explains what his childhood was like. He tells me what his father forced him to learn and see, but mostly he talks about his mother and how kind and caring she was. How she always made chocolate chip cookies when he had a rough day and how she made him feel cared for.

I'm not sure why he is telling me so much about his past. If I were to guess, I think it is because James is trying to explain why he is the way he is. Still in my mind, I don't blame him for the whipping, especially after seeing him cry last night.

James looks happier than I have ever seen him when he talks about his mom, and it makes me feel connected to him in a new way. We both find joy in remembering our mothers.

Besides his parents, he also tells me of his relationships with his brothers. How David and him used to be really close, but once

James was the chosen heir of the cartel, his brother resented him. Will is always the quiet one and is the one that continually tries to keep the peace. Will is the peacekeeper, David the fighter, and James the leader of the three.

After a half hour discussion, we finally pull onto the runway. A white private plane, similar to the one that I was kidnapped on, waits for us. We were the second to arrive, right after David's own van filled with soldiers. When David sees James giving me a hand while getting out of the van, he glares like he wishes he could kill me with a single look. It strikes me as a bit odd, but I ignore him.

Climbing the stairs of the plane is absolutely exhausting. Eventually my escorts come to my rescue, the two each taking one arm to hold and a hand on the back to steady. James is in front, looking back at me the entire time. David is stalking up the stairs behind me, probably trying to use his eyes as lasers to put holes in the back of my head.

The inside of the plane is quite luxurious, with silken, plush chairs and couches. Dark oakwood tables stand between sets of chairs. I take a seat across from James. He grins at my choice of sitting next to him. I open my mouth to say something, but David interrupts.

"James, is the girl bothering you?"

Confusion passes over James's face, then a cold, cunning smirk, "No, but she must be bothering you."

"I have no idea what you're talking about," David says angrily, disbelief in his eyes.

"I think that you do. For your information, that you should've already gathered by now being trained as you have, I am enjoying my time and company with Alena. If you have a problem with that then the door is behind you and still open. You're always free to leave."

I try to cover my laugh with a cough, which catches David's eye. I'm again met with an evil, chilling glare. He doesn't leave the plane, and instead mutters his retort and dejectedly finds a seat on the opposite end of the aircraft.

I turn my attention back to James.

"Why did you do that?" I ask.

"Because David was being rude," James states. "And because I am following my heart. Besides, his ego needed to be knocked down a peg or two."

My face heats up like a thousand fires have been lit in front of me and I feel the warmth all the way to my stomach. The implications of what he said are not lost on me. I try to suppress the smile that grows on my lips as we fall back into conversation.

Everything you could ever think of, we talk about: high school parties, families, jobs, friends, the food when we get to order *on* the plane—James laughs at how dumbfounded I am at the whole private plane thing—and lastly about brothers.

"No way, my brother is much worse than yours," I say, trying my best to convince James that Jeremy is worse than David and Will.

"At least your brother didn't shoot an arrow at you when you were eight," James replies.

"No way!"

"Yep, father grounded him for a week. Something about endangering his heir."

"Which one?" I ask.

James gives me a look that says *you are dumb if you don't know.*

"David it is then." I say with a grin.

"Yeah, I don't think that he even remembers it, but maybe. He hasn't left me unguarded since. Or shot an arrow at me." Mischief fills his words.

"Can I ask you a question?"

"But of course," James answers with a side of dramatic bow. If you can even call it that, because I don't think bowing while sitting works.

"Why do you hate my family so much?" I quickly add, "I know it is probably a touchy subject, but if we really are going to see my mother I want to know why you are so against each other. I want to understand the reason for your rage."

"You're right, it is a touchy subject, but I do think that you should understand what is happening." He says, followed by a long pause and a sigh, "My parents were at war with yours. A month before they left, my father started acting frantic, pulling my mother into a fight she wasn't prepared for.

"Not only that, but my father started muttering about stuff that cannot exist and how he must end a threat before it becomes too powerful. He started ordering the soldiers to watch a certain house and to report everything they said. He became obsessed with your parents' cartel and lives. My father even went to the point of trying to follow your mother everywhere she went, writing down family homes, places that were visited a lot, doctor names and addresses.

"He was obsessed with everything your parents did. And when my father went completely insane, he attacked your family, killing what we thought was the head of the Amarum Cartel."

"What do you mean 'killing'?" I ask. My mind was thinking about only one thing.

"I'm sorry, it isn't my place to say."

"James. Tell. Me." My words are clipped, but in my heart I already know.

"The head of the cartel was your father."

My heart drops.

My mother told me that my father died protecting innocent people, that he died stopping a bank robbery. My dad was an honorable man, and he died that way.

"You're telling me that my father died not from stopping a bank robbery, but because of a cartel war?" I had started to tremble.

"Yes, but he died protecting something important, that is what I know. I don't know what it is or why my father thought it was a threat, but your father was honorable."

Now it isn't just me that is shaking.

"Alena," James's voice is full of warning.

James isn't the only one that is feeling the vibrations that the plane is undertaking. All around me—guards, escorts, higher ups—they all feel the sudden change in the air. Will comes to my side and turns my face toward him.

"Alena you need to calm down. Don't let your emotions get the best of you," Will says as he bores his eyes into my soul.

James chimes in, "Just breathe. Deep breaths."

I try, but then I glimpse David and his hand going to his gun at his hips. I can't stop myself as I think of him hurting me and wishing for someone to stop it.

Instead of fire, it is water that attacks David. It flows from off of my skin, water in cups and the water in the chemicals used to clean. All of it combines into a huge water-like figure, and as I picture myself being harmed by David once again, it attacks him. When David's gun fires at the creature, it absorbs it, and continues to advance.

It ends too quickly to be human, David is pinned to the floor, the gun five feet out of reach, and the creature transforms into chains. Huge chains hold him in place, as the rest of the guards try to free him. Everyone witnessed what happened, but only a few understand how the creature came to be.

"Alena, it's fine, he isn't going to hurt you," James comes and bends down infront me.

"Alena, listen to me, the more you get angry or scared the more that your magic is going to flare. Think of something calming," Will suggests.

James tells me about his calm place, "When I think of calming myself, I always think of a waterfall. The way the water cascades down the rock, falling like leaves in autumn. A place where your worries are far away. Close your eyes and imagine it. The smell of the blooming flowers, the cool misty air, the sound of the water hitting the rocks."

I listen to what he says and imagine every detail and then some. The flowers turn red like blood but glow like golden sunshine. The sky is bright with stars, each making up constellations unique to the ones that were taught to me when I was young. The water, instead of rushing down the cliff, falls slowly like leaves as James described it. And when the water touches the lake below, it sends bright colors that seem to dance like the fireflies on the flowers.

When I open my eyes, I realize that the lights in the room went out, replaced by the bright lights in my imagination, and fireflies, each a different color than the other. The water that was fighting David before, now floats in the air in different shapes, the colors reflecting off of them making breathtaking designs on the wall. Everyone in the room is enchanted by the scene unfolding before them. I want to stay here all day, but I release the breath that I had been holding in, and the lights go back on and the water returns to its rightful place.

James turns to me in absolute astonishment. My body collapses against the seat. When my mind is finally clear enough that I can think, I realize that David is now standing behind Will, careful not to get too close. My body tenses as I understand how near David is. James follows my gaze to his brother and uses his hands to make his General stand down. A pause from him, but eventually he does.

"What was that?" I ask, my voice a little shaky.

"That," James starts, "that was magic."

Chapter 18

We exit the plane, no longer silent from the events that occurred on the aircraft. James and I resumed our conversation, surprisingly a little more easily than before. It was as if the lights and water revealed something important about who I was, and perhaps it did. Ever since then, I have been trying to get just a drop of water to move, but nothing happens. I think that it might have been my imagination, but that was way too real to be fake.

We are walking down the stairs of the plane when I realize that I don't need any help. More bizarrely, there is no pain in any part of my body. Because I can't see my back to see if it's still full of gore, my arms reach uncomfortably behind me to feel my wounds. The only thing I feel remaining is lines where dried blood should be, like scars.

"James, what did you give me?"

"What are you talking about," James turns around and asks me.

"My wounds...they're gone."

Everyone stops descending the steps and turns toward me. Will is the closest one to my backside, and he lifts up the back of my shirt to find my skin has healed.

Will sucks in his breath as he takes in the sight, "Your back is completely healed."

Everyone's eyes widens at his announcement, but I don't care as the information is done processing in my mind. I burst down the rest of the steps, the people in front of me moving to the side. And I run. Not away from my kidnappers, but I run for the joy of it. I relish in the feel of my feet on the ground, my lungs pumping out air to just catch up with the speed I am going. I am running so fast that it feels like I am flying. In circles, squares, and spinning, I run just to feel the ground beneath my feet. My legs gobble up the pavement as I fly through the air back toward the plane.

And when my lungs finally cannot take the rush anymore, I slow my roll. As I am walking, I yell out a joyous laugh, I feel alive. Like I could run around the world four times and I would never tire.

"You done with running around like a maniac or are we going to have to delay our meeting?" James asks, an amused smile on his lips.

I reply with a wild smile, my body free and light like wind during the night.

We are riding in four black SUVs. This time, James decides to go into his own vehicle. He mentioned something about maintaining an image. The only thing I truly remember was me snorting and he coughed his own laugh. I smile now thinking about the memory.

The private airport we came into was not far from the town I grew up in.

Sure enough, within minutes my hometown comes into view. The old brick buildings stand tall in the rising sun. Evergreen Lake reflects the sun, gleaming like a giant mirror. The neighborhoods still look well-kept as ever, but there's something missing and I can't seem to put my finger on it.

We continue to drive through the familiar streets. With the blacked-out windows, no one on the sidewalks can tell that the missing child they have been looking for is inside, eager to come home to them. I even sit up a little straighter as I lean toward the window as we pass by my old high school.

I missed graduation. I wasn't able to leave high school with a degree or celebrate with all of my fellow classmates. Perhaps I wasn't all that well liked, but I still might have been accepted by my peers, if only for that night. Soon all my old schools pass, and the malt shop at the center of them, along with the memories made in each.

Before long, we are out of town completely, and heading toward Briars Cliff, Ava, and my favorite place to sit and think. There was a rock that was shaped like a throne that sat atop the hill that Ava and I could both sit in.

We arrive near the top of the sloped land to find nothing. No cars, no people, no traps, nothing but trees and rocks. All I hear is a whistle from within the car ahead of me, and there forms a small army. Each soldier is clad in black, in contrast with the bright and sunny morning.

The SUVs park in a semicircle, and mine is the one closest to the exit road. James comes up to my car and takes my hand to help me down. I look to where the opposing side is and find a wall of guards of our own, and symmetrical to our own. No one notices yet another kind gesture from James, save for the jerk brother of his.

I look back at the other wall. Whoever is behind it is important, and I find myself silently hoping that my mother is a member of this cartel, not the leader. I scan the other group's faces and recognize a few. From where, I am not certain.

James is at my side, Will next to him, and David behind Will.

"I'm sorry for this," James whispers into my ear, hand on my bicep, as two guards come up from behind me and take hold of my arms, James letting go. "It's just for show. I need your mother to believe my threats."

"Surprisingly," I turn back toward him. "I'm not mad about this. My mother lied. Let her believe this."

Instead of responding with a smile, as he usually does, James walks to the front of the unit, keeping a stony expression. Will stays to his left, and David now takes up my spot at his right. *Strong family indeed*, I think to myself. The guards hold me back, and I stop moving along with them.

I observe as our wall of guards breaks to let the brothers out. It closes before I can see who the real leader is. It isn't long before my request is answered with a cold version of my mother's voice.

"James, welcome to *my* town," my mother says as she walks through her own crowd of guards.

"Well, I can't complain, I was so wonderfully welcomed, Karen." James says with faked sincerity.

"You called, and I am here to consider your offer," my mother replies, her tone sounding almost bored.

A chuckle answered, "Consider?"

One of the guards creating our wall shifts enough so I can see all of my mother. Her face is covered in cuts and wrinkles of worry. She doesn't see me as I watch her face drop into a death stare.

"Where is my daughter?"

My heart drops, why did I forget that this is the reason we are here.

"Don't you want to hear my offer first?" James asks.

"I want to see her."

James sighs at the demand, but gestures for my guards to bring me forward.

Before my mom can see my face, Will creeps into the back of my mind.

"Act like you're struggling," he orders.

I obey as I twist in the boys' arms. They seem to understand what Will and I are trying to pull off, because they don't yank on my arms as hard as they should.

I pass our boundary, to see my mom standing in front of me, hands hanging so they are within arm's reach of her guns. I look alarmingly at James who just gives me a slight jerk of his chin. My mom also senses my unease and drops her hands to her sides.

"Now that Alena has joined us, would you like to hear my terms?" James asks once again.

Mother removes her eyes from me, and goes to the powerful man standing before her, who is not much older than me.

"I want a word alone with my daughter."

Why won't she say my name?

James laughs, "Do you think I'm stupid? What, so you can snatch her without having to pay the price?"

"No. So I can make sure she is unharmed, because that was a part of our deal."

"Alright, I'll allow it. But I think you will find that Alena has taken care of herself. I am sure you understand what I mean."

Mom narrows her eyes, then walks away from me.

Chapter 19

My guards guide me through the woods as we follow my mom. More soldiers follow us, each from one side or the other of this war. We come to a clearing. The ground surrounding it has been disturbed, as if it had been dug up. I must be the only one that notices it, because no one else tenses up.

Mom brings me over to the center of the clearing. I come to a stop only when I am a few feet away from my mom, who is standing in another center of another turned up circle.

"Leave us," Karen instructs my guards.

"You don't order us, Karen."

"And you don't have the luxury of calling me that. Now let me talk with my daughter. Alone."

I look at my guards, to find them staring at me. I am not sure why they are, but then I realize they are waiting for my permission. It is my choice.

"It's fine," I say, my voice weak against my will. "Just stay close."

A nod of their heads, and they let go of my arms. When I step into the circle, the soldiers continue to back away but eventually stop a few yards out.

"You could at least look at me," My mom draws my attention back to her.

I snort and look at her, "So I have to look at you, but you can't even tell me the truth."

"What are you talking about? What lies have they fed you?"

"How about the fact that you run a cartel? Or that you and Jeremy knew about it the entire time and didn't tell me?"

"You don't know what you are talking about."

"Really? Then why don't you tell me how my father actually died. Because we both know that it wasn't an armed robbery."

Hurt. Betrayal. Longing. Surprise. All of it passes through her eyes, then vanishes without a trace.

"How did you-" my mom tries to recover.

"James told me. He said that he probably shouldn't and you should, but I made him. You've lied to me enough."

My mother turns around, unable to look at my face, "Oh Alena, ever the believer. You can't make assumptions without hearing both sides of the story."

"I don't want to hear your side. You don't deserve it. Do you know how much you've put me through? How much pain you've caused me?"

"You did the same to me!" She throws her hands up and turns back around to me. "I have been worried sick about you, doing everything that I can to get you back, which is why I am here. I am taking you home."

"What if I don't want to go home?" I ask, despite feeling unsure of what it is I truly want.

Mom's eyes turn icy cold, "That's not your choice to make."

Within seconds, the ground bursts open like a lion breaking free from its cage. From the ground rises fire, fed by gallons upon gallons of gunpowder. The heat almost sears my skin, but I am already on the move.

I jump through the small ring of fire that encloses my mother and I, just before it rises too high. I hit the ground, sprinting for the second and last wall of fire that attempts to cage me inside with my monster of a mother.

Inches from the fire line, the flames leap up toward the open air. I stumble back at the sudden change of height. My mother seems to have followed right after me because she now towers over me.

"Are you done yet?"

My breathing comes in short pants, elevated by being trapped in a cage. I hate cages. I am not an animal to be kept away, hidden under lock and key. I'll be damned if I let it happen again.

I get to my feet, brush off the dirt, and lift my chin. I say the words that I will always live by from now on.

"I will not be caged. I will not break."

"You are coming home." My mother pulls out a syringe.

"I will not be chained down to the ground. I am not an animal for you to control."

Then I feel it, that surge of power. It is majestic and has the potential to pull apart every fiber in my being and reconstruct it, all at my fingertips. It is like a black hole, it never ends. But this is not black. Oh no, it is full of sun and starlight.

Something snaps behind me, and I seize that power bellowing to be set free. I free it into the outside world, enclosing myself in gold and white hot flame. My power reaches and crushes the syringe, making my mother jump. The palm of my hand pulsates, and I look down at it to see my black star birthmark has now turned gold. It too seems to flicker like my flames.

My eyes go straight back to my mother.

"You lied to me. My heritage, my life, my name, all of it. Lies. You never told me who I was. I had to figure it out by this," I gesture to my hands. "I was locked away with chains on my limbs and scars on my back. I was whipped until I was numb. And still on top of it all, I forgave the man that did it. He never lied to me, he apologized and swore to live the way he wanted to.

"James is not evil; he was made into something he is not. Give a slave too many lashings and they will not feel the pain. He is starting to not feel that pain. He grew up into something monstrous, corrupted by his father. Only now is the real him starting to show."

"You don't know what he has done."

"No, I don't, but I'll ask him. At least I know he'll tell me the truth."

My mother's eyes fill with fury and she whistles a signal. Behind her, I see my two guards, lying down on the ground motionless—dead or unconscious, I don't know. But I don't have time to think about that as a gun goes off and I feel that familiar ping of bullets come off my body. Except today I will not be weak. I am not weak. The bullet doesn't meet its mark. It falls to the ground in a ball of flame.

"Go ahead mom, shoot me again. Except maybe this time, *you* shoot me. Don't make others do your dirty work," my voice shows my strength.

She tries a softer approach; she reaches out her hand. "Please, just come home with me."

"Tell me the truth and I will."

"I can't. Not here, not now."

I shake my head as my answer.

"I want to know. I don't want to hear your excuses. I just want the truth. Right here, right now," a pin-prick of tears forms in the corners of my eyes.

Mother returns my head shake, "I can't."

The expression on my face turns to stone, "Then I am not coming home."

It wasn't only that my mother never told me the truth that is keeping me from coming home. But like I told Ava, I won't put those I love at risk. Even if it means not telling my mom that.

She would come up with some reason or excuse as to why I could come home. I can't listen to any form of hope. If I am getting out of

James clutches it will be after I strike a deal. It will be on *my* terms. Then, and only then, will I come home.

And maybe I can use that time to my advantage. I could learn more about my heritage and my power.

"The only way I am coming home is in a body bag as you just tried to do."

"It wasn't going to kill you."

"Are you really willing to bet my life on that?"

With no answer coming from her lips, I step forward.

"I'm sorry mom, but I need to know more. I hope that you'll understand one day."

She doesn't answer me, and I continue to come for her until I am only a hair's breath away. She breathes fast and shortly, so much so that I am worried that she might faint. Mom looks at me and turns her fearful breaths into a rageful puff.

I hold out my palm so she can see what—*who*—I have become, and perhaps who I have been all along.

My star glows brightly, illuminating my mother's face. All of her pain and worry are no longer concealed, they show through every shield and wall that she put up. All of her attention is on my palm and what it displays.

"*Alena*," James yells from a distance.

"I can't stay long," I say. "I have to go back, and you cannot follow me."

"Please, you don't have to do this," My mom begs, her eyes not moving from my birthmark. My birthright.

"You don't understand. I am not going to explain this again to you. I am not going home, I can't."

"Stop saying that," My mother cries. "You can. If you think that he will find you, that he can hurt you, then you're wrong. I can protect yo-"

"You can't protect the world! Not everything and everyone I love and care about."

"Alena! Where are you?" James continues to yell for me.

"I have to go."

My mom reaches out for me, "Is that why you won't come home, because you think you are protecting us?"

I turn away from the truth she has discovered, "Goodbye mom."

I back away as I hear my mother break down into tears. I don't turn around, I can't. Because if I do, I won't ever leave, I would stay until her tears dried and she was okay. But as long as I am gone, she won't be okay, so I keep walking right up to the wall of flame.

James stands on the other side, "What are you doing?"

"Coming back with you," I reply. "You're welcome by the way. She was trying to bring me home without making the deal."

"I told you she's a liar," James says, no smirk on his face.

"Don't, just don't. The only reason I am coming with you is because I know that you'll give me answers. I want to know my heritage."

"I can't guarantee anything," he says with fortitude.

"I would be surprised if you could," I move my arms up to chest level. "By the way, I think I figured out how to grasp my magic."

I move my arms outward, like I am parting a curtain. The fire in front of me follows the movement. The flame reflects like a mirror in James's eyes, making him look fiercer than before. When the white-hot veil is split apart large enough for me to pass through, I sense something wrong.

"James, did your guards follow you?"

"No, they are restraining your mother's clan. Why do you ask?"

I look behind me to see my mother rise to her feet, vengeance written all over her face.

"You made your choice," she whispers, more to herself than me.

That's when I realize the strange smell is gasoline.

"James get down!" I scream at him, just before a bomb hits.

My magic understands what is happening and throws out a shield, encasing James and me. I ask for it to add extra protection to our backs, to hide from my mother's rage. Instead of obeying, it gives itself to me, showing the threads of energy all around us.

I yank on them, pulling the fire to my will, asking the wind to feed my flames. I move away from my mother and close the veil.

"Follow me closely," I order James and stalk forward.

Bombs, bullets, and arrows come barreling down upon my shields of hard air. With each attack, I send out golden flame as an answer to its call.

I don't run, I walk slowly, carefully, welcoming the fight, embracing the anger from deep inside myself. My mother wants a fight, then I am going to give her one.

From the trees comes most of the battle, in which I ask the plants to help me. They answer my plea by enclosing around the shooters.

James continues to follow my lead, ducking at the blasts all while watching me fight.

Eventually those in the trees come down and turn into lines and lines of warriors, each with the intent to capture and win, but they don't stand a chance.

Not with my fury feeding my power.

I continue to rip through the men and women in my path, making them run from my rage. These people know who I am, and yet they fight me. Let them fight and be afraid, because when the ash settles, there will only be me left.

Soon, we are close enough to the meeting point that I can hear the complaints of the fighters. There are only a few people left standing, and I make a dramatic flare, literally as the heat and fire rise. That scares the few left in the remaining army that stands between me and the real fight.

James comes to my side, "The big fight isn't even here yet, how long can you hold on for?"

"I'm fine, don't worry about it. Tell me what you need done."

A wicked smile appears on his face, "Show them what you're made of."

Chapter 20

I create a path, lined with bodies. I command my power not to kill them, but to hurt them enough that they won't be an issue as we pass. When I walk by, their eyes are closed, eventually I worry that they aren't breathing. I keep the faith in my strength, never faltering my step. James walks beside me, matching my strength with his own kind.

Out of the corner of my eye, I watch James as we walk. Before he was mischievous with his smirk, but I see how upset this is making him. I don't miss the way his eyes cloud over as he looks at the bodies of his fallen people. A part of me wants to reach for him, to help him in his sorrow, but I don't, I focus on the task at hand, knowing that I'd rather him be alive than dead.

Our guards that we pass fall behind us, each fighter I give a space in my shield, stretching my power out over many meters. I feel the power wearing on me, but my adrenaline blocks out the brunt of it.

Many of the opposing side comes for our army, only to be thrown back by a mixture of shield and flame. Wind and earth continue to aid in my battle, feeding my fire and growing thorns under the enemy.

When we get into the thick of the fight, I find Will and David fighting back to back. A circle of deadly soldiers stand around them. Blood and dirt cover their faces. Four more soldiers advance against them, but two fall down to the brothers before I shove the rest away with wind.

Will looks at me and gives me a strained smile, while David only grunts his thanks. I simply nod my head in acknowledgement.

When no one goes for the brothers, James rushes to them and the army follows. Within seconds I am in the back of the unit.

I turn around to the path of pain I left in my wake, to see an army advancing toward us, my mother at the head.

I flare my nostrils in frustration. Why can't she leave me alone?

20 feet stands between my mother and me. I hear James suck in his breath behind me, but I pay no attention. I hear the shuffling of feet as he fights his way to me, but I take my own step forward. 19 feet.

I steel my answer with my voice, "I made my choice, now respect it."

My mom chuckles at me, "You didn't think I would just let you go like that, would you? You know me better than that."

I force my flames to spread out around and above me, enforcing my shields on the warriors behind me.

"No, but I had hoped you would have. It would make this a lot easier."

My mind pushes everything out of it, leaving me with my emotions of pain and betrayal.

"Mom, please, just let me go," I plea to her, which comes out as an order.

"No."

I take two more steps, 17 feet.

"I won't come home, not until I understand why," tears shine in my eyes.

"I will tell you when you're home."

"Liar. Have you not done that my whole life? Is all you say a lie?" anger continues to control my words.

"Don't be dramatic, Alena," my mother rolls her eyes, finally uttering my name.

"Now you say my name?" Another step, 16 feet. "You won't listen, then this is on your hands."

My hand pulses again, like a heartbeat in my palm. I show my hand to the open sky, my arm not adorned with fire. I send a spiral of flame to snake up my arm.

If she thinks that I am dramatic, then I'll prove her right.

I feel the threads of energy around the sun, and I draw them in, using the hand pointed at the sky, bathing in the power that swarms around me. I bring my arm back down and face it toward my mom.

"You won't let me go, then I'll free myself."

I call upon wind, earth, water and fire. Earth will weaken them, water will protect me. Fire will bring them to their knees, wind will feed my rage fire.

My mother, of all people, is the one who shoots first, I compress the bullet with air. I don't throw the bullets back, I let them fall like rain on asphalt.

They don't stop shooting, no matter how much of their ammo turns to dirt. Those behind me stare and stare and stare, not a movement in the crowd. They let me fight for them, so I will.

That is, until they realize that the army is forming a circle around our own. My energy wanes, but all I have to do is look at my mom and my emotions fuel me.

The soldiers split into three, each group knowing exactly what to do without a word. One group goes to Will and David, another to the front lines, and the last to me. I can't see James anywhere, so I go back into the fight, only to find him standing by my side.

"What are you doing here?"

"Fighting alongside you," James says. "That much force upon your body without training will drain you. Let me help."

I huff my reply, "You won't be helping much if you're dead."

"I'll be fine. Go, I'll finish this."

That was my mistake.

I listened to him for a split second, and it cost me. My shields slip at the idea of taking a break. In that single moment, a bullet passes through to mark James in the shoulder.

Time seems to stop for a second before James's scream brings me back to reality. His scream is loud and terrifying, so much so that I can literally feel his pain.

My shields shoot back up into place, and I command the wind to push James behind a few lines of warriors.

Get him out of the fight, that is my job.

My power is fueled by something other than anger at my mom. Now, it's rage at myself for the stupid mistake I had just made.

I take more steps forward; the army follows me. I send a wave of heat to the opposing side. Dehydrating them will make them sloppy. Sloppy is exactly what I need.

Roots grow from the earth to trip them, and those that don't fall are either blown down or shoved into a river. I release my command on water and earth but continue controlling wind and fire.

Wind doubles my shields, while fire feeds my army's swords. A group of fighters come for me, all at once. I battle them with fire until I am able to grab a sword from one of their scabbards.

Swords are from olden times, but it is well balanced enough that I can fight with it.

I swing and blast until they are all down. More advance and I dispatch them quicker than the last.

When their army starts to thin, reinforcements come out to help rebuild the fight. I assumed mother's right-hand man would lead the charge. Instead I find my brother, coming for his only sister.

I shouldn't be surprised; of course mom would tell him what is happening. My heart hurts, either from the energy I am forcing out or my brother turning against me.

Out of everyone, Jeremy is the one that comes to fight me. He only uses his armor, no weapons. At least *he* isn't trying to harm me.

I don't use my fire on him either, only shields. He dances through the maze of thorns and mini lakes created by the elements.

Death, danger, and mischief laces his movements, all directed at those who hurt me. And when he is close to me he stops, but I keep my shields up. I won't be making that mistake again.

"What are you doing here, Jeremy?"

"I could ask you the same of you, little sister."

We stand there for moments of silence, staring at each other.

"You're not going to let me choose, are you?" I ask.

"Nope."

I break, "Did you know that when I refused to come home, mom shot me? Or at least tried to."

"Are you mad? This is mom we are talking about; she would never do that. Besides, you are not even bleeding."

"That's thanks to this," I show my fire. "Were you aware that we are royalty? That I am an heir to the throne."

"Alena, we can expla-"

"Wait," I stop dead in my fight. "You knew?"

"Let me-"

"No, no, no. You are *all* the same. You scheme and lie and think that you can get away with it. Well you can't."

"Alena, you don't understand why we did it."

"I don't need to. I've heard enough from both of you," I say to my only family left in this world, as my mom comes and stands beside my brother. I can't keep doing this with them.

"I'm done with this—with you," I wave my hand at my family. "Please leave me be."

"No, I won't allow it," Mom tries again.

"Mother-" Jeremy turns to her.

Mom only moves her head to look at him, "Do you want your sister back or not?"

Before Jeremy can answer, ice spreads to their feet. It is exactly like it was with Ava, but when I try to reign it back in, it doesn't work. It doesn't stop growing, no matter how hard I try.

I breathe, focus on calming my mind, relax my body, but nothing stops the growing cold. My fire doesn't melt it, my sword doesn't break it.

My family gets spooked and starts backing away. Even if they are leaving me alone, the ice still scares me. I want it gone.

The next thing I know, Will is knocking on the walls of my mind. He doesn't calm me.

The soldiers fall back, afraid of the ice too. I try to pull on the threads of energy, reach into the black hole, but it only grows. I'm trapped within my own power.

I panic and do something dangerous. I send my power out in all directions, releasing every part of my being into the world.

It takes so much of me, the release of the magic. My heartbeat quickens, my hand pulses more and more. I am surrounded by this golden light, like I am inside the sun. I can't see the outside world, only bright, blinding light.

Only a speck remains of my magic, and I hold fast. Blood starts to trickle down my face, from my nose, my ears. A figure starts to emerge from the light. Afraid that it is my mother coming for me again, I let go of that last grain of power, and my consciousness goes with it.

Alena falls hard and fast. For a time, blinding lights surround her. They only disappear when she falls to the ground. Her mother is far away from her body, covering her head from anything that might come flying at her.

I run to her, the girl on the ground. There's no movement when I call her name. And that army that was fighting alongside her is not even close to her. I am stuck in between them. I had been pushing my way back to her the whole time since she sent me here.

The wound in my shoulder isn't bad, it won't kill me. She should've listened to me; should've left the fight to me. I brought her here, this is my fault.

When I am close enough, I see the blood in the cracks between her teeth, coming out of her ears and nose. Unlike the bullet, she didn't pass out from an injury, she fainted from her magic.

"Dammit, Alena," I mutter under my breath.

I sink to my knees to assess her more closely. Her face, like last time, is pale as the moon. The color from her lips is the same as always, and her face is set to a peaceful sleep.

"Alena? Come on. Wake up."

"Alena?" The voice is one that I don't recognize.

The boy that walks toward us has familiar features, but a foreign face all the same.

Alena, that's what is familiar about him. Her brother then.

Will and David step up on either side of Alena and I, guns drawn.

"Not a step closer, boy." David orders.

"Please, she's my sister."

"You must be Jeremy then," David replies.

"Yes, sir. I just want to make sure she's okay."

Will explains, "You don't need to worry, she'll be okay. The magic wore her down."

"It doesn't help that you showed up to take her home against her will," I cut in. "Your mother shot at her you know?"

"She what?"

"Why don't you ask her yourself," I turn my voice ice cold. "Wil-"

"She's going to be fine, brother," Will answers my question knowing it was coming.

"We'll take her off your hands."

Jeremy counters, "She's my sister, she needs to come home with me."

"You really are going to call that a home? You tried to shoot her, bring her home against her will and lied to her." All of which have happened with us, but at least we didn't lie to her for her entire life.

Alena's mother starts to come our way, finally realizing where her children are.

"Get away from my daughter!"

"I don't think so," I reply. "Like I told your son, I'm taking her home with me. You shot her."

Karen pushes back, "So did you!"

Ava said more than she should've.

"You're right, I did, but I am also not her mother. I'm allowed to. I'm the big, bad wolf remember?"

"And that makes you entitled?"

"No, what makes me entitled is that I'm rich and powerful. And because I'm the boss."

I scoop Alena up in my arms and carry her away. Putting my back to Alena's mother is not only dumb, although I have protection, but is a sign of disrespect. A sign that this leader does not take lightly.

My eyes drift down to Alena as soon as my face is out of Karen's sight. She's limp in my arms, her head cradled against where my shoulder and chest meet. I sigh to myself and her, this was not how today was supposed to go.

Granted, I had no intention of giving Alena back. I actually was hoping that Karen would accept my offer, but she was selfish, trying to take Alena instead of just giving herself over. It is a difference that I am starting to notice between Alena and her mother, one will do anything it takes to keep others safe, while the other couldn't care either way.

It surprised me though, Alena actually decided to come back instead of me having to take her by force. She protected my people and I even when we have done everything to hurt her. I know that I shouldn't care what happens to her as long as her mom is suffering, but what she did, I can't help but feel grateful. I hold her closer as I continue walking to the car that will take us home.

I don't hear any footsteps following, only those that are backing away. My brothers will be the next to follow me, they are the second ones to protect.

In clans, soldiers are regarded as lessers who can die and not be missed. It was one of many of my father's rules that I disagreed with. Many of the soldiers had shown pity on me over the years, back when I was bullied by my own father. When they died, which eventually they all did, I mourned them. Quietly and secretly, of course. I would sneak into the gardens at night to light a candle.

Lighting a candle or fire of some sort is a sign of respect and of the honor that person had. Though that tradition has been abandoned in many families, mine included. Only was it reserved for the leader, important people, and relatives to them.

It's another thing that I have always wished to bring back, but never got the chance or guts to do.

We arrive at the SUVs. I climb into mine, Alena still in my arms. I won't leave her side until she wakes up. I'm getting to the point of not caring about my bad guy image in my clan. Let them think me weak. Their opinions do not matter to me, not where Alena is concerned.

We are pulling out when a figure pops out from the tree line and in front of the car. We skid to a halt, guards yelling out an alarm. Protocols are put in place for instances like this. They are playing out now to deal with the idiot that decided to mess with me.

I place Alena gently down on the other bucket seat, silently promising myself to hurt whoever is delaying my trip back home.

I get out of the car when I know that the person is detained. I am informed that the person is a teenage girl before I move further. A look on the soldier's face puzzles me, and when I ask what else, he replies with something even stranger.

"It's the royal's friend."

I stroll over to Ava, my guess as to why she came is simple. It's a noble way of buying Karen time to save Ava's friend.

"You are either incredibly stupid or have a death wish," I announce as I round the corner of the car to face Ava, two soldiers holding her down by the shoulders.

"Where is she?"

"In the car that you just tried to get hit by. I don't know what good that does for you, though."

Ava struggles to come to a standing position.

I wave the guards off of her and send them into the car to protect Alena.

"What do you want, Ava? I have places to be and someone to check on."

"I want Alena back."

"You know my answer to that already. What do you actually want?"

Ava takes a deep breath, "To come with you. Alena, I mean. If I can't take her home, then I'll go with her."

"So honorable of you, but you don't know of what you're asking for," I assure her.

Ava stands a little straighter, "Actually I do. The possibility of never seeing my family again. And being able to be there for my friend when she needs me most."

"Loyal to Alena, I respect that. I admire you for that actually."

"Do you accept my deal?"

Karen screams from a distance, "Ava! Where are you? I swear to the gods if you don't-"

"Deal," I smile as a bag slides over her face.

Chapter 21

W   e only arrive at the plane after evading cops for an hour. Though quite secluded, the forest did not hide Alena's flames.

The fire trucks that we passed will not find anything other than thousands of scorch marks. Thanks to Alena passing out, the elements went back to normal, with nothing flying in the air or anything growing, within seconds.

She still hasn't woken up, even when we are on the plane. That is also the first time that Ava sees her. When she did, she screamed, or more like squealed. Ava hasn't let go of her hand since, not even when Will came to check on the little princess.

The power initially caused damage to her internal organs, specifically her brain, but there are no tears. No broken bones, or internal bleeding currently. Her mind is functioning normally, even though it was bleeding before. It has already healed despite the blood running down her face. We have not figured out how, but our best guess is due to the Starfire blood running through her veins.

Everyone is silent on the way back, even my brothers. The only sounds are the clearing of throats here and there and the clinks of glasses being set back down on the table. Everyone is either stunned, ashamed, or exhausted from the day's events.

When we arrive back at my personal airport in Michigan, Alena still hasn't awoken, in spite of the hours of flight that have passed.

Two days pass the same way. Sounds only come from eating and the hourly updates on Alena's condition.

Only on the third day, late afternoon, does she make a movement other than the rising and falling of her chest. I was holding her hand at the time, with Will's dawns, the maids, and Ava all in the room. Alena's fingers curl around my hand.

I rise from my chair in surprise as Alena takes a large intake of air. All heads in the room turn toward the sleeping beauty. Her eyes flutter open and everyone jumps to their feet, coming to crowd around the bed.

"If I had known that I had so many fans I would've woken up earlier," Alena croaks.

A mixture of tears and laughter follows the comment.

"Talk about comical relief," Ava breathes out as she wraps her hands around Alena's own.

"Should I ask why you're here?"

"Not unless you want to be upset."

"James?" Alena looks to me with accusing eyes.

I put my free hand in the air, "Don't blame me! She's the one who jumped in front of my car."

The conversation doesn't go further. Only looks of curiosity and anger pass between the three of us. I ask the girls to leave Alena and I for a moment, and they obey.

"You are the dumbest person I know," I start.

"Thanks for the compliment. I'll take that as a thank you as well."

I move to sit down on the bed next to her.

"You scared the living hell out of me. Out of all of us. I told you to leave the fight to me."

Alena's eyes shine with sorrow when they drift to my shoulder, and she says, "And the moment I listened to you, you got shot." A pause, "Are you okay?"

"Do I look okay?" I ask.

"Yeah."

"Then, there is your answer," I resolve.

Alena changes the subject, "Did everyone make it back okay?"

I inhale, "We had a few losses, but not as many as we would have had you not been there."

"One minute you are yelling at me for being in the fight, the next you're thanking me. That was a thank you?" She asks again.

I chuckle deeply, "Yes, that is a thank you."

My heart is beating so fast that I swear Alena can hear it.

"My mom?"

"Alive. For now, at least. So is your brother."

Relief floods her eyes, "And they'll stay that way?"

"I'll think about it," I reply, knowing very well that they are going to pay for what they did.

I try to sort through the best way to hurt the two idiots, my anger boiling. Trying to calm it down is easier when I'm around her. Just looking at Alena subsides it completely.

When I do look at Alena, I can see the anger and hurt in her.

"Are you okay?"

"Does it look like it?"

"No," a long pause follows.

We sit there so long that my body goes numb, a good numb. One that makes me feel safe and not in danger of humiliation or rage being thrown at me. Alena has that about her, the calming aura, but today it is tinted with something related to sorrow, but deeper than can be put into words.

"She tried to shoot me," Alena breathes, eyes staring off into space, mind afar.

I don't reply, only wait for her to say what she wants when she needs to.

Instead of speaking, Alena bursts into tears. I stand up, roll the covers back, sit back on the bed and pull her towards me. She allows it to happen, crying into my chest. I sit there and hold her, brush the hair out of her face, and wait for the tears to slow.

It takes a while, with Alena murmuring "How could she" and "She's my mom" into my grey shirt. Eventually, we get to the point where we sit there in silence.

Alena is the first to break it.

"She hates me."

My heart seizes. Even with my awful father, he still loved me. With his twisted ways, I still knew that deep down in his hateful, cold heart. Every child should know that, especially a girl who just gave up everything.

"She doesn't hate you. Karen just wants you home."

"You don't blame her for what she did?"

"No, of course I do. There are other methods out there."

"Would you have done it?" Alena looks up at me.

"Done what?" I question, unsure of what she means.

"Left your home if they lied to you," she shutters out breathily.

I sit there in deep thought, "I don't know. Maybe, but I don't know if I would have the strength. Not everyone is as brave as you, Alena Starfire."

"It sounds cool. My real name. Much better than Alena *Nightglade*."

I huff a snicker, "Yes, so much better."

We sit there in more silence, sadness and anger hanging in the air. Alena moves her head onto my chest and curls her body around mine.

"You tired?" I ask gently.

A series of movements on my chest turns into a yes.

"You should go to sleep then."

"The girls want to see me," she protests.

"They'll wait. I'm sure they will understand."

"Okay," she gives up. "Will you stay with me?"

Something comes to life in my chest. A thing that hasn't been alive in a long time.

"Of course, as long as you want."

Chapter 22

The next several days consist of sleeping, talking, and lots and lots of food. I don't think I've ever had so much food in my entire life. Every meal I am convinced that I gain ten pounds.

Breakfast is filled with pastries and fruits, my favorite being the raspberry filled danishes. Lunch usually is a type of sandwich and soup. The chef makes this amazing soup with all these vegetables and potatoes and tops it with lamb meat. Every time I come near it, it's gone before others get the chance to even look at it.

They all seem to know and are fine with it because eventually no one touches the soup. James sometimes hides it on the days I know it's out, just to mess with me. And I always yell at him. Everything is fun and games about it.

And then there is dinner, dessert, and heaven all in one. They have a chocolate souffle and macarons. At least those are my favorites. James was with me the night I tried them and saw my glee. I know that they are made every night now. Secretly, I think James ordered that it be done.

He and I have hung out a lot lately. Almost every night, actually. Sometimes Ava is with us, or the brothers, and even the Dawn girls. But every time, James and I end up in the same room each night.

Tonight, instead of eating in my personal dining room, I tell James that I want to eat with everyone else. After a few minutes of laughing from James, telling him I was serious, and then the confirmation about it, we start to head down to the dining hall.

Only a few guards are on duty. The rest have already gathered for dinner.

Just as I'm descending the stairs, I hear laughter drift up from the level below. I pause to listen more to the men and women's voices.

James takes it as me being hesitant.

"We don't have to do this if you don't want to."

I shake my head, "No, I want to."

I finish the staircase and walk to the right, toward the dining hall. Many conversations stop the moment I step in. It isn't my outfit that makes me stand out, just jeans and a t-shirt. Not my shoes, which are the exact same black combat boots that everyone else is wearing. Maybe my hair that might be in all different directions behind me. It might just be me.

I continue forward, fully aware of the many pairs of eyes tracking my every movement. Trying not to seem too uncomfortable in front of everyone, I advance to the kitchens, passing table after table of servants and guards.

When I reach the kitchen, I walk right in and find the chef. Alfenzo, the chef, greets me with a smile—a hard luxury to find these days.

I've only met Alfenzo recently, and as soon as I did I loved him. At first he reminded me of Santa, with a big round belly and red cheeks from the sweltering kitchen. He is a charming fellow and knows how to brighten up a room.

"Mi amor, welcome, welcome! Looking for more desserts?"

He's Italian.

"Here for dinner actually," I reply with a giggle. Of course Alfenzo would think that.

Confusion covers his features, but eventually, "Of course, of course! Let me get you some soup, madam."

I head back into the dining room where conversation has only gone partly back to normal. James leads me to the only empty table near the windows on the east wall. He pulls out one of the chairs facing the rest of the dining hall and motions for me to sit, which I do. He then sits down next to me on my right. I notice he moves his seat slightly closer to me.

Food is brought out to us, and I eat slower than normal.

"Everyone is staring at me," I murmur to James between bites.

"That's because you saved their lives."

I choke on my soup. "What?"

"When you came with your magic, you protected them and fought their battles that they were about to lose. They don't take that lightly."

"I only did what anyone else would if they were in my position."

"Fight their families, pass up the chance to go home, and defy their mothers? Not many would. In fact, I don't think *any* of them would."

I sit there in silence, at a loss for words, until a group of soldiers walk up to our table.

"Mind if we sit, sir?" One of the men asks.

James points to the seats across from us. They sit with their food but don't touch it.

"I'm not going to kill you for eating your food in front of us," James says, trying to break the tension.

But they aren't worried about James. They're worried about me.

I put my hands up as they look at me, "I'm certainly not. I don't even have access to my magic at the moment."

"What are you saying?" A maid in passing asks.

"That I can't access my magic like *that*," I snap my fingers, adding emphasis. "It comes when I need protection or when I'm mad or scared."

"Did your mother really try to shoot you?" A guard at our table asks.

"Yes, my mother did."

"Is she always that cruel?" Asks the one to his left.

"That's enough," James stops them. "What happened between Alena and her mother will stay their business unless shared. Don't push her."

I blush at the respect and protection given. But I want them to know my mother's true colors, and why I did what I did.

"No, no it's fine. It feels good to talk about it. What do you guys want to know?"

James smiles surprisingly at me as questions are asked from every direction of the dining area. Apparently, the entire room was listening in. I answer the questions one by one. When one is answered, another begins. Some have stories about them, while others are only yes or no answers.

We talk for so long that after hours of eating desserts and conversation, the topic turns to my personal opinions.

"Okay, so current president," a soldier starts. "Do you like him?"

"Politics now," I reply thoughtfully. "Okay, in some ways, yes, but like most every other president, he focuses on his values instead of others. It's good to have them, just don't force them on others."

The 20 people crowded around the table shake and murmur their agreements.

"I have another one on politics, and you don't have to answer," a maid in her mid-twenties asks. "Are the rumors about you being a Queen true?"

Like before, when I walked in, the room goes quiet. I look to James for an answer, only to find him staring at me for one.

I clear my throat, "Umm, well my mother never told me about my heritage or who I really was, but supposedly there is a legend about this birthmark," I show my palm, and look at it as I continue to talk. "I don't know if I am queenly material anyway. Besides don't you guys like your freedoms?"

No one answers.

"I think that me becoming your Queen would harm all of you. There would be a lot of clans coming for me, and you would be caught in the crossfire."

One lady starts laughing. She has dark, short hair, with an equally dark complexion. Scars pepper her face.

Her brown eyes fix on mine, "You say that you're not very Queenly and yet, what you just said was the exact thing a Queen would say."

I once again am stunned by this clan and its ability to believe. Conversation keeps on going after that, a little uneasy though.

Once I'm sure it is past midnight, I utter a good night to everyone and head to bed. James doesn't follow, instead he sits and speaks to those that have been loyal to him for so many years. I leave him behind and go to the grand staircase to find Will sitting on the bottom step.

"Are you alright?" I ask tentatively.

He doesn't say anything, but stands up, spins around, walks up the stairs, and motions for me to follow.

After a minute he says, "I heard what you said in there, about not knowing your heritage. I would like to show it to you."

We walk up three flights of stairs and down a few hallways until we meet ancient looking doors. Will turns to me before using his body to shove the doors open.

Inside are books upon books, shelves upon shelves, levels that go up and up, maps framed on the walls, and mystical tapestries nailed in stone.

"This is the building's original library," Will explains. "Every time I go on a vacation, I look for books or information on the Royal Family. Everything that has happened with your bloodline, is contained within these pages. You want to learn about your heritage? I'd start here."

I take a second look at the contents of the room. Centuries of stories and legends about my family are all within my reach.

I wonder if James knows that there is a room dedicated to me on the third floor of his fortress. I walk in through the doorway and go to the closest bookcase. I run my fingers along the books spines as I read title after title. Behind me, Will picks up a random book lying on one of the reading tables.

"What is that?" I inquire.

"It's the legend of your family's rule. How Allura gifted Gianna and why. If I were you, I would read this," Will's pointer finger lands on the leather casing of the story.

I don't bring my gaze to Will; I keep it on my family's book. I trace the letters on the front of the book that reads *Starfire Legend*.

Flipping open the old protection of the book, sit down at the table, and start to learn about my heritage.

It's well past 1 a.m. by the time I leave for my bedroom. I had been caught up in conversation with my fighters. For a long while, I have been distant, and speaking with everyone tonight made me feel ashamed.

I suppose I have Alena to thank for it. She is the one that convinced me to go down and eat food with everyone else. She disappeared during one of my conversations, and I hadn't noticed until 10 minutes later.

When I reach the entry to my bedroom, I pause. My cool down from my day has somewhat of a routine. It's a shower, some music, night clothes, paperwork, then bed.

But tonight is something different; I don't want to enter my safe haven. I don't want to do my routine or go to bed. Instead, I head to Alena's room. It doesn't take long to get to the East wing of the estate.

My brothers and I like to refer to it as an estate, even though it's more of a castle. It has that look of a castle to it, but it feels weird to call it that. Everything we keep in here you would find in a palace.

When I knock on her bedroom doors, a sleepy-eyed Ava answers the door.

"Alena? Why are you knocking so lo-" Ava stops as her vision clears of sleepiness.

"Good evening to you Ms. Smith."

"It's morning James. What are you doing here so late?" She questions.

"I was hoping to talk to Alena."

Ava doesn't answer, but glances back at what looks to be a pile of sleeping girls, some awake and staring.

"She's not here."

"What do you mean she's not here?"

Ava sleepily shrugs her shoulders.

"Well, where is she?"

"I don't know. If I see her, I'll tell her you stopped by. Now I want to sleep."

"Alright, have a good night's rest, girls."

A genuine smile is given, "Thanks. And… you too, James."

I blink at myself, did I just say that? I turn to walk down the corridor. I am totally taken aback by the act of kindness, that I don't notice the red-haired mess until she runs into me.

"James! I'm sorry, I should watch where I'm going."

I smile at Alena's rambling, "Alena! It's fine, don't worry about it. What are you doing in the halls at this hour?"

"That's a funny story actually…" Alena starts.

We walk around the estate as Alena fills me in on her recent knowledge. She starts with Will meeting her on the stairs and ends with spending an hour pouring over her family's history. Only when she got to her great grandmother, did she shut the book, promising herself to come back the next morning.

Now in my own chambers, we lounge on opposite loveseats, each angled at the blazing fire.

"Can you feel it?" I ask Alena.

She answers, knowing what I'm referring to, "Sort of. It's like a pull. I can feel the energy, but I can't move it, I don't want to."

"Are you afraid of it?"

Alena's eyes go distant, "I'm not afraid of it. I'm scared of what I can do with it."

When the confession comes, an uneasy silence falls between the two of us. We sit unmoving for what seems like hours, making it look like to others, on the outside, that we're dead.

"Would you help me? To learn how to use them?" I ask.

"Come over here," James pats the spot on the couch next to him.

I do what he suggests and sit down next to him. James takes a deep breath before turning to me and taking my hands in his own, "Let me make you a promise. No matter what happens, I am going to help you find a way to control your magic. And if you ever want to leave," James pauses. "I'll let you go."

"What about the others?"

"What about them? They are not you and me."

"So, you and me?" I don't face him.

"Till the stars fall," that was promise enough.

"I should head back to-"

James puts a hand out, "Stay?" A plea.

I respond by putting my head to rest on his shoulder. As I close my eyes from the outside wonders, I hear James lose a breath. I wasn't sure if it was the dream I was being pulled into or real life, but I heard someone say, "Goodnight, princess."

Chapter 23

When I wake up, I am no longer on the velvet cushions; instead a fluffy mattress envelops me.

James is nowhere in sight. I almost believe he isn't in the room, until I notice the sound of running water coming from what I presume to be the bathroom. My ears are confirmed after hearing a faint hum, also coming from that direction.

I roll back the covers and place my bare feet on the fuzzy rug next to the bed. Not a moment later does James walk out of the bathroom, with only a towel around his waist. He stops dead in his tracks.

"Alena-" he stammers. "I'm sorry, I didn't mean to... I mean I-"

"James, just go put some clothes on," I put a hand up to my eyes.

Instead of trying to find an excuse he replies, "Um yeah."

A minute of rummaging in the closet, a few curses here and there, a slam of something, and finally James emerges in a black t-shirt and navy-blue pants. His hair is in disarray, and his cheeks are still red from the heat of the shower, or pure embarrassment.

"I didn't think you'd be awake yet," James tries.

"Sorry to disappoint," the heat in my own cheeks still hasn't settled since seeing him as he was.

"You fell asleep on the couch last night," James changes the subject. "I moved you to my bed, I thought you'd be more comfortable."

"Yeah, thanks," I respond a little awkwardly.

We both start at the same time, "I should-"

We burst out laughing.

"See you at breakfast," James says as I move for the door.

I echo the sentiment and move from his room. My pace is brisk and silent as I pass hallway after hallway. Servants that are busy and about hop out of my way. Some say "good morning", while others yell at me to slow down. I pay no mind to them; my thoughts are somewhere else.

Whatever was happening between James and I was getting pretty serious. I'm digging a deep hole, and I'm not quite sure where it is leading to. Soon enough people are going to start noticing, which would be awful for James.

I shouldn't care about his image, but I do. Maybe that's just the loving side in me. Lately I've been noticing a certain twinkle in his eyes when he smiles. Maybe it's something that's always been there, and I've just never noticed.

James also has been working out with the soldiers in the gardens. I wouldn't have thought that weird if it wasn't for the fact that I never see James train.

A few mornings ago, I went on a walk with Ava, and James ran by with another soldier. Drenched in sweat, the bastard still managed a smile and a hello to Ava and me. When he had gone past, Ava giggled and nudged me. I just smiled and acted like nothing happened. James had also come to the secret library with Will and me today to study my family's origins.

There's not much on my magic; mostly family trees, sacred objects, castle blueprints, safe houses, transaction records, and royal decrees. So basically, everything but magic. The only thing that talks about my powers comes from a diary of Gianna's daughter, Natalia.

She subjected herself to a multitude of tests to try to awaken her magic. A trigger. She found it after she froze the doors to her room shut. It took her days to reign it back, in order to get out. Even after reading that aloud, the two idiots that have become my study buddies still thought it would be a great idea to try.

"This is stupid," I say to James, as Will reads aloud from Natalia's diary, totally ignoring me.

"It says that using a traumatic experience from the past should trigger something."

"What would be traumatic?" James questions.

I interfere, "How about nothing?"

"She nearly died from being shot?" Will inquires.

"And her mother shot her," James continues.

"She shot *at* me, she missed remember?"

"Let's shoot her," James says pointing a gun at me.

I'm dumbfounded, "Are you insane? What if Natalia was crazy and I end up dead?"

James just shrugs and points the gun, head level, "Better not fail then."

A shot fires. I close my eyes and put my hands up in defense, and on reflex, my magic surges forth. I crack one eye open to double check that I'm not on the ground, and I find the bullet three feet from not my face, but James'. I laugh and lower my hands. The bullet moves with me.

"Bet, you didn't expect that," I giggle out.

James' face goes neutral, but a hint of a smile dances on his face.

"I aimed for your shoulder at the last second, but yes, I am insane, love," James winks at me.

I roll my eyes, a blush creeping up my cheeks.

Will is all business, "Can you see them? Here it says there should be string-like light beams."

"They're called *threads of energy*. And no, they are not here."

James starts walking past me, "I've got an idea."

It's a two hour drive, half hour hike just to get to a massive, stupid lake that, I might add, is on top of a 6,000-foot mountain. The worst part: I'm supposed to get in the freaking water.

"Absolutely, not. No, I'm not doing it. Forget it."

"Do you want to find your magic?" Will asks.

"Yeah, but a lake is not the answer."

James rolls his eyes, "A lake is a giant form of water."

"And?"

"And it would make sense that you connect with magic when you're close. When you were fighting your mother, one of the first things you used to fight was water. Now if I'm correct, water should be one of the easier things you can call on."

"I'm not walking into that water," I state.

Without so much as caring about what I said, James throws me over his shoulder and strolls to the lake.

I pound on his back, "James freaking Ashburn, put me down this instance!"

"Well, that's a new one," James laughs as he is about to chuck me in. "Come on, you have to have a better one that that."

"I mean, if I had to-" I don't get a chance to finish as water hits my face. I yell out in frustration when I break to the surface.

I shoot James a glare.

James only shrugs, "What? You said you didn't want to walk into the water, so I helped you out."

"Hypothermia kills hundreds of people every year," I say.

"Then you better start with fire," a soldier in the back calls out, and the rest of the group chuckles.

I go underwater to drown out the sound of my misery. Everyone is quiet by the time I come back up for breath. Will must've told them to shut up.

"Focus on your breathing."

I do as Will suggests, close my eyes and breathe deeply.

"Notice the feel of the water."

That is the last thing I hear before I drown everyone out. I had already noticed the silky smooth feel of the water. The crispness it gives to the air above. Thousands of organisms underneath are all working together to make the water come alive.

I turn away from the shore and swim to where I can no longer touch the bottom. Faintly I hear the boys' warnings before I go under. The farther from the surface I am, the more I feel the water.

Lights spark behind my eyes. My neurons start firing out in beat with torrent blasts. Then I feel it, the black coming to the surface, a light filling the darkness. It's so close I can almost reach it. There in a sea of light, is my trigger. Hidden in a star, I sense the switch to my gifts.

I open my eyes as I push it. Underwater, I see the thousands of lights. In my ears I hear the heartbeat of the centuries old lake. I pull on my hold of the water, creating waves on the surface.

I go topside to see what I've created. Waves like mountains move across the freezing liquid. Just before the wave in front of me starts to crest, I put my hand up and freeze it where it stands. My focus is only on keeping the wave solid. I undo the wave, and flatten the rough surface, hoping that I don't drown.

I swim to where I can touch the rocks beneath. My mind is exhausted from the concentration and use of magic. Not even noticing, James comes up behind me and gives me his arm to balance on. I turn around to face him. His eyes are filled with fear, lips parted ever so slightly, face outlined in water. I take an extra moment to enjoy his beauty before remembering where I am. Behind him, I see Will headed toward us, the soldiers still on land.

"James, you're going to get cold," I warn through my chattering teeth.

"Well, it's better than me worrying about you."

I lean more into the warmth of James as Will finds his way to us.

"You alright, dear?"

"Fine, thank you, Will," I respond.

"It's getting late, maybe you want to build us a fire," Will suggests.

The sun is already starting to set, making hiking back nearly impossible. Not to mention that hypothermia will set in before we even reach half a mile.

I don't need to hear Will's way of calling on fire. My breathing evens out as I focus. I hang on tight to James' arm, just so I won't plunge into the water.

I picture in my mind the way fire moves; the crackle of wood popping, the heat it gives off. I imagine it small and contained, a shelter against the growing cold. When I open my eyes, on shore, a small light burns, fed by nothing.

I can no longer feel my legs, my nerves numb to the bone. When I try to walk out, I trip over my own legs. James catches me and carries me to shore.

Tents are set up around my fire before the sun sets. With the water fully calm from the magic before, the clouds are in the perfect position. The sunset it creates warms my heart; the beauty of the colors and the way it signifies life. Blue, pink, yellow, and red paint the sky like a canvas.

My tent is closest to the lake. After it was put up, I turned it to face the lake. The view entrances me, grounds me to the earth. I don't go and talk with the soldiers. My exhaustion wears too much on me. So instead, I grab my portion of dinner and go to the edge of the water.

Beside the distant chatter of the soldiers, the simplicity of the silence clears my mind. I eat my food slowly, savoring the warmth of the bean soup. It's not the best tasting dinner I've had while being here, but it fills my stomach.

"I remember a lake, much like this one, that my mother and I used to go to," I say to the crunching rocks behind me.

"Where was it?" James sits beside me.

"Somewhere in Minnesota. We camped there and I always liked to look at the stars. They were the brightest by the lake."

"Sounds beautiful," he agrees.

"I want to show it to you sometime. To let you know of a time when my mother wasn't evil," I look to James.

He stares back at me, eyes boring into mine. Something in his eyes flicker, a detail that I can't quite place.

"I've realized something, being around you. I was always taught that what one person does, they all do. The mistakes, the choices, all of it. It's the reason why I blamed you for killing my parents. I know that your mother did, but I couldn't harm her unless it was through you. Now I see the error in my ways. And… and I'm sorry for that."

I don't move my eyes from his downcast face.

My mouth is hanging open when he starts to speak again, "And don't say you forgive me. What I've done is… unforgivable. I don't deserve to even speak to you."

James walks away before I can respond. I don't follow him either, stunned into shock by what James has just laid out in the open.

I finish my dinner hastily, eager to go do something to distract me. My final bite is taken as I set my bowl in the dirty dishes pile. When I look up, I find James wandering off into the woods. Not allowing him his freedom, I follow, making sure to make no sound. He walks well away from camp, his form slouched over, head downcast.

10 minutes we walk, all the while making sure I don't make a sound. When he finally stops in a clearing bathed in moonlight, my legs are exhausted. As I lean against a tree, just outside the clearing, a branch cracks beneath my feet. James' head whips around to face my general direction, gun drawn and pointed.

"Who's there?" He calls out.

Taking a step into the light, I put my hands up, "It's just me."

James' gun retreats to its holster, his grim expression doesn't change.

"What are you doing here?"

"I needed to talk to you," I continue to go toward the center where he stands unmoving. "You don't get to say something like that and then walk away without giving me the chance to answer."

"You can't say it."

"Why not? Because you think you're unworthy?"

"Because I am!" James yells at me. "You're not."

"If I'm not then you're not. A person doesn't understand what they are doing is wrong until they are shown what is right. So, quit being so hard on yourself and just forgive," I say.

His eyes float to mine, a glimmer there.

"So, despite what you might think," I close the distance between us, until I'm only an inch away. "You are worthy of forgiveness. You've always been."

"I'm not going to keep this up," he whispers.

"James, has anyone ever asked you what you want? Not as a leader, but as a friend?"

His eyes lock with mine, a hunger there, "No."

"Then what do you want?"

It would be crazy to say I expected what happened next. The following words that he says make my heart glow.

"I want you," he says to me, just before he places his lips on my own.

Passion, needing, wanting, waiting, all of it pierces through me.

He pulls away too soon, his body tense and unsure. Myself, unsure of what just transpired between us.

For whatever reason, I grab his head and pull it toward me. Unconsciously, my body arches up against his, his arms snaking around my waist. Kissing him made me sure of what I wanted. What I wanted wasn't to go out in the world to my freedom. I had already been given that. For the first time in forever, I had been given the choice to do what I wanted. And in this moment, I wanted James. I needed him.

When I pulled away from the magical kiss, our breaths entangling, foreheads touching, I was free.

"I want you too," I tell him. A dazzling smile was his response.

We walk back together, closer than before. I was okay with it. I wasn't afraid. For what felt like the first time in a long time, I felt happy.

Amazing, fierce, breathtaking—the kiss was all that and more. My mind is unable to focus on anything else. We walk back quicker than I wanted, but the night is coming to a close and I need sleep.

When we arrive on site, the fire has died and everyone is asleep. Alena and I part ways. Smiling, I watch her go to the tent by the lake.

When I can no longer see her silhouette, I dip inside my tent, eager for sleep. I change into more comfortable wear, making sure that it also keeps me warm. Sleep greets me as soon as my head hits my pillow.

When I wake, everyone is already packing up camp, Alena included. The bags beneath her eyes are smaller than I expected. Her face is alight with joy, her eyes carved out in it.

My tent is the last to be packed up. As we start the trek back to the cars, Alena stays far back, her eyes wandering all over nature's canvas. Disappointed that she isn't walking with me, I stay back till I'm by her side.

"You seem happy this morning," I greet.

"Morning to you as well. And yes, I am," she says back.

"So, I've been talking to Will-" I start.

"Oh boy, I don't like where this is going."

"Relax, it's all good. I just told Will that you might want your room back."

It was true. For the past couple of days, I had been speaking with Will about giving his Dawns their own rooms. He reluctantly agreed, unsure at first. He had brought up the issue of Alena trying to run. That was when I explained to him that I had given Alena her freedom to leave. Astonished into silence, Will agreed with a nod of his head.

"Are they okay with that?" she asks.

"I'm sure that all of them being in one room is getting old."

Alena nods, "Yeah, that's true."

"And besides, they can stay with you whenever."

Alena brings up the one left out, "What of Ava?"

I'm unsure how to phrase it, so I just say it outright, "I was thinking of making her your lady's maid."

Alena pauses for a moment before putting the pieces together, "I have to be a Lady to do that. Not to mention that is a Medieval practice."

That was true, lords and ladies were very Dark Ages. That being said, those titles were still used in clan families. Surprisingly, more often than not.

"That's true but making you a Lady would solve a lot of my problems."

"Oh yeah? Like what?"

"Glad you asked. It would be easier to present you as a Lady at the ball."

Alena chokes on the water she was drinking.

"I'm sorry ... ball?"

"Do you know how to ballroom dance?"

"James!"

"Well we have two weeks, you could learn."

"In two weeks?"

"But we still have to find you a ball gown."

"Ball gown?"

"And all the rules with the other cartels-"

"James! I am not going to a ball."

"Well, why not?"

"Because too many things can go wrong," she tries to explain.

"Name one," I challenge.

"They could figure out I'm a royal," she says flatly, and she wasn't wrong.

"Okay, good point."

"But?" she says, sensing my next retort.

"But, you're still going."

She huffs her reply, "I hate you."

"No, you don't."

She just shoves me with her shoulder and walks onward.

An hour passes in the car. The soldiers are much more talkative than usual. Despite my complaints, the next hour of the car ride, James starts to teach me about each and every clan that will be at the ball. To my knowledge, most of them hate the Royal family. But due to weapon trades, few non-haters will be there.

One of the clans is actually one that killed my great grandmother. I was told not to kill the head honcho. Although, he did add that if I really wanted to, I would have to wait until James left.

I return to a completely clean, and wonderful smelling room. It is also empty. It's kind of spooky how silent it is, but after yesterday I really need a bath.

Much to my dismay, as soon as I fill the bathtub, put the bubbly soap in, and change into my robe, I hear a knock at my door. Pretty convinced that I shouted loud enough at the intruder, I go and answer the person ruining my bath.

As soon as I answer the door I say, "I hope you know you are ruining my bath time."

"Is it bad that I don't care?" David answers.

"David I-"

"We need to talk." He barges in.

Before I can even answer he fires off a question.

"What is going on between you and my brother?"

I scoff. I actually scoff at him. This is what he is wasting my time for.

"Why should you care?"

"How about he is my brother, and I don't trust you."

"How about, it's none of your damn business. Go ask James if you want, not me."

"Listen to me, girl." He looks me dead in the eye. "If you don't stop whatever you're doing, you're going to regret it."

"If I remember correctly, you are the ones who kidnapped me."

"Fine. Tonight, you are going to get out of here. I'll get the guards out of your way."

I laugh in his face. He doesn't know. Wait 'til I drop it on him.

"He didn't tell you, did he?"

Confusion is written all over David's face, so I explain, "He set me free. Let me go days ago."

"Then why are you still here?"

"Because I'm learning my powers here. And in case you haven't noticed, my mother shot at me."

"I know you don't like me; you've made it clear. But being here gives me a chance to learn who I am. And I would never ever do anything to harm you or your family. I just need time to figure out mine."

He's silent for a while, contemplating what I've said.

"I still don't trust you."

"Same here. What can I do to earn it?"

His answer is surprisingly fast, "I want you to train with me. Every morning, five o'clock in the gardens. If you're late you have an extra mile."

He doesn't say anything else, and instead walks out the door.

Before it closes, I yell a "thank you."

When I return to the bathroom, I slip into the semi-warm water. At this point, any relaxation that I had planned was gone. I sit there for hours, using my mind to make waves in the bubbly water. I get into a rhythm of moving the water, then stopping it.

Once my hands are covered with wrinkles, I get out and wrap myself up with a cozy towel. It's well past nine o'clock. Dinner has passed but the kitchen is still open. As I'm emptying the tub, I hear a knock on my door.

"Come in!" I yell, exchanging my towel, for a robe.

"Alena?" James asks.

"Yeah," I call back, entering my bedroom.

His face flushes a strawberry color, struggling to think of what to say.

"What's up?" I ask, going to my closet to change.

"I wanted to talk to you about dance lessons tomorrow."

I laugh at the thought of something so simple happening here.

"They start at 8 a.m. Dance for two hours, then lunch for one. Clan studies for three, then magic training afterwards. Dinner then whatever you want," he finishes as I come out in matching silk pajamas.

"I can do that for a day."

"No, every day for two weeks."

"No."

"What do you mean no?"

"I mean no, I'm not doing that."

"Alena, come on," he begs.

"Look, every girl out there has dreamed of going to a ball. But I can't. I will see people that I have been hidden from my entire life. They hate my family, and I..." I pause. "I can't dance."

"So, you've dreamed about going to a ball, but now that you have a chance to you aren't because you don't want to meet people and you supposedly can't dance. Correct?"

I nod my head.

"You realize how dumb that sounds, right?"

I start giggling. Listening to my reasons does make them sound stupid. His face lights up when I laugh, scrunched up from trying not to join in. I shake my head. When my joy slowly stops sounding, I go to sit on the new sofa added to my room. James comes to relax next to me.

"Want to have breakfast tomorrow? Just before dancing?"

"Is that a date?" I question.

James stutters, "No...no. Okay, yes."

I see his surprise when I explain, "Can't. I'm training with David tomorrow."

"I must say that I didn't see that coming."

"I'm trying to earn his trust," I also add the other fact. "He tried to get me to leave before I told him I was already free."

"You told him that?" He confirms.

I nod my head, "I did. But he seemed okay with it."

"Keyword: seemed."

I shrug my shoulders and go out onto the balcony, needing some cool air on my face. The tiles beneath me hint at the coming fall, with green and red leaves lying on the floor. With the sun already set, the stars start to reveal themselves.

James grabs a blanket from the chest at the end of my bed and drapes it over my shoulders. The gesture brings tears to my eyes. I miss my mother at that moment.

Maybe it is random and sudden, but my heart aches for her. In spite of everything she's done, I still can't let go of the woman I used to know, the woman that used to stay home whenever I got sick, just to keep me company. The one who would get me ice cream after every play; who gave me advice on how to deal with bullies when I came home crying. She would build me a leaf pile every year, no matter how old I got.

"You're thinking of her," James states, leaning against the railing.

I nod my head and look at him questioningly.

"Your expression changes when you think of her."

I don't respond, and instead just stare at the awakening sky.

"It's gorgeous," I say.

James hums his agreement.

I stand there, watching the stars twinkle. The only sound is our breathing.

"I don't know if I can face her again," I tell him.

James arms slip around my middle, holds me close, and lets me know that he's here. I lean into the warmth of the man that comforts me. A few minutes pass until I'm tired enough to sleep. I'm silent as I walk, my mind milling about.

Crawling under the covers, I curl in on myself, saddened with thoughts of my past. James goes to the chairs by the fireplace, watching my mood worsen. Time passes without my knowledge, James' steady presence the only constant. When I finally start to drift, I hear someone come into the room, but my body is too exhausted to wake. So, I go into darkness and let the unknown person walk freely.

Finally, she drifts to sleep, awake for hours in her own memories. Will enters just as she leaves the real world, face blank.

"What?" I ask, still watching her.

"David made a deal with Alena."

"She told me," I respond.

"How are you not concerned? You know he doesn't like her."

"Well, he doesn't like me when I'm angry even more. Besides, it's a way for her to gain his trust," I confirm.

Will does a "yeah sure" sigh and comes to sit down on the chair opposite of mine.

"All things considered; she would make a fine Queen."

"Agreed. I don't think she will do it though," I say.

"Have you asked?" Will challenges.

"I suppose I will," is my only response.

He says one more thing before he goes, "If she says yes, send her my way. I have a special something for her."

Chapter 24

The next two weeks are absolutely awful. I was late by thirty seconds my first day, earning me an extra mile of running on top of my already five given. I'm still not sure if David is trying to make my heart burst or if this is an everyday thing with him. David occasionally would strike conversation with me to really push my limits. When I gave him short answers, he yelled at me and said that I wasn't giving him enough information.

Dance class wasn't much better. My first day there I fell so many times that James actually came in to watch. I flipped him off when he started laughing at me. Never, since being here, had I seen James truly laugh. It was deep and full of joy, and so contagious that I laughed along with him.

I had done his schedule for a week, including David's training. I had gotten so into training I asked some guards to teach me fighting techniques at night. Trusting that I wouldn't tell, I got three nights in before James confronted me.

He wasn't as mad as I thought he'd be.

"You're training behind my back?"

"No, I am training to protect myself. I need to be prepared at the ball," I explain.

"Nothing will happen."

"Better to be safe than sorry."

"Fine, but you won't learn much from them. Mind if I tag along?"

"Makes no difference to me."

"Come with me, will you?" James asks, motioning me out the door.

I follow, unaware of where we are headed. To my surprise, he brings me out into the gardens, and doesn't stop walking until we get to the Panther fountain. Its teeth seem to glean in the moonlight, eyes alight with life.

"Creepy, isn't it?"

I shake my head, "Just misunderstood."

"Listen, Alena. No one has asked you and you've never truly answered," he pauses to take a deep breath. "Do you want to be Queen?"

I'm stunned by this hard question. Being Queen takes responsibility, sacrifice. From everything I've learned, everywhere a Queen went, death followed. The decisions they made, the image they have to uphold; all of it seems like too much, and I'm not sure if I'm ready for that.

People I love would be targeted. Every move I'd make would be watched and judged. I would be a celebrity in power, constantly on edge. And the worst part, I would have to make those decisions that could change or take someone's life, and I don't know if I could do that.

"I can't decide that. At least, not yet," I recover.

"Take your time, you're in no rush."

I shake my head and continue to stare into the eyes of the Panther.

"Okay, so maybe it is a little creepy," I say aloud, to break the tension.

James chuckles deep, the sound vibrating through my bones. We talk lightly on our walk back, our conversations lifting my heart up.

For the first time in what feels like forever, I sleep alone in my room. The only company is the fire crackling. My mind is quieted by the sound, the big question barely a buzz in my subconscious.

The dream I have that night revolves around the question, my mind giving me a display of what it could be like. Being a Queen takes responsibility as well as helping people.

When I wake from the peculiar dream, I feel motivated. I even show up early to training and run an extra two miles. When I see David, I stop in my tracks. He holds two swords, and James, standing next to him, holds one.

"What is this?" I ask.

"Training," David responds as I come closer.

They explain how they are the best teachers here, and they are who I should learn from.

"So, what's first?" I say, happy to agree.

"This," David answers, tossing the sword at me and advancing, sword point at my heart.

I twirl out of the way, only to end up face to face with James.

"Two on one, that's not fair."

"Battles are not ever fair," David says from the sidelines, waiting for the moment to pounce. "The sooner you learn that, the better prepared you'll be when the real thing happens."

James strikes with perfect precision, power laced in every blow. I play defense, meeting his hits with my sword, careful not to get hurt. Blow for blow, I match, James born for this fight. His skill is hard to put up with. Out of the corner of my eye, I see David joining back in.

I look for that trigger inside me, the threads. David doesn't notice the flame growing from my heart to my sword. The metal goes white hot, my mind getting into the fight. Fire races up my left arm, filling the space that is unprotected. Now I've got a chance of winning.

David gives a displeasing smile, while James looks excited.

"Bring it," I breathe.

James is the first to challenge. His form is picture perfect as he brings his sword down. I push him off with the edge of my weapon. David circles to my back side, searching for a weak point. I bring a wall of fire to meet him, as I continue this dance of death with James.

I duck as he swings right. He jumps when I go low, and he follows back with his foot holding my sword down. Flames snake up his leg, just enough for me to recover with my sword. David circles around my wall of fire and swipes for my arm. The weapon misses after I push my way to an open area.

When I turn to face my opponents, I only see one. James is nowhere in sight. Once I figure it out, it's too late.

My head hits the ground first, after James sweeps my legs out beneath me. And when I catch my breath, the point of James' sword scraps my throat. I'm breathing hard from the workout. This is a much harder fight than the soldiers gave me.

"Done?" James asks, steel hovering over my heart.

I blow him back with my fire, rise to my feet and smirk.

"Cheater."

"You have an advantage," I try.

"*I* have an advantage?"

I only shrug at his point.

"I need to practice my ball dance," I pronounce brushing off my clothes.

James steps up, "Need a partner?"

I smile and stroll into the estate, letting James decide whether to follow or not.

The lesson ended quickly for a 'fitting'. That's what rich people call a tailor coming in to measure your body for clothes. In this case, a ball gown. Which, much to my pleasure, is absolutely gorgeous.

James was kicked out before he could see what the masterpiece looked like. The dress is lined with millions of fabric shaped stars. The dress only stays up by two straps close to the end of my shoulders, leaving my chest bare for whatever jewelry I choose. The bodice is filled with swirls of white. The dress itself is a deep navy blue, to bring out my eyes.

When I move to put it on, several people have to help. It's lighter than I thought, the cloth still full of volume. My hair isn't fixed up. They only show me pictures of an updo bun in a ballerina fashion.

What I love most about this dress is the back. Despite its openness that goes down to my lower back, the way it shapes my body is astonishing.

To finish it all off, my feet are placed in white plain heels, I'm given white ball gloves, and white pearls that will be woven into my hair.

To be honest, this whole ball thing is a little intimidating. It is clear from how calm everyone is about this that this ball is not an unusual thing. Everyone makes it seem like it's a typical high school party. Meanwhile I am over here freaking my ass off.

It's dinner by the time the fitting is done. My torso is sore from being poked and prodded for hours. In the workers' defense, the dress was totally worth it.

I eat my supper quickly, eager to get to bed. When I reach my chambers, I do what has become my routine: bathe, change, do my homework for my classes, read my history, and then go to bed.

Five full days of the normal routine, with some added ball gown lessons. They actually teach you how to wear it; how to sit and stand, move in it without tripping. It was all preposterous in my opinion.

The rules about wearing the dress made me even more nervous for the ball. Instead of telling anyone how I am feeling, I kept my true feelings hidden. Partly because I did not want to make anyone upset, and I was secretly excited for this ball.

It wasn't until I was explained all the rules of the ball that I understood why all the dress lessons.

"No slouching, no fights, and absolutely no magic. They will kill you on the spot," James says.

I only laugh and say, "I can take care of myself."

"I've seen that, but you lost against two people. I can't fathom 20."

"I've been practicing," I counter between mouthfuls.

Breakfast was pounded with rules. Not that I minded, it gave me an excuse to eat more food than usual: boredom.

"Anything else?" I ask, sure that they could pump a gallon of food out of my stomach.

He nods and laughs, "Had enough to eat?"

I moan my discomfort from a food induced coma.

"Want to go on a run?" He asks.

"I thought we weren't supposed to stress our bodies."

"We can spare a mile. Unless you are too lazy."

I scoff at his attempts to get me up, but I give in.

The run is over relatively quickly, partly because I was about to throw up by the end of it. I was, however, lazy enough to not change into workout clothes. When I return to my room to shower, I find an army of maids waiting for me.

Ten girls scurry around my chambers, eager to start the real work. I was not prepared. They surround me immediately, scolding the sweaty clothes sticking to my body. They herd me into the bathroom and put me in a pinkish water bath, which smells so much like roses I think I might cry.

I sit in the bath for an hour while the maids polish and prime my skin until it glows. They don't let me dry off with a towel when I get out. Instead, they wrap me in a robe and put me in front of what looks like to be four giant fans. They leave the bathroom after they instruct me to turn on the contraption and "dry off." The wind power the things make is quite astonishing, drying my hair in a minute and my body in less.

I take a glance at my body in the mirror. The person who stares back could be my twin, if I glowed. My skin shimmers in the sunlight filling my bathroom. Any cuts or bruises don't show. The bags under my eyes are completely gone. And my birthmark stands out more than ever. When I smile, I find pure joy in my face. I wrap the robe back around myself before I can squeal.

When I emerge from the bathroom, I find my masterpiece of a dress waiting for me. The sunlight that pours in elevates its beauty tenfold. I still have two hours before I have to leave. Eating is only allowed to take twenty minutes, because apparently makeup takes an hour and a half to put on.

To much of my surprise, there isn't a whole tub of makeup waiting for me when I finish lunch. There's only a tub of paint. It has more of a glitter look, but it is painted into my hair. The bun pictures they had shown me earlier isn't exactly what they do. It's messier because of the tons of woven hair they thread through the pearls. When my hair is finally collected on top of my head, they put another thin layer of the "paint" on.

Next, the maids move onto the makeup. My face is a lighter shade than normal, which miraculously looks like my normal skin tone.

My eyes get the best treatment of all. They are turned white, then filled in with a blue and pearl blend. My eyelashes are not fake, but the type of mascara they use makes them look longer.

With only 15 minutes remaining, the crew finish the touch-ups of sparkles on my face and hair, and then move onto the dress. It takes three people to pull the dress onto my body, one of them holding me for balance. A small zipper in the back is the only thing that keeps the entire dress together. My back is totally exposed, my smooth skin shown for all. They don't add sparkles to that. Something about how it has to look "authentic."

My shoes are easily slipped on. The last piece is two simple, white, elbow length, ball gown gloves to cover my birthmark and for the simplicity of it. I had been practicing how to walk in these heels for days, so when I head out of my room to get to the entrance, I have no issues.

James doesn't greet me at the stairs. The host wanted to have drinks with the leaders before the party arrived. Instead, Will and David wait for me. Descending the stairs was easier than imagined. Will and David both take an arm as my escorts. They inform me that at the ball it will be a soldier that will wait for me at the bottom.

I ride in not the standard SUVs, but a black limo. The vehicle is only for me. David and Will will ride in the other limo leading mine.

Ava gives me a hug before I climb into my ride. James, Ava, and I agreed it would be hard to fit Ava into the family image. She opted to stay back so we didn't have to make up a story.

She cries when she sees me and calls me the most beautiful angel she has ever seen. She waves me off, and in turn I send a small flamefly toward her.

During my extensive practice, I learned how to shape two of the elements. Fire is my main power, easiest to access, and I have a lot of it. I can control other things too, but it isn't necessarily the easiest of my power. Will said that after the spell my grandmother cast, everyone's power has either died or, like me, been greatly reduced.

The house we arrive at is grand, almost as grand as James' house. This one is much more modern, with quartz pillars and marble steps. A guard takes my hand to help me from the limo, my dress easily slipping out of the car to gather around my ankles.

For only having started 30 minutes ago, the party is bustling. If the red carpet was a party, it would be this. Girls and guys everywhere are dressed up like me in gowns and tuxedos. Will and David are already inside, so I head in with curious glances in my direction.

The guard that brings me into the mansion leaves me alone just before a grand staircase. If I ever thought there'd be a moment that I would feel like Cinderella, it would be now. Just before I go into the light, I check to make sure my gloves cover my birthmark.

The room seems to quiet when I reach the top step. Like before, many eyes drift to me. Despite my dress being magnificent in every way, I was confused on how I was the center of attention.

I pick the skirt of my dress up off the floor, place my free hand on the white granite railing, and descend. I search for that familiar face in the crowd. In the back, lounging with the other leaders, I find James. Like me, he is dressed to impress in a classic grey blazer and pants and a black button up shirt, which makes him look striking.

At the bottom of the staircase, as promised, a soldier in a tux waits. He offers his arm when I reach the bottom.

"Why is everyone staring?" I ask him.

"They don't know you. And pardon me for being outright, milady, but you are the most beautiful Lady here."

I blush at the compliment as we weave our way through the crowd. The guard leads me to the area where James and his buddies lounge. James' face is like it was when I first met him, a mask of mischief and all.

"Gentlemen, this is the Lady Alena. She's been staying with me for the past few months."

I curtsy to the five men staring at me. Just like calling people Lords and Ladies, curtsies are still a thing, done only to higher ups. Old court customs were kept within leader families.

"Lady? What might she have done to earn that?" The one to the left asks.

"Other than being absolutely sexy, nothing," James answers, his old facade cemented in his words as well as his face.

"If she's nothing more than that," the one to the right says. "You won't mind if I take her for a dance."

Alarm flashes in James' eyes for a split second before dissipating.

"She's all yours, Aaron."

Aaron Casestate, leader of the Miami clan. Notorious for kills, Aaron is considered quite the ladies' man.

Aaron stands and descends the few stairs that separate me and the rest who sit on a raised platform.

He bends down to kiss my gloved hand, "Mrs.-"

"Jackson."

"Mrs. Jackson. May I have this dance?"

I answer with an incline of my head. Aaron leads me out to the dance floor. We both do the starting bows before the ball dance and begin. The tempo is a tad slower than normal, making it easier to have a conversation.

"Pardon me for my manners, but there seems to be more behind that pretty face."

"I could say the same for you, Mr. Casestate."

"So, you know who I am?"

"Clan leader of Miami. Known most for your charms with women and your death toll," I list off my known information.

"More than a pretty face," Casestate laughs. "You and James..." He says, looking back and forth between James and me.

"No, no. James doesn't like me in that way," I try to recover.

"I saw the way he looked at you when you entered the room."

"I just cleaned up well, that's all."

"If you say so."

"I do."

We continue dancing to a second song, before he asks another question.

"You look familiar. Remind me how you met James?"

I don't have time to recover from the blow. I fumble over my words for a few seconds before responding.

"A coffee shop. He was on a mission and he needed coffee for the morning," I say, repeating Ella's story of David and her.

"I see."

"May I steal her back from you, friend?" My relief says.

Aaron smiles, as we bow goodbye to each other. When James slides in to take his place, I let out a loud sigh.

"Thank you," I say to him.

"What? You weren't enjoying your time with the womanizer?" I laugh as we bow to one another. "Now, now. Don't make me look weak in front of them."

"He said that I looked familiar. Do you think he knows?" I whisper to him.

"I wouldn't worry, he has slept with so many women their faces are probably bleeding together. To make the most stunning of them all," James says, making me blush.

"If you keep flirting with me, I might have to flirt back," I tease.

"No, that would ruin your reputation."

We both laugh at our sarcastic conversation. We continue to dance and talk for an hour. We only break our dance to grab food and drinks. Well, in my case, chocolate. David and Will help point out their favorites. James' favorites, however, were the most delicious. The four of us spend the hours at the ball together, laughing and talking like a family. During the time, I couldn't help the smile that was glued to my face. Family. That's what they are starting to feel like to me. When we all agree that we should stop eating sweets, David offers me a dance.

The typical waltz we dance to is tinged ever so slightly by beat. To my surprise, David's feet move with the music impeccably.

"I don't know what this means for the future, but you've earned my trust."

I miss a step hearing the unexpected news.

He looks out at the audience with a chuckle, "Careful there, don't let your training go to waste."

"I can't believe this," I say. "What? No ridiculous course to run and pass?"

David only shakes his head.

He leans in 'till I can feel his breath on my ear and whispers, "You've earned it."

I beam at the accomplishment I made.

"Good, I can't do another morning of training."

"Oh no, you're still training. I didn't waste all that time for nothing."

I laugh my agreement, just as the song ends and James steps in.

"I've earned his trust," I tell James, in awe of everything around me.

"I knew you would."

"About that thing before, you do look handsome."

"Dear me. Princess, you best watch it. Don't want others getting any ideas."

I laugh, "I don't mind."

"Speaking of, have you come up with an answer?"

I know what he's talking about. It has been on my mind all week, but I knew what I wanted; who I wanted to be.

"Yes. I want to be Queen," I say firmly.

James' smile is different than I expected.

"I'm glad because-" he didn't finish.

Before I could realize what was happening, James starts to fall. I catch him just before his head hits the floor. A scream starts, then 10 more follow. I throw up a shield around James and me.

When I look up, I see a sniper reloading his gun, acting as if what he just did wouldn't cost him. I catch Will and David running over, so I pass through the shield and enter the fight.

Cartels and clans from every angle protect their leaders. On the balcony surrounding the ballroom stands an army dressed in all black.

Mother's voice booms over the chaos, "Alena!"

I look up to find her standing, on the leaders' raised dais, beside Aaron. Little bastard.

"You ready to come home? Or are you still trying to be something you're not?"

When I break through the crowd hiding me, I find my mother with tears in her eyes.

"I've decided who I am and there is nothing that will change that."

To prove my point, I send water to collect her sniper. Water from glasses and faucets mix together as one. In one swoop, the gunman is taken and put in front of me, back to my mother. When I see the fear in his eyes, I am reminded of who I am.

"If I ever see you touch a gun without my permission, you will never see the stars again. Am I making myself clear?" I say softly.

A simple nod is enough for me and I tell the water to let him go. I let the water fall to the ground, just to replace it with fire. Only then do I realize that I had just exposed myself. It's probably not the best way to reveal myself, but they would know eventually.

"She's... she's..." Aaron babbles.

I can feel the fire in my eyes, the burn in my soul. The threads of energy reveal themselves to me, allowing me to take full control. Fire goes in all directions, keeping everyone in the room and away from rivals. I bring my mother's cavalry to James' soldiers, their guns dropped to the floor.

"Let me make myself perfectly clear," I address to everyone. "There will be no fighting here today. If any of you even so much as breathe the wrong way, you won't like what comes next."

No one answers with words, they only nod with shock on their faces. I bring my fire back to me, surrounding myself in my birthright. I shape the fire star around my body, embracing me with its warmth.

"Is this clear enough, mother?"

My hand pulses in delight with my performance. I find no pleasure as my mother, moves away from the dais, walks up to my symbol and drops to her knees, tears splattering her face. Walking to the edge, I put my hand out for my mother. She takes it and rises.

The world is made up of those that push and pull. The causes and effects and the consequences at the end. Whether it is regretting something you never fulfilled or having an unexpected child, every decision we make creates who we are.

In that moment, with everyone's eyes on me, I have to make a choice. The choice for them and for myself. I just hope that even though it will eventually cause me more pain than not, that it is the right choice.

I smile as I take both her hands and say, "I forgive you."

I don't expect her to be okay with the choices that I made, but I need her to know that I forgive her, if only so I can move on with my life.

Mom takes her hands and cups my face, "My beautiful daughter. I'm sorry for how I treated you. I didn't listen to you. What I did was wrong. You need to do what's right for you. Look out for #1."

I was genuine when I told her that I forgave her. This moment now just proves it. She didn't want word getting out that I existed, that our family still lived. So, I can forgive and I can live on, being who I am.

"Alena?" A voice calls from behind.

I turn to see James, still kneeling on the floor, watching me. I go to him, the boy that destroyed and saved me. I smile, fully aware of all the eyes trained on me.

"Are you sure?" he wonders.

I bend down and place my hand against his chest, feeling that beating heart.

"I'm ready."

Chapter 25

Unlike before, James and I drive home together.

Home.

It is weird that the place that once held me in chains is now what I consider home. I suppose that is thanks to the brothers.

James was hit with a paralytic bullet, only meant to last 15 or so minutes. He quickly recovered by the time we exited the party. Much to my relief, might I add. After the night that we just experienced, I wanted nothing more than to spend time with James.

James offers me his hand as I exit the car, my dress gathering around my ankles. My mom is being brought over in an hour, as soon as David and Will deem her safe enough to be around James and I. I don't mind either, I need a moment to breathe before I see my mom again.

After my announcement, people stared at me like I was Jesus, or the Devil, it depended on who was looking.

My mom initially tried to hold onto me, but I brushed her off and allowed James' clan to sweep me away from the scene. As soon as I was behind the door of the car, my breaths came out shaky and short. James just sat there, hands holding mine, waiting patiently as I tried to gather my thoughts.

The entire ride home, I both scolded and praised myself. I never planned to reveal myself that way, or at all an hour before that.

James was silent on the way home, I think we were both stunned about the turn of events. Me most of all.

Because of the sheer force of power I called on, and so fast, I am drained. My magic isn't meant to be used so forcefully, it is supposed to be there like an extension. However, like everyone else, my magic has its limits due to the curse. At least that is Will's explanation for it.

Ava is sitting on top of the steps when the front doors open, her body bowed over her knees. She stands ramrod straight at the sudden change in sound. I don't know what she has been told, if anything at all, but I am sure the commotion was enough to send her nerves on edge.

She has always been worrisome, and always overthinks every-thing. I do that too, but her anxiety compared to mine is in a whole other universe. Where I would maybe stress over finals, she is physi-cally sick and up all night, anxious for the sun to rise.

We run to one another, both wanting the comfort that only a best friend can provide. She crumples against my shoulder when she realizes that I am perfectly fine. I tell her as much as she voices her protests about not going. I get her off my back with the excuse of exhaustion and the promise of my fireflies. She relents, not easily might I add.

I escape up the stairs before she can change her mind, send-ing the promised firefly into another room for her to follow. James trails behind me, a knowing smile on his face. He is as unhappy with the night's events as I am. It's bittersweet really, for I am hoping that maybe this will offer a chance for both my mom and I to rekindle that broken flame.

The door to my room shuts with comfort and protection, James doing all the work. He doesn't follow me in, both of us needing to get out of the night's attire and into something easy to walk around in. He promises to come back later, I simply excuse him.

Even with the beauty of my dress, I can't wait to escape it. An almost silent woosh sounds as my dress collapses to the floor. I wrestle the pin, holding my hair together, off letting my hair fall down in bouncy waves. The pearls stay stuck, they only come off as I run my fingers through my hair, and let them fall into a bowl.

Free of the night's decorations on my body, I quickly change into a set of black pjs. I build a fire in the fireplace and sink onto the new sofa in my room, surprisingly more comfortable than the last one.

When I hear the doors open and shut, I immediately think it's James. So I call out.

"James."

"No, it's me."

My mom comes into view as I turn my head away from the fire. Her face is drawn, regret graces her features. She no longer looks like the woman from before. She doesn't look quite like my mother either. She is a mix of both, and I don't know who I want more, the one that I would slap or the one that I would hug.

Mother drops on the couch opposite of mine, her shoulders drooping, folding in on herself. A story shines in her eyes.

"I am not here to start trouble," she starts, and pauses, thinking about what she needs to say.

"I told you this is where I want to be."

"I know, but you asked for the truth. I want to give it to you." I don't answer, so she starts the story that I've always wanted to hear. The story that would break me if I let it.

"You already know that your father didn't die protecting a bank," I already don't like this. "He died protecting something much greater."

My mom takes a deep breath and begins.

"You were four, so little and fragile. We had come home from dinner, your brother had just left for a friends house next door. I checked on you, saw that you were still asleep, and we went to bed like we normally would. I remember hearing a creak in the floorboards, and the scuffling of two sets of feet. I immediately woke up your father. At the time, he was in charge of the cartel. I knew what he did and I was partially involved but I never led them.

"He loved you so much, would come home just to watch you play-"

I cut her off, "Mom. What happened?"

"He got up, grabbed the handgun in his nightstand, and went to check on you. He never heard the creak, and I started thinking that maybe I had just imagined it. But I let him go anyway. That's when I heard the arguing. I grabbed my own gun and followed him, into your bedroom. The door was already ajar and I saw your dad there, pointing the gun at old friends of ours, the Ashburns."

I shake my head, "Mom they wouldn't-"

"They came for you. Margaret looked so regretful, but Edward, looked perfectly at peace with a gun pointed at you. I couldn't believe that you were still asleep. Edward finished saying something to your dad, and he turned back to you. It all happened so quickly I didn't even realize what happened until Margaret started screaming. Your dad, he shot Edward, trying to protect you. Margaret, that woman was not who I knew years ago. She was perfectly calm, stopped screaming, as she raised her own gun, and shot your dad. I thought I had beaten her, I fired my own gun at her at the same time. I remember feeling so triumphant, but then I saw your father fall. Margaret fell at the same time, but the damage was already done to both of them. When she shot your father, a bit of the bullet ricocheted into my shoulder. I was so focused on your father that I didn't even realize.

"When I reached your dad, he was already dying, there was nothing I could do. He could barely speak his goodbye to me, but I already knew what he was saying. He was staring at you. You were starting to wake up and he didn't want you to see. When I looked back at him, he was gone and I ran to you. I shielded you from them, and I took you from the room.

"When I got downstairs your dad's second was already there, and he ordered the others that were with him to get us out of there. When we left the house everything else was a blur. The bullet in my shoulder had caused so much blood loss that I lost that memory."

"Does Jeremy know?"

"Yes, I told him," she answers slowly, the emotion in her eyes fading.

We sit there in silence for what feels like eternity. Only one thought circling my head.

"Why me?"

My mom lets out an exasperated sigh, "Because Alena, you were, are, a threat. You are the only thing that could bring the clans and cartels together, pull them away from their way of life. And, your powerful, more than even maybe the first Starfire, and people may want that power for themselves. That's why I never wanted you to know. I know how you feel about your father dying and-"

"Does James know?" my voice comes out low.

She pauses before answering, "He-"

"Does. He. Know?" my voice staying at a calm, even growl.

"Yes."

And I am out the doors before she says anything else.

Chapter 26

My mind is a blur now. I am lost in the memories, the anger, and the hurt. As soon as one thought forms, it slips through my fingers only to be replaced by another. The next thing I know I am running into David in the hallway.

"Alena, what's wrong?" He asks, sensing my rage.

I do not look at him in the eyes, "Get out of my way, David."

"What's going on?"

My walls break ever so slightly.

"Did you know?" I whisper.

"Know what?"

"About how my father actually died?" I make eye contact with him.

I don't wait to hear his response, I back away. Before I realize what I am doing, I'm running. The energy to my legs is comforting, it takes away from my mind.

I sprint down the hallways, to the stairs, and out to the garden. It isn't until my feet are on the grass, that I realize I am barefoot. I run anyway.

The voices in my head start to grow, shards and fragments of memories pulling at my attention. I sprint fasting, trying to outrun the tidal wave that is about to crash down on top of me.

It doesn't matter.

The wave has already fallen, and I can't bear it any longer.

I scream out my thoughts, my lungs burning at the sheer agony of my emotions. It isn't enough. I let my voice continue, only stopping to bring in breath. I pull on my power, needing to distract myself. If the pain isn't burning my throat, my fire is. It pours over my senses, like a hot acid that I need to survive. It soothes and pains me all at once.

I am dimly aware of David's presence catching up with me, and then sprinting away. But I don't care, not about anything.

For what feels like eternity, I sit there and wrap myself in fire. My screaming slows, my throat sore from the pure effort of it. I lose myself in the flames, until a hand lands on my shoulder.

I shake away his hand, and scoot away, but James follows. That must've been where David went, to find James.

"Alena, I-"

I scream at him, "You knew! You knew all of it and you didn't tell me!"

"It wasn't my place-" James kneels down next to me.

"It was because I asked you! You should've told me. You should have told me why," my voice breaks.

"Alena, I never knew why. I still don't know why."

He sits there and waits for me to answer.

"Me."

My fire starts to dim.

"What do you mean?"

"I was a threat. So your dad came to take care of me." I say it so calmly and softly, for a moment I am unsure that it is me talking.

He doesn't answer, and I don't glance at him. I can't, I may not know what Edward looks like, but James is his son.

The son of the man who killed my father.

The son of the man whose father came to kill me.

A man that I have trusted and opened up to.

And yet, I still see only one person to blame.

"It was supposed to be me," I pause.

I let my fire flare, wrapping my nerves in the fury of it. When that doesn't satisfy, I punch at the ground, wishing for the pain in my hands to be enough, to bleed. James attempts to pull me away, and I throw my hands at him. He takes it, surprisingly, the way I attack him.

The pain, the betrayal, and the knowledge tear at my soul. I can't think past my anger, the fury at myself. My fire doesn't harm me, no matter how much I ask it too. It just burns my energy away.

James turns me around, my back to his chest, pinning my arms against myself. No matter how hard I try to pull away, he holds me in place, not letting my hands do more damage to myself. There we stay, kneeling on the grass, clutching onto one another.

"I'm sorry. I didn't know," James whispers into my hair.

My sobbing has quieted, and my fire has dimmed. The sun is already falling away, only the crest of orange showing over the trees in the distance. My breaths come out in uneven waves, slowing as I relax. James just sits there, waiting until I'm ready to move, to decide when to take that step of letting go.

When I attempt to go, James steadily turns me back towards him.

"It is not your fault. You're father would've said the same," he stares at me dead on.

I return the gesture, "This whole thing, the blood in my veins, the responsibility, the power. I'm scared James. I can't be who you need me to be."

"I don't need you to be anyone other than you. But if you are not going to be Queen because you don't want to, that's fine, but don't do it because of my father. We'll figure this out. It's your birthright, so make the choice for yourself, no one else."

I know what I had said to James at the ball, about how being Queen was what I wanted. But what if I hurt them? Hurt him? But maybe James is right, maybe this is his father talking.

"Stay with me?"

He seizes my face with his hands, "I'm not going anywhere."

And we kiss.

Chapter 27

M y ceremony takes place at James' choice. Ironically enough, it was the lake that I found my powers at. Mom, James, Will, David and the Dawns were all present.

Ava helped me get ready. I am dressed in white, gold, and red, the colors of rebirth and of my family. My mother is the one that performs the ceremony, being the only other "royal."

My brother leads me to the edge of the water where Will, James, and David wait for me. David winks and Will smiles as he sends a picture of a rose into my mind. James' smile is the brightest of all of them; pure joy.

"Till the stars fall," James says, reminding me of his promise that he fulfilled.

When my foot enters the water, I don't feel the cold, my fire warming it. I wade out to my mother who waits to crown me Queen. When I reach her, tears fill my eyes.

"Bow my child," Mother demands, starting the ritual.

Water flows up to my waist as I sink to my knees.

"Do you swear to guard this kingdom and its people, no matter the consequences?"

"I swear."

"Do you swear to give your life to guiding the kingdom to safety and prosperity?"

"I swear."

"Do you accept your role as Queen of Astraea?"

"I do."

"Then, let these waters be a witness."

Mom pushes me underwater, then raises me back up.

I stand up and turn toward those gathered as the final words cement my fate, "I pronounce Alena Benazir Starfire, Queen of Astraea."

Cheers erupt in front of me. One does not cheer. Instead, he is on his knees, bowing to his new Queen. James' gesture means more than respect, it's an apology. When everyone follows suit, I walk to him, pull him to his feet, and kiss him.

It is a promise that I am never going to let him go. So, when I break away, I am ready for what comes next. Because in the end there are two things I know for sure: that I am a Queen, and that this world is going to know my name.

Until next time...

Acknowledgements

There are so many people in my life that I have to thank for making this book possible, so this is going to take awhile!

First off, always have to thank God first! Thank you God and Jesus for everything that you gave me to continue writing this book, and starting it. Thank you for the tragedies that started this, pushed me through this, and made me feel for this book. Thank you for the love and the profound joy that reminded me to laugh and that sometimes laughing at dumb moments or pieces of writing is always the best of times.

Thank you to the BookBaby team and Avery my publishing agent. I couldn't have done any of this without your help. You guys have such a unique system that allowed me to keep my book my own which, going into this, was something that I was afraid I wouldn't have.

Thank you to Mrs. Traynor. I would've never found BookBaby if you hadn't recommended Amazon to me in the first place. As well as the entire English Departments, middle and high school, for encouraging me to continue.

Thank you to my cousin Rachel, for editing my entire 70,000 word book, without pay at the beginning! Glad we were able to at the end! For that alone, and many other reasons, thank you! Honestly, the editing part was the most stressful part, but you made it a lot better.

To all those at school that had little inputs here and there. Special shout outs to Autumn, Lexi, Liz (for book 2), Sawyer, Jordan, Karlie, Abi, Abby, Kami, Anissa, Chloe, Maddie, Dawson, Mallory, Destiny, Marisa, and Love. There are so many others but you guys really helped with inspiring me in certain moments, whether you were aware or not, in the book. As well as editing parts of chapters and the book cover.

To my family, who supported me in mostly every aspect, save for the kissing scene haha. Mom that was meant for you!

To my parents, thank you for listening to my messed up storylines, kissing scene (again, directed at my mom who thought it was going to get rated R really quick haha), your time, money, inspirational speeches, and patience with me. I know that I am not the easiest teenager but you allowed me to detach so I could write this, and for that I thank you to the stars and back.

To my sisters, Ali and Katie. Ali, for reminding me that there is more in this world than that of America, and that this world needs love in it, and that adventures take sacrifice as well as a willing heart. Katie, for understanding me at home when literally no one else would. You are my crutch and the reason that I am alive enough to accomplish something like this. Thank you to both of you.

Thank you to my grandparents, especially Tom and Donna. For opening your home when mine was no longer standing, buying me books upon books when this world was too much to bear, and paper and pencils so that I could create one of my own. You may not believe me, but your talks, effort, protectiveness, understanding, and love got me through a time when my world was falling apart, and is pretty much one of the sole reasons this book is even alive. For that I will never be able to thank you enough.

To the other authors like me. Without you guys I wouldn't be able to understand my own book. For allowing your characters to reflect parts of yourself that you keep hidden, something that I understand completely now. For giving me worlds to escape to and characters to learn from.

To those characters in the books. For teaching me how to fight to survive, ball dance, about art in every shape and color, worlds beyond this one, to love and how to love every bit of yourself. For teaching me that scars and burdens are rough and messy, but in the end the reward is worth every bit of it. Especially for teaching me what love really is. That the bad guys can be loved, because they were once the good guys. That love feels like you've known the person forever, that it can be selfish, that nothing compares to that one specific person, and that we shouldn't waste time because we only have a little bit until it runs out.

Thank you to myself. This may seem selfish, but years from now when I come back to this, I need to remember that I could have all this advice again and again, but I could've chosen to not listen. So thank you me, for fighting for us and dreaming even when everyone at one point said to stop. Thank you for your belief and love for me. Thank you for being me.

And finally to you, my readers. You are another cornerstone in making this book. Because even if everyone hates this, but it saves just one person from their own bullshit life, it was worth it. To those that read until midnight, knowing that indeed there is magic in the world, that know that you just have to be brave enough to look for it.

Thank you.

CHAPTER 1:

The Beginning of an Era

A day. That is how long I had of being Queen before I was overtaken with problems. Cartels everywhere are rising up with anger against the new monarch. I had already heard the death threats, expected them actually. They didn't scare me. But they did scare James.

Demands had been made for my removal, in which I had declined, along with the old supporters of my family. No one came for my head, at least not that I had heard of. My family stayed in my hometown, while I resided in James' estate.

It wasn't really allowed, but James and I stayed with each other most nights. Mostly we just slept, other times we talked for hours about what I should do.

When I got back from the ceremony, James had gone off before I could talk to him. I didn't see him for hours, mostly because I was too busy being bowed to. The dawns didn't come and speak with me, but I had found them and told them that me being Queen changed nothing.

I was rushed around during that first day, learning about old traditions. One thing that the brothers made clear to me though, that because I was the first person to come back into power, I got to change the rules. They warned me against totally altering a rule, more adding. Too much change could cause an uprising, but I had pointed out that one was already starting.

For that reason, I called a meeting with all the clans and cartel heads. Friend or foe, I wanted them all there. James, however, I did not. He would be threatened just as much as me. But to my dismay, he disobeyed and weaseled his way into going.

The location was completely my choice, an isolated and abandoned house on the outskirts of New York. It was the middle ground for many of the major clans. It was the first building that I actually bought for myself. Well, it was more of a safe house for anyone that needed it.

Only twelve of the sixty-three cartels, in the United States, showed up. Two supernatural, both witches, and the rest were of human origins. I had used the giant dining room for the meeting, a round table that went around the entire room, sat the heads and they're second in command. Because I was in charge, I had James to my right and Will to my left, David stood at the door, guarding who came in and out.

I was the last to sit, the head of the table saved for me. When all threats were assessed, I entered, fully aware of everyone.

The day before, I had been taught in the image I needed to show. Powerful and a leader. I didn't wear a suit, but a dress. The ends of the sleeves going out in ruffles, the back and front a plain red. My hair is pinned to one side, curls framing my face. Simple, elegant, powerful. It showed my status and hid my secrets.

The room becomes instantly silent when I sit, everyone finally believing that the Starfire lives. I look at each leader in the eye, calculating their move, trying to decide to make mine.

"Thank you for coming. I am to assume you know who I am?"

"We know who you are, bitch," the second to the man directly in front of me speaks.

Each of my members stands in defense. To both me and my honor. I smile at myself, I knew this wasn't going to be easy, but I enjoy a challenge. I motion them to sit, and when I rise, I make myself clear. He doesn't see the fire that grows around me, snaking up my chair, around my legs.

"Mind your tongue," I respond, letting mischief go across my eyes.

His leader speaks, voice smooth as silk, "What my sentinel meant to say, was that you are nothing more than a child. And you are not a Queen."

When I sit, I extinguish the fire surrounding me, creating myself to look human. Almost.

"Some would say differently," I answer, forcing calm into my voice.

As I do a second look around the room, I realize that they are not looking at me. Instead, their focus is on James. He sits as calmly as me. But unlike at the ball, he doesn't put up a mask. He shows his certainty in me, his belief in who I am. They will look to him for acceptance.

James responds next, "You all don't know who you are dealing with. Ever since the last Queen fell, we have dwindled."

"We also have had peace and freedom," a leader speaks.

"You call war peace?" He asks.

A different one pipes in, "We are not at war!"

"No, but you will be," I say, getting in on the debate. "I have seen the records. The casualties from each side. You are going to tell me that won't spark another, bigger war?"

"You can't predict the future," the man across from me counters.

"You're right, but I can read the past. The past has always repeated. Unless we change our course."

"*Our* course? You are not part of this," the man across again challenges.

"Yes. She. Is." David fights.

"She is nothing more than a petty child."

"She is your Queen."

"Enough both of you," I cut off the argument. "If you think I am not worthy, then let me prove it to you. Challenge for my position."

The man once again comes for me, "We are not the werewolves."

"I never said you were, but this is a fairway. You use all of your resources. All who wish to challenge me can. If I win, you obey me. If you win, I'll sink back into the shadows."

The two witches that haven't even spoken do, and creepily in unison speak my name, "Alena Starfire. That name still means something to our kind. We will not fight. We recognize your position, and we are willing to stand by you. Just as we have done before."

"Your acceptance is appreciated, thank you," I look to the older one of the witches.

"You want a challenge," the man across from me says, as his second stands and draws a gun. "You'll have one."

A shot fires.